THE MOON'S LAST FORTRESS

Christopher Bulis

THE MOON'S LAST FORTRESS

Chapter 1
Amber Warning

I was falling through endless night.

I really wanted to stop falling but I could not.

A flash of blue was seared into my retina and my head throbbed and I felt sick. Why? How had I got like this? And if I had been falling for so long why hadn't I hit anything yet?

What could I remember? Oh, yes. Something about danger... a warning? A blue warning? No, not blue...

* * *

When the most D-DG (that's Drop-Dead Gorgeous) girl in Stapleforth school began telling me how much she admired my work as an amateur journalist, alarm bells should have started ringing. Then I would have begun an orderly evacuation to a place of safety, just like they tell you to do in a fire drill...

Anyway, I didn't do the sensible thing. Any tinkling bells I dimly heard I put down to the background music of my... well let's call it *infatuation* (look it up if you have to) because it was not really a mature enough emotion to be called *love*, which is a word I think is grossly overused today (and doesn't saying that make me sound *so* mature... I wish!). So, I was fourteen and I was infatuated... all right: *hopelessly* infatuated with the D-DG in question, whose name, by the way, was Amber Cavendish.

Amber was also fourteen but had the poise and self-possession of somebody five (possibly ten) years older. She was in addition (by overwhelming agreement) seriously hot! If that wasn't enough she was an Einstein in the science lab, a Shakespeare in literature class and an Amazon on the sports field. I, on the other hand, was plain unprepossessing Tom Mallory who was (by the agreement of those who could be bothered to express an opinion) bearable if taken in small doses. Unlike Amber I was an occasional test-tube breaker in the lab, a tabloid writer in the lit class and a "came in fourth again" on the track.

I'd only really begun seriously noticing girls in the last year or so, and thinking maybe it would be interesting, sort of, to get to know some of them a bit better... you know? And then Amber came to Stapleforth and I was lost. Why? Well apart from her physical hotness and brilliance, she didn't spend all her time on her phone texting and she wore this chunky multi-function diver's watch, which not many girls did, which suggested (to me at least) that she'd done lots of exciting things. She was different, right?

Yet despite her numerous plus points, so far Amber had appeared oddly boyfriend-proof. Several of my more confident contemporaries, and quite a few senior boys, had launched themselves at her only to bounce off what you might call the Cavendish emotional shield. There were even stories circulating of a couple of girls who also had a thing for Amber and hoped she might secretly be gay, but they had no better luck. Amber was friendly enough and obviously she was a star to the teachers and a boost to Stapleforth's academic ratings, being a sure thing for Oxbridge, but there was a kind of distance about her. It was not actual arrogance but something that set her apart from the rest of us lesser beings, which only made her seem more desirable. Many times had I looked on her from afar (by which I mean the other side of the classroom) and dreamed of what would never be...

Then came the day when my world had been turned on its head. Until ten minutes earlier I wasn't sure Amber even knew I existed and now here she was telling me that not only did she know that I lived and breathed, but actually approved of the fact!

We were in the office of *The Gazer*, which is Stapleforth's school newspaper. I sat at a computer terminal trying to look as though I was in charge and not just a junior reporter while Amber perched on the edge of the desk idly swinging her legs (such amazing legs!) in a way I'd never seen her do before while we talked. Actually she did most of the talking while I burbled semi-intelligible replies in between grinning foolishly and trying not to stare at her bare knees.

Yes, I know that makes me seem like an idiot, and right then I suppose I was. But then if I hadn't been I wouldn't have had the most amazing adventure of my life, etc, etc... see above.

'That was a good article you wrote on the Science Museum trip,' Amber said. 'You took the trouble to get all the facts right. I hate careless reporting, don't you?'

'Oh... yes, hate it,' I agreed, feeling that this was not the time to mention that I'd copied half of it from the handouts they'd given us.

'And your photos were well chosen and neatly composed.'

'Er… well, you know, I try my best…'

'That's why I thought you might be interested in doing a feature on my Father. He has a new invention that he's going to be demonstrating in a few days' time. It would be an exclusive for *The Gazer*.'

Amber got at least half her impressive IQ from her Professor father, who had been a sort of celebrity scientist until a few years ago, one of a handful who had achieved a popular profile. His field was some highly specialised branch of physics.

'Umm… yes, that sounds great.'

'The only thing is it will involve some travel. We'll have to be away from Fulchester for a day or so. Could you come this Friday evening and stay over to Sunday morning, if you've nothing else on?'

Two essays, French test revision and clearing the junk from the garage that I'd been promising my father I'd do for the last three weeks.

'Uhh… no, I'm free.'

Amber smiled and my heart skipped several, probably unimportant, beats. She handed me a card with her father's name and address and, for some reason, a matrix bar code printed on it. 'You'll have to show this at the gate to get in. See you on Friday at seven, then.'

The door closed behind her, leaving only a waft of fragrant perfume in her wake, while I sat there in a happy daze marvelling at my luck.

Sammy Khan, a sixth-former, talented wordsmith and the actual editor of *The Gazer*, came in.

'Was that Amber Cavendish I saw leaving?' he asked.

I swelled with self-importance. 'Yes. She... uh, was just asking me to do a story on her father's latest invention. An exclusive, you know.'

He did not look as impressed as I'd hoped. 'You're brave. Prof Cavendish is crazy, you know that. Don't you know what happened at his last public demo?'

'Uh... no, what?'

Sammy clicked his tongue reproachfully. 'Do your research, Tom! You'll never make a good reporter if you don't do basic background research...'

The thing is, although I've never admitted it to Sammy who's a great guy, I don't particularly want to be a reporter. I haven't really got it straight yet what I want to be. I only joined *The Gazer* to try to improve my school cool rating (which had been pretty low) and make myself seem a bit more interesting to people like... well, like Amber. So call me cynical but it worked, right?

Anyway, I turned back to my laptop and hit the internet.

Did I wonder at that moment why I, an amateur reporter for a school paper, was being asked by the daughter of a noted scientist to an exclusive preview of his latest invention? What about the national media or specialist scientific press that you'd think would be invited first? What was this invention and why did it involve travel? All these were very good and sensible questions that I entirely failed to ask myself because I was not thinking at all sensibly at that moment.

A search on James Edward Cavendish came up with a huge number of references and articles, from which I extracted the following.

He was forty-three years old and an F.R.S. (that's Fellow of the Royal Society) plus an alphabet soup of other letters after his name representing a dozen other awards, qualifications and memberships of learned societies. He worked on the higher peaks of theoretical physics so rarefied that mere mortals would need oxygen to get beyond base camp. I read the title of one of his research papers three times and still had no idea what it was about. There was also a list of about fifty books he'd written, ranging from the popular to the totally obscure. But Cavendish was no slope-shouldered, lab-bound academic, also being a practical engineer, a qualified scuba diver and light aircraft pilot. Photos of him showed a tall, wiry man with a leonine mane of greying hair, a determined chin and very sharp eyes. The other half of Amber's brainpower and an even higher proportion of her striking good looks obviously came from her mother, Professor Myra Russell, who was a big name in her own right in the field of zoology.

The more I read, however, the more I began to suspect that childhood could not always have been easy for Amber.

The process of bringing Amber into the world seemed to have exhausted whatever romantic reserves her parents had started out with and now they had a pretty loose relationship, with her mother spending a lot of time abroad doing field research while Amber lived with her father. Up until a couple of years ago Cavendish had been the undisputed star in his field and a popular if sometimes controversial celebrity intellectual. Then things had started to go wrong. There was a bitter argument over some scientific papers he had submitted for peer review, followed by a practical demonstration that had literally blown up in his face and singed the eyebrows of several reporters. He'd lost his temper in a big way during a televised interview and insulted several of his fellow scientists. There were rumours of him having a mental breakdown. One reporter who went after him sniffing around for something sensational got a punch on the nose from Cavendish for his efforts. It was around then that he dropped out of the public eye and moved here to Fulchester.

And this was the man whose latest brainchild I'd so casually agreed to review.

* * *

My parents were a lot easier about the prospect of my spending much of a weekend away covering the Cavendish story than I'd imagined. Of course I didn't mention the schoolwork backlog and promised I'd clear the garage on Sunday after I got back, which may have helped. They were also better informed than I had been about our local ex-celebrity scientist.

'James Cavendish was always on TV a while back,' Mum said. 'Never short of an opinion on anything. Didn't matter if it was his speciality or not, or cared what anybody else thought about him either. Always entertaining, though.'

'What about those Royal Institution Christmas Lectures he did?' said Dad, slipping into cosy

11

reminiscence mode. 'I liked them. Once he attached a whole row of people to that electrostatic generator and made their hair stand on end. Then he blew up a solid bucket of ice with the same machine to show how much power it had.'

'And of course Myra Russell wrote and presented that big natural history series,' Mum added. 'She did that very well.'

'Remember when she smacked down that crocodile when it made a lunge for her?' said Dad with a glint in his eye. 'You had to admire her nerve for keeping so cool.'

'It wasn't her nerve you were admiring when she wore that tight swimsuit for those scenes diving with a whale,' Mum observed with a grin.

By now I was feeling pretty inferior to the whole Cavendish family. I mean I was just about holding my own at school, my father ran a driving school and my mother had a physiotherapy practice. They couldn't be more solid and respectable than they were, but they were not what you'd call exciting professions. On the other hand, at least my parents were still together, while, for all their brilliance, Amber's were not. Maybe she was secretly looking for a bit of comfort and companionship from somebody with a stable family life? No? Well, I could dream, couldn't I?

* * *

Friday finally arrived. I hurried home from school, showered and, more out of hope than necessity, shaved. Afterwards I dabbed on some of the aftershave my Aunt Sandra had given me for Christmas that stung like hell but which I hoped smelled sophisticated. I wasn't sure about the right

12

way to dress so I tried for smart-casual, with a jacket and open-necked shirt paired with my best jeans. With laptop and camera charged and ready I slung my carefully pre-packed overnight bag across my shoulders and rode off to my fateful rendezvous.

I know! A cub reporter trying to impress the girl of his dreams should not arrive on a pedal bike, but I reckoned it was better than being dropped off by a parent or taking a bus. I could just say I was a dedicated environmentalist travelling green, which might actually impress Amber. Was she eco-conscious? Of course, she had to be...

Professor Cavendish lived in Rawsleigh Woods, which occupied a slight hill at more exclusive end of Fulchester. From the road all you could see of his house was its roof peeping over a high boundary wall topped by spiked railings. The solid entrance gateway was guarded by security cameras. By an outside mailbox a small brass nameplate read: *Continuum House.*

I punched the call button on the gate intercom. It was answered by a woman's voice speaking with a gentle Scottish accent. 'Yes, who is it?'

'Tom Mallory, to see Professor Cavendish,' I said, trying to sound as though I called on famous people for interviews every week. 'Amber invited me. I've got a card...' I held it up to the intercom camera. A laser lens underneath it twinkled as it scanned the barcode.

'Oh yes, you're expected, dear,' said the voice. 'Do come in...'

The gates swung open and I wheeled my bike through.

Continuum House was a large Georgian mansion with sash windows and a lot of tall chimneys, surrounded by lawns and thick belts of trees, with the end of a tennis court showing to one side. Apparently there was money to be made from being both brilliant and controversial.

Feeling totally overawed and with my stomach tying itself in a knot, I parked my bike by the big main door and rang the bell.

The door was opened by a comfortably plump, fiftyish lady, with greying hair and bright blue eyes. 'Come inside, Tom,' she said with a friendly smile. 'I'm Ellen Whittle, Professor Cavendish's housekeeper. I've told Amber you're here. She'll be through in a moment.'

The hallway was as imposing as the outside of the house with a double flight of stairs leading up to a large landing. There were several framed photos on the walls which all had a common theme. There was Professor Cavendish receiving the UNESCO Kalinga Prize, next to Cavendish shaking hands with the Prince of Wales, followed by Cavendish addressing a House of Parliament committee discussing scientific research policy. Apparently he was not shy about his success. Fortunately Ms Whittle's welcoming, motherly presence had eased my nerves a little.

I realized she was looking me up and down searchingly. 'Now, are you quite sure you're ready for all this, dear?' she asked.

'Oh, you mean reporting on the demonstration?' I said. 'Yes, thank you, I've got everything with me.'

She looked concerned. 'But are you ready for the journey?'

'Oh, the journey,' I said vaguely. 'Is it far?'

Just then Amber appeared through a door in the back of the hall.

It was the first time I'd seen her out of school gear of some kind. To my surprise she was wearing a one-piece long-sleeved blue jumpsuit with an elasticized waist band fitted with lots of Velcro-flap pockets and handy loops. Her hair was now tightly combed back, curled up and pinned into a bun. She was carrying bundles of blue and grey fabric under her arm together with a pair of Converse blue canvas sneakers similar to those she had on.

She flashed me a quick smile. 'Hallo, Tom. You're prompt, that's good.'

'Well I wouldn't want to miss it, would I?' I burbled back, grinning foolishly.

Miss Whittle was fixing her with a stern gaze. 'Amber, have you told him everything?'

'Father said not to, Mrs W. Anyway he probably wouldn't have believed me if I had, but he'll find out soon enough.'

'You must explain the risks.'

'You know they're negligible. We've done all those tests. Everything will be fine.'

'Even so, is he.... suitable?'

'He's the best I could get in the circumstances. Father was very insistent.' Amber handed me the bundle of clothes and sneakers. 'You'll need to wear these. They should fit.'

'Why do I need these?' I asked.

'They're more practical, and they've been fireproofed.'

15

'What? Why?'

'It's just a precaution. You can change in there,' she indicated the way to a downstairs bathroom. 'There's a hanger for your clothes behind the door. Then I'll take you through to meet my Father and he'll explain.'

I know! How arrogant of her to presume I would simply do as I was told even after hearing I was only the best she could get "in the circumstances" (and just what did that mean anyway?) My self-esteem and infatuation had taken a knock but I said nothing. The fact remained that Amber, for some reason, wanted me here and I wanted to be where she was. Besides, it now seemed that this demonstration might be dangerous which meant there was no way I could back out now.

'Okay,' I said, trying to sound nonchalant.

I took the clothes and went into the bathroom. So much for my smart-casual look, I thought.

The blue bundle was a jumpsuit of the same pattern Amber was wearing. The grey bundle was a close-fitting once piece thermal base layer with elasticized cuffs at the wrists and neck and integral padded gripsock soles that covered everything except for my head and hands. Apart from a fly flap it had a slightly comic panel round the back that could be opened up to allow full use of the toilet without having to peel the top half down. I shrugged and put it on. It was actually quite comfortable to wear, but why was it necessary? Where were we going that required a special set of fireproof underwear?

Still with the jumpsuit and sneakers on it did not show except about the collar and as I examined myself in the mirror over the basin I decided I looked pretty good. I was all kitted out for doing something dynamic and exciting. But what?

Amber was waiting alone in the hall when I came out. She led me back through the door she had used, along a corridor and out into the back garden. Nestling amongst the trees on the far side of a large open square of lawn was a big green-painted steel portal frame building clad in corrugated panels. It had large sliding double doors that were currently drawn shut and looked like a light aircraft hanger with an extension built onto one side. Amber took me across the lawn and along a path to a smaller man-sized door set in the front of the extension.

Inside was a workshop running from front to back which was partitioned off from the main body of the building. Nearest the door were benches supporting several computer terminals linked by tangles of cables, while above them were shelves packed with assorted electronic components. Further back, through a plastic strip curtain, I could see the bulky forms of what looked like heavy machine tools.

Seated at the computers were two men also dressed in blue jumpsuits and sneakers. Professor Cavendish I recognised from his pictures. The other was a younger man, perhaps thirty, tall, blonde and I suppose you'd have to admit, quite handsome. Both men looked up as we came in.

'This is Tom Mallory,' Amber announced. 'Tom, this is my Father and this is Oliver Vance, his assistant.'

Vance frowned at me while Cavendish's face lit up almost boyishly.

Stapleforth positively encourages old-fashioned good manners and at times like this a little formality helps. 'Good evening, Professor Cavendish,' I said, stepping forward and holding out my hand. 'It's a pleasure to meet you.'

'Ah, so you're the reporter,' he replied, springing to his feet and shaking my hand with a crushing grip. He was wearing round wire frame glasses and he blinked through them at me looking alarmingly like a predatory owl. 'This is going to be a unique privilege for you, young man. Your article is going to make history. That'll teach those hacks from the gutter-press a lesson!'

Cavendish finally let go of my hand, allowing me to massage some life back into it. I then offered it to Vance. 'Good evening, Mr Vance.'

He stood and shook my hand as briefly and coldly as the Professor had been hearty. 'I suppose you've already been blabbing about this to all your friends,' he said accusingly.

I blinked. 'Excuse me?'

'He doesn't know anything yet, Oliver,' Amber said, 'just as we agreed.'

'I've made my views clear about this, Professor,' Vance said, glaring at Cavendish. 'This boy will only be in the way. We can document the trip perfectly well ourselves.'

'This has got to be done properly, Oliver,' said Cavendish. 'Besides I want an independent witness to prove that we can carry an entirely untrained passenger without any special preparation. People have got to realize the scope of this advance.' He chuckled as though enjoying a private joke. 'After all, it's going to put everything that's gone before it in the shade!'

'But we don't need him along to prove it,' Vance persisted. 'Your fame is already guaranteed. Let's not take any unnecessary risks.'

'There are no risks, Oliver,' the Professor admonished. 'Don't you agree all the tests have been perfect? Do you think I would allow Amber to participate if there were any doubt?'

'And you know my feelings on that matter as well,' Vance said. 'It would be better if we went alone, this time at least.'

'Amber has important functions to perform.'

'But not vital ones. And this boy has none. It's also unfair on him. I think Amber agrees with me.'

Amber chewed her lip unhappily. 'I got Tom here as I promised, Father. But now he has to make up his own mind. Oliver's right. We are taking a step into the unknown. There's still a small chance something might go wrong. Tom may not want to do this.'

'Of course he will!' the Professor said incredulously. 'Who wouldn't?'

Then they all began talking at once while I started at them stupidly. I'd obviously got caught up in an argument that had been simmering for some time and although I was the subject of it I had no idea what it was actually about. What was this "step in the unknown"? Was it the same as the "trip" we were going on? Why was I to be an "untrained passenger"? Well I'd had enough of being talked about as though I was a dumb stooge, Amber or no Amber.

I took a deep breath: 'Will you all please be quiet!' I shouted. I think I caught them all by surprise, especially Amber, because they actually shut up. 'Now can someone tell me what all this is about? What's this "demonstration" I'm meant to be covering? Where have we got to go to? If I don't get some straight answers I'm leaving right now!'

I'm not sure if I would have done but drawing the line had the desired effect.

'I suppose we have been expecting him to take a lot on trust,' the Professor admitted with bad grace, the animation draining from his face. 'Show him the *Eclipse*, Amber, and ensure he understands what is expected of him. We've got the flight profile to check.' He turned back to his computer, apparently dismissing me from his thoughts. Vance scowled at me again and then did the same.

'And what's the "*Eclipse*"?' I asked Amber.

'She's what all this is about. And she lives through here…'

Amber led me through a door in the partition wall into the building proper. Now I could see it really was a hangar because there was a vehicle sitting in the middle of it. But it was no light aircraft. What it most closely resembled, and there was no other word for it, was something very like a classic UFO: *a flying saucer*.

'This is the *Eclipse*,' Amber said, with thrill of pride sneaking into her voice. 'And tonight we're going to fly it to the Moon and we want you be our

20

reporter on the journey.' She grinned. 'Well, I did promise you an exclusive.'

Chapter 2
The Eclipse

I was still falling…

If I hit something from this high I'd just go splat like strawberry jam on a dropped piece of bread landing butter-side down. But I really didn't want to go splat. I was too young to die. I had so many more clichés to split… or did I mean infinitives?

I wish I could remember what had happened!

There were distant voices. I felt I should know them. One at least was really important to me. That was what this was all about…

* * *

I didn't reply at first to Amber's amazing offer to join her on a flight to the moon (which I agree did have certain old fashioned romantic associations). Instead I took a minute to walk round the *Eclipse*, examining it from all sides.

It was a compact, gleaming white craft, a little like a pair of Frisbees joined rim to rim, standing on four wide-splayed retractable legs that extended from its underside with fat metal mesh tyres on their ends. It was not actually a true saucer but elliptical, measuring about twelve metres long by eight across and a bit over three deep at its centre. There was a deep groove running round the ship where the upper and lower halves joined. Recessed into the groove was a long silver tube wound about by complex coils of wire. The whole assembly had then been sealed in behind thick glass or clear resin that ran flush with the curve of the hull.

This groove was broken in two places. Set in what I took to be the leading edge of the saucer were the transparent panels of a cockpit canopy, while at the rear, framed between a pair of stubby vertical trailing fins as deep as the ship was and cut into the hull, was a kind of hatchback and tailgate arrangement that had been flipped open so that a ramp extended to the ground. On either side of the cockpit three sets of forward facing oval ports were recessed into its sloping sides, two on the upper curve and one between them below. Currently the *Eclipse* was connected to a thick bunch of cables that ran from a socket by its rear hatch back towards the workshop.

Amber was frowning, evidently disappointed at my muted reaction. 'You did hear what I said?'

'Yes: Spaceship, Moon, fly to. Um, who built it?'

'Well, Father designed it. Most of the specialized parts were prefabricated by outside contractors who had no idea what they were for, of course. Father and Oliver did the actual assembly, with a little help from me.'

'I see.'

Why was I not more wowed or punching the air in excitement? Because I'd already half expecting something like it when I saw the thing. I'll explain...

The *Eclipse* was obviously a backyard spaceship, which is one of the oldest clichés in science fiction and which has been a long time dead. The scenario runs like this: a brilliant, if slightly wacky scientist, aided only by his beautiful daughter and possibly a loyal assistant Igor, builds a spacecraft in their garage and flies off to the moon… or Mars, or Alpha Centauri. Occasionally there's also a square-jawed hero involved with more muscle than brain… anyway you get the picture. It's a lovely fantasy but real life does not work that way.

When Project Apollo sent a crew to the moon for the first manned landing in 1969 they were launched on top of a massive multi-stage rocket as tall as St Paul's Cathedral that weighed around three thousand tonnes at take-off, most of which was fuel. The system had taken a huge team of scientists and engineers nearly ten years to develop at a cost of billions of dollars. Almost the whole rocket was used up in flight and all that came back was a cramped capsule carrying a three man crew, the world's most expensive set of holiday photo album snaps and a crate of moon rocks. The space shuttle that followed Apollo was slightly more efficient but it could never have reached the moon, let alone returned, and the privately financed craft they're working on now still need large companies to fund them and big rockets to boost them out of the atmosphere. The *Eclipse* didn't look like it could ride on anything.

'So?' Amber prompted me. 'Do you want to come?'

'Sorry. I'm just living up to my name and being a real doubting Thomas. It's a long way to the Moon. How is it supposed to get there? I don't see any rocket nozzles. What kind of propulsion system does it have?'

'It reacts against the continuum, the fabric of space-time itself, by means of the Cavendish Effect.

24

Father discovered it so he has the right to name it after himself,' she added almost defensively. She indicated the coils and silver tube set in the hull recess. 'It's generated in here. Only father really understands how it works, but basically it distorts the geometry of reality, creating a kind of pressure differential which provides a propulsive force. It's powered by batteries which are recharged by solar panels in the hull.'

I looked for the usual glossy black segmented panels. 'I don't see any.'

'You won't but they're all over the hull. They're set in a liquid crystal matrix and only become black and light absorbent when they're activated. It's another of father's inventions.'

'Even so you can't have enough power in batteries to lift a thing this size to the moon!' I said.

'Oh, the batteries only energize the drive field. The actual lift comes from the continuum itself. Like the energy needed to turn on a tap has no relation to the force of the water that comes out.'

Just for a moment I felt drawn to the wonder of it. This was another SF cliché: the fabled clean, compact, space drive. If it was real it would be the biggest breakthrough in physics for a century. If it was real...

I admit I enjoy SF stories and fantasies, even the trashier ones, but deep down I knew these things didn't happen in real life, at least not to people like me. Of course I wanted to believe everything this girl I felt so intensely about was telling me, but I was secretly afraid that she was being strung along by her father who really had lost his grip on reality a while back.

25

Sensing my continued doubts Amber said: 'I know this must seem unbelievable but can you just go along with it for another couple of hours? If we're all deluded then what have you got to lose? If we're not, do you want to miss a free trip to the moon?'

I didn't know about that. All I was sure of was that would mean I'd spend two more hours with Amber, who, despite the dents she had recently inflicted on my self-respect, was still paying me more attention than most other girls I had known. I tried not to let this selfish and/or pathetic piece of calculation show on my face. 'Okay.'

Amber smiled warmly and I felt that deep disturbing inner thrill again. Please don't let her be crazy like her father, I thought.

'Let me show you round inside...'

We entered through the rear hatchway. Beyond it was a pair of pressure doors with round ports set in them that obviously served as an airlock, which opened onto a short corridor. Folded up into the roof was a light extending ladder giving access to a clamped and sealed circular hatch with another round port set in it. On each side of the corridor was a pair of doors.

'Emergency escape hatch,' Amber explained, pointing up. 'Stores, spacesuit locker, sanitary facilities and air plant,' she continued, opening up the doors on each side one at a time to show me.

There were shelves full of spare parts, cartons of pre-packed food and plastic carboys of water all clamped down against free fall. On folding hangers were four white pressure suits that looked rather slimmer than the Apollo moonwalk designs, with a rack of life-support backpacks hung opposite them. There was a tiny washroom with a covered flip basin, paper towel and wet-wipe dispensers, first aid cabinet and an over-plumbed toilet bowl with a sealable lid and a set of operating instructions posted up beside it. Finally there came a device that was a complex mass of tubing, cylinders, precipitators and filter packs.

I had to admit it all looked very comprehensive and functional, but it only proved Cavendish had fitted out his fantasy vehicle well, not that it could fly.

Another pressure door at the end of the corridor opened onto the flight deck, which occupied the front third of the craft. This was even more impressive.

There were five aircraft-style chairs mounted in an arc following the curve of the hull. Each had safety straps and headrests and was set on lockable swivel mounts. The middle chair looked out through the cockpit, which with its clear roof and floor panels gave a wide field of view. Set in the arms of the chair were control pads, a lever and a joystick, while there were pedals built into its footrest. They reminded me of helicopter controls. Hung in the apex of the cockpit blister in front of the chair was a transparent heads-up display screen.

The seats immediately to each side of the command chair were fitted with swing arms with laptop-sized displays and keyboards mounted on them. They looked out through the pair of upper oval ports adjacent to the cockpit. On either side of these ports, hung on the inward curving hull where it ran up to form the ceiling, were big flat screen monitors, currently dark. Outside of these control chairs were the single ports set in the lower curve of the hull, currently giving a view of the concrete hangar floor. Then came the outer pair of seats set next to the second pair of upper ports.

Amber sat down in the chair to the left of the pilot's station. 'This will be where I'll be when we take off. I control the environmental systems and monitor the external sensors, general ship status and communications. Oliver will be on the other side running the power and drive systems. Father will pilot, of course.' She indicated the outer chair. 'You can sit here next to me.'

On one side my chair had a swing arm fitted with adjustable clips to hold a laptop, while on the other was an extendable pivoting rod with a very good quality digital camera mounted on its end. Beside it were an instruction booklet and a thick white padded slipcase to fit over it.

'That's what you'll be using to document the flight,' Amber explained. 'The mount is to steady it during take-off and periods of weightlessness. There's the manual and its protective thermal cover for use during our moon EVA. Everything you image or record on it remains my father's property, of course. He'll say what you can use afterwards. Obviously you can make what notes you like but you'd better okay what you plan to write first. He can get a bit... upset if reporters get their facts wrong.'

I recalled the reporter with the broken nose and said nothing. I tried the chair out instead. It was very comfortable and even reclined.

'We'll be sleeping in the chairs as well,' Amber said, 'but we'll only be gone two nights.'

Naturally, they were just going to hop up to the moon and back in a weekend. It was less time than travelling to Australia and back. The Apollo craft had taken three days one way.

'The hull's very tough, self-sealing and insulated against micro-meteorite penetration and radiation, both thermal and ionizing,' Amber continued, apparently trying to reassure me. 'The cockpit and all the ports are lead glass and quartz composites with polarising and UV filter layers and they're augmented by full coverage external hull cameras. Most of the control systems and basic fittings were bought practically off the shelf and have proven reliability. The air recycling system was originally developed for mini-submarines, for instance. The batteries are quite standard as well. They're in a compartment under the deck. There's also a reserve hydrogen fuel cell if we drain them faster than they can re-charge. All the vital systems have backups. Everything's been thoroughly tested. It'll be perfectly safe.'

'Yes, it all looks great,' I agreed. 'Even a bit like a *Star Trek* shuttlecraft. Of course *Star Trek* props don't actually fly... sorry.'

She sighed. 'I've got the pre-flight environmental systems check to run. Why don't you stow your bag under your seat and set up your laptop. Then begin by taking some pictures of the *Eclipse*.'

'But why me, really?' I asked. 'And why this moonflight stunt? If this thing is as wonderful as you say then a simple flypast over London would be all the demonstration you need.'

Amber frowned. 'Maybe you'd better ask my father that. But wait until we're on our way. He's rather preoccupied with last minute preparations now. He'll be more approachable later.'

I sighed. 'Okay.' I tried to sound casual as I added a phrase I never expected to utter for real: 'And when do we take off for the moon?'

She checked her watch. 'A little over an hour. We're taking off at ten o'clock BST. We want it to be fully dark so people don't see us. It might cause complications. This isn't exactly a scheduled flight.'

An unpleasant possibility occurred to me. 'What about air traffic control radar? Suppose they track us and call up the RAF? They're nervous about strange aircraft after 9-11. Is the hull insulated against air to air missiles?'

'No, but it is almost totally radar-invisible, like a stealth fighter. And we've got another trick to stop us being seen in-flight... well, you'll have to wait and see. Father's not stupid, you know.'

Maybe not, but was he crazy?

* * *

I set up my laptop as Amber suggested. I had a small plug-in hand held mic I could use to make audio notes which would also be transcribed through a voice writer programme. Then I read through the camera manual to be sure I could work it. Unclipping it from its mount I left Amber working in the cabin and went back out into the hangar and walked round the *Eclipse* taking some still images. I even got Amber to wave at me

30

through one of the ports and snapped her. It looked impressive from some angles but did it actually work? Amber had all the answers but the *Eclipse* was apparently going to be propelled by something only a step away from pixie dust. I moved in to get a close-up of the Cavendish Drive tube and coil assembly in its recessed perimeter groove, then ran my hand over its transparent seal. Could this really make rocket propulsion obsolete? Was the *Eclipse* a work of genius or sad self-delusion?

Just then Vance came through from the workshop carrying a small carton under his arm. 'Don't touch that!' he barked so sharply that I jerked back.

'No need to shout,' I said.

'Why were you so interested in the drive coils?' he asked suspiciously, striding up to me with an angry scowl on his face.

'Just doing my job as the mission reporter,' I said defensively.

'He wasn't doing any harm, Oliver,' Amber chided, emerging from the rear hatch of the ship. 'I said he could take pictures of the ship for the record.'

Vance took in a deep breath and then forced a rueful smile. 'Sorry for that, Tom. It's nothing personal, it's just I've put a lot of work into getting the *Eclipse* ready for this flight and I don't want anything to go wrong at the last moment. You understand?'

'Understood,' I said. Then added, not entirely, truthfully: 'No offence taken.'

Vance nodded and climbed on up the ramp into the ship.

'You see,' Amber said. 'He's normally very friendly and he's been a fantastic assistant to Father over the last few years.'

I was not actually thinking about his qualities as an Igor but how "friendly" he'd been to Amber. If only he was not so good looking... On the other hand he must be twice her age. What was I imagining? Oh God, was I that jealous? I had to get a grip on reality. The trouble was right now reality was insisting I was about to fly to the moon...

Professor Cavendish strode in, heading for the *Eclipse* and rubbing his hands together. 'Forty-five minutes, Amber,' he snapped impatiently. 'Time for internal power-up and final checks.'

'Why don't you get some fresh air?' Amber suggested to me as she followed her father into the ship. 'I'll call you when we're ready.'

* * *

Standing on the big back lawn I realized how late it was. Apparently time spent in Amber's company passed at a different rate than normal. The sun had long set and the twilight was fading into a fresh night with a scattering of clouds drifting across the sky. Through the trees that ringed the Cavendish estate I could see a pale glimmering half disk. You fall for an unattainable girl and next thing you know she's inviting you on a trip to the moon. As my dad often said, not terribly originally, it's a funny old world. But was I laughing? No.

Mrs Whittle appeared along the path from the house carrying an insulated picnic box.

'And how are you feeling now, dear?' she asked.

'I'm okay, thank you, Mrs Whittle.'

She glanced up at the Moon. 'Are you sure you want to go?'

Apparently she believed it all as well. Was the whole household crazy or was I being really slow on the uptake?

'Um, yes... I think so.'

'Well don't let the Professor bully you. He can be a wee bit overbearing at times.' She tapped the box. 'Shepherd's Pie, one of his favourites. Make sure he has some on the way. That should mellow him.' She continued on into the hangar.

Of course, I thought, we couldn't go to the moon on an empty stomach and what better than Shepherd's Pie? I sniffed approvingly. Actually not a lot, I had to admit. This weird mixture of the homely and high-tech was getting hard to get straight in my head, which was beginning to ache.

Was I going to witness a staggeringly brilliant triumph, a possibly tragic disaster or a sad humiliation? I knew what I secretly wanted to happen, however I also knew what was more likely.

From the hangar came a whine of electric motors. Wheels squeaked and rattled along metal rails as the hangar doors began to slide apart, revealing the *Eclipse* looking suitably unearthly under the strip lights. Slipping into reporter mode I snapped a picture of it. The power cable had been disconnected and the twinkle of live displays now showed through its cabin ports. I could see Cavendish in the pilot's seat while Vance and Mrs Whittle were standing outside.

Amber stepped out onto the lawn and came over. She was carrying a plastic beaker of water and couple of pills which she offered to me.

'For space sickness,' she explained. 'We'll be under drive a lot of the time but there will be some periods of free fall so it's best to be prepared.'

'I don't get airsick,' I said.

'This will be different. Don't be proud. I've already had mine.'

I took the tablets.

'You'd better come in now. We're almost ready. We're just going to test the shadowmask.'

'The what?'

'It's a piezoelectric-induced change in a film of long chain polymer fibres coating the surface of the photocells,' Amber explained. 'The photo crystals turn black while the polymer fibres align perpendicular to the hull, creating a microscopically super rough surface, still allowing light to pass in but not out, making it almost totally non-reflective. There's also a fibre and liquid crystal layer in the cockpit and port glass. Watch…'

Cavendish signalled to Vance through the cockpit canopy and Vance acknowledged. I saw Cavendish reach over to Amber's chair pad and then the ship turned black.

I mean dead black, landing legs, ports and all. It was like looking at an almost perfect silhouette with hardly any sense of depth. You could only tell something solid was there by its ground shadow and contrast to the brightly lit background of the hangar.

Vance gave a wave and thumbs up and the portals and cockpit reappeared, seeming to be floating in the black shadow. Another wave and the whole ship snapped back to normal.

'It should reduce the risk of anybody seeing us in the optical wavelengths,' Amber continued. 'Near-earth orbits are monitored for space junk. We'll occult a few stars but that's all. Activating selected sections of the hull also helps with temperature control.'

Slightly dazed at this casual display of scientific genius, I said: 'So in addition to every other spaceship that's ever flown, the *Eclipse* even puts itself in the shade.'

'Father rather liked the double pun,' Amber agreed.

I realized the ship was positioned to roll out onto the lawn. 'Er... is there enough room to take off?'

'We don't need a runway. The *Eclipse* has full VTOL capability.'

'Of course...'

The Professor had emerged from the ship and was standing talking to Vance and Mrs Whittle. Amber and I joined them.

'You know what to do if we're... delayed for any reason,' the Professor was saying to Mrs Whittle.

'I do, Professor,' she said solemnly. 'Good luck to you all.' Then she reached up and kissed him on the cheek, and then did the same to Amber and Vance. Even I got a quick motherly peck. Then Mrs Whittle glanced at Amber. 'And mind you bring him back safely,' she added sternly.

I actually I thought I saw Amber blush.

Stepping back from the ship Mrs Whittle crossed to a switch panel on the hangar wall. We climbed aboard the *Eclipse* and Amber closed and locked the external hatch shut behind us, and then sealed the airlock chamber.

The main cabin lights had been dimmed and the now active display screens glowed colourfully with graphic scales, virtual gauges and ranks of numbers. We took our respective seats and strapped in. I screwed the camera back onto the swivel mount on the chair arm which would keep it steady while still allowing me to swing it round to cover the entire cabin.

'Internal air mix, pressure and temperature control now active and all reading normal,' Amber reported. There was a soft whisper from a duct above my head.

'Now, young man, this is an historic moment.' Cavendish said to me. 'Record everything properly with full details, times and dates. We shall use a 24 hour GMT clock during the flight. Note the display on the screens and adjust from BST accordingly.'

'Yes, Professor.'

With a dry mouth I panned the camera across the cabin and command chairs. My heart was beginning to thud in my chest. I saw Amber glance round at me and mouth: *Say something!*

'Er... the time is 20:58 GMT on Friday the Twelfth of April on-board the space ship *Eclipse*. Pilot: Professor James Cavendish, crew: Amber Cavendish and Oliver Vance, reporter: Tom Mallory.'

The Professor made a sign through the cockpit to Mrs Whittle and all the lights in the hangar went off. The windows of the main house were already dark.

Cavendish punched some keys on his panel and then took hold of the joystick and control levers. Smoothly the *Eclipse* rolled out of the hanger onto the big shadowy square of lawn.

'Hull shadowmask on,' Cavendish ordered.

Amber worked her controls. 'Shadowmask on,' she confirmed.

'Begin the launch sequence,' Cavendish said.

'Safeties disengaged. Main power to drive,' Vance reported. 'Batteries at ninety-nine percent.'

'The *Eclipse* is about to lift off…' I gulped '… destination moon!' Let me tell you that is a hell of a phrase to utter for real and also a classic Fifties SF film. But was it true?

'Activate the main drive,' Cavendish said.

'Main drive activated,' Vance confirmed, tapping at his controls. 'Cavendish field building…'

A low humming steadily rising in pitch seemed to pulsate through the frame of the ship. The hair on the back of my neck was standing up, whether from anticipation or some static discharge I was not sure.

'Field stabilised and locked,' Vance declared.

The Professor eased back on the joystick and ship seemed to shiver slightly. Motors whined and things went clunk a few times underneath the hull.

'Landing gear retracted,' Amber reported.

The timer display flicked over to 21:00 GMT. The ship wallowed momentarily and then tilted sharply backwards. The blackness outside was disorientating and my stomach flipped. Despite the pills I thought I was going to be sick.

It was then I discovered that even foolish pride had its limits. Was it through fear that this crazy machine was actually going to work or thought of the shame the Cavendish's would suffer if it didn't? I don't know. It wasn't heroic and I wasn't proud of myself but I just knew at that moment I had to get out of there.

Letting go of the camera I fumbled with my straps. 'I'm really sorry, but I don't want to do this anymore. I'm getting out...'

'Tom, you can't get out!' Amber called back to me.

'Yes I can!'

'No you can't... *because we've already taken off!*'

I looked down through the lower side port. Far below me and shrinking fast were the lights of Fulchester.

Chapter 3
From the Earth to the Moon
(with apologies to J. Verne)

I just wanted to stop falling!

If I was going to hit something then get it over with! Anything but this endless drop. It couldn't go on forever... could it? Was it a nightmare with no end?

Then there was pressure on me. Something or someone was holding me, pressing me down against something solid.

But here there was no down.

But before that there had been a lot of up...

* * *

Lift-off had been so smooth that in the darkness I had thought the *Eclipse* was still resting tipped backwards on its tail on the lawn. Actually we were already climbing at an angle of about forty-five degrees, onward and upward without levelling out. The lights of more distant Leahampton and Wychford joined those of Fulchester, and then they also dwindled into the distance.

There was no vibration and hardly any wind noise, except for the deep background hum of the drive field. I was being pressed back into my seat firmly but not uncomfortably. My mind spun and not all in one piece as bits of it were having trouble keeping up. The *Eclipse* really worked! It was no fantasy. I was actually flying in a backyard spaceship, complete with mad scientist, beautiful daughter and Igor. Eat that cliché for breakfast! We really were going to the moon!

My sense of light-headed elation was crushed like an eggshell as I saw Cavendish glancing round at me with a mixture of annoyance and contempt. Even worse was the sight of Amber studying her control panel intently and pointedly not looking at me.

The truth was that in the face of the wonder of all this I'd panicked. I'd been a coward and now they all knew it.

Unexpectedly my spirits were lifted slightly by Oliver Vance. Aloud he said: 'Drive field still stable, batteries at ninety-seven percent.' Then he glanced across at me, but instead of a look of disgust or an "I told you so" to the others, he grinned cheerfully and gave me a quick thumbs-up.

That helped… a little.

The pressure of acceleration seemed to ease off, although we were still climbing rapidly. 'Holding at eleven hundred kph,' Cavendish said. 'Entering cruise phase through troposphere.'

I took a deep breath. 'Sorry,' I said to the cabin at large. 'Feeling better now.'

Amber reported: 'All environmental systems still green, internal pressure normal.' Then she looked at me scathingly and hissed: 'Do you always react like that during a simple take-off?'

'Maybe, if it's the first flight of something radically experimental!' I protested feebly. 'How could I know it would even get off the ground in one piece?'

'What do you mean the *first* flight?' Amber said incredulously. 'We've flown dozens of test flights in the *Eclipse*. This is just the first time we'll be leaving the atmosphere.'

'Test flights?' I exclaimed. Indignation began to replace my shame. 'You never said you'd flown actual *test flights* in this thing before!'

'Of course. I told you everything had been tested thoroughly.'

'But not that you'd actually *flown* it!' I knew it was a thin excuse but I was desperate to salvage some shreds of self-respect.

'Well perhaps I didn't say so because I never imagined anyone could think we'd attempt a moonflight and a maiden flight at the same time!' Amber retorted. 'Who'd be that dumb?'

'Only people who think in clichés,' I muttered, thinking: idiot, idiot, idiot! That was only how they did it in *stories*... More loudly I said, trying to make up for my behaviour: 'Congratulations, Professor... incredible spaceship you've built...Nobel Prize in the bag.'

Amber rolled up her eyes and shook her head and turned back to her controls.

'Thank you for that commendation, young man,' Cavendish said tersely. 'Now perhaps you will cease distracting my daughter with further irrelevant chatter and perform the task assigned to you.'

As I took control of the camera again I wondered what my companions now thought of me. They had every right to distrust me now. I mean would you travel to the moon with somebody who was likely to lose his nerve so easily? True, they had been prepared for it while I'd been thrown in at the deep end with hardly any warning. It was also true that it had been a strange and potentially frightening situation. But I'd still let my

41

imagination get the better of me. I took a deep breath and told myself I'd simply never ever let it happen again.

'The *Eclipse* is climbing steadily through the lower atmosphere,' I reported. 'All systems A-OK.'

Outside the port I saw a ragged deck of ghostly moonlit clouds far, far below, overlaying a dark land. Or was it sea? I'd no idea how far we'd come. All I knew was we were heading east and a bit south into the night. How soon would we be crossing the channel? I angled the camera out of the ports to make the most of the spectacle.

Cavendish checked his readouts. 'Entering stratosphere,' he announced. 'Prepare for orbital ascent phase...'

The hum of the drive increased and I was pressed back into my seat again harder than before. I had no trouble breathing, although my chest felt heavy and I was grateful for the padded headrest. I would not have been able to hold the camera for long if it had not been for the bracing rod. Now we really were going up like a rocket. What was our acceleration? Three g's? Four? We must have already broken the sound barrier some time back but any sonic boom had been left far behind us.

Vance reported on the drive status and power levels every half minute. The drive was fine but the battery reserve was falling steadily. Nobody else seemed concerned, however, so I assumed it was at the anticipated rate. Now I'd got my mind around the reality of the Cavendish drive I understood the need to move fast. The *Eclipse* might not be burning tonnes of rocket fuel but it could not fly without expending electrical energy to keep its wonder drive active. Every second in the atmosphere meant power spent overcoming its resistance while also fighting the drag of gravity. The batteries could only hold so much juice so speed was the answer. Get clear of the atmosphere as soon as possible and go into orbit where the force of gravity could be balanced by its velocity. The *Eclipse* was a spaceship and its natural home was a vacuum.

That wasn't a bad phrase and I hoped I could work it into my article.

In between Vance's reports, Amber advised on the state of the ship. Everything was in the green... so far.

'We're on our way up to orbit,' I said for the benefit of the record, my voice sounding a little tight as I fought the pressure on my chest. 'The ship is still accelerating steadily. Being night I can't see much below us but I know the ground is a long way down.'

'We're crossing over Turkey,' Amber said helpfully, reading off the navigational display in front of her. She touched a button and a view from what must have been a forward facing hull camera appeared on the screen. 'There, you can just see the Arabian Sea in the moonlight ahead of us.' That sounded rather romantic, I thought. Being Amber, however, she had to qualify it. 'Our altitude is now just over one hundred kilometres.'

'As I said, it's a long way down.'

We climbed like this for about seven minutes in all. Then, still accelerating, began to level out.

'Entering orbital insertion phase,' Cavendish announced, checking his readings and making small adjustments to our course.

Simply grabbing altitude was not enough. If we wanted to stay there we needed the correct horizontal velocity. In my mind's eye I saw us flying along a great arc in the sky, the upper curve of which would reach out into space. Through the ports the dim grey mass of the Earth lay far below us, softly illuminated by the half moon. Everything I'd ever known was down there and now I was leaving it behind. I shivered. Terrestrials were not evolved for life in space and deep down a primitive part of me was still terrified. But, now I'd got over my initial panic, I realized I would not have missed being here for anything.

According to Amber we were somewhere over the Indian Ocean when the hum of the Cavendish drive slowly faded. It felt like the ship was dropping away from under me and I was grateful for the comforting pressure of the chair straps holding me down. I swallowed, trying to keep my stomach under control. I knew this was not falling in the normal sense but an endless free fall curve mirroring that of the Earth's surface beneath us. I checked my watch. Incredibly, just fifteen minutes ago, we'd been in a back garden in Fulchester. Now I was in orbit like a real astronaut!

All right: *amateur* astronaut.

Cavendish swung his chair round to face us, his eyes sparkling in triumph. 'As planned we are now in an equatorial orbit at a mean height of two hundred kilometres,' he declared.

'With fifty three percent battery power remaining,' Vance added cheerfully, 'exactly as projected in the simulation.'

'All environmental systems operating normally, cabin pressure constant, shadowmask functioning,' Amber said. I saw a tear grow in her eye as she added: 'It's all worked perfectly, Father.'

I managed to take the initiative in the right way this time by beginning to clap loudly. Amber and Vance joined in. Then Amber slipped out of her seat straps far enough to lean across and kiss her father on the cheek.

Cavendish visibly swelled in response to this attention, beaming happily as he acknowledged our praise. He was undeniably a genius but I was beginning to suspect he also had a rather childlike ego that fed on attention. My reporterly instincts might be poorly developed, but they prompted me that now would be the moment to repair some of the damage I'd done to my credibility earlier. As the applause died down I turned my camera on Cavendish.

'Congratulations on this fantastic achievement, Professor. The *Eclipse* has just made conventional rockets obsolete,' I said, flattering him shamelessly. 'Now please can you tell me, for the official record, how long we shall remain in Earth orbit and when we will set out for the moon?'

'We are in a low orbit, a temporary parking orbit, you might say, with a period of a little less than ninety minutes,' Cavendish explained amiably, slipping into lecture mode. 'We shall stay here to recharge our batteries and check the ship is performing as expected in vacuum. If there are any serious problems we can swiftly re-enter the atmosphere and return home. If all is well we can depart for the moon after we next pass into the Earth's shadow, which will be in a little over an hour's time.'

'Then I'll let you get on with your check's, Professor,' I said, winding up rather neatly I thought.

The Prof, Amber and Vance turned back to their control panels and began checking the ship's systems. I filmed them for a few moments and then dictated some notes of my own, trying to capture my first impressions of being in orbit. Then I just sat quietly.

Inside twenty minutes I had run the full range of emotions, from anticipation through to terror and then wild elation, with a generous side helping of deep shame. Now I wanted time to collect my thoughts and acclimatize to a whole new reality.

Hundreds of people had ridden up to space on rockets, of course but none the way we just had. Regular space capsules are cramped! One of the early astronauts said you didn't so much ride inside one as wear it! The space shuttle had only been slightly better.

By contrast the cabin of the *Eclipse* was large and comfortable, so that I was not overwhelmed by the spectacle outside. The cabin lights washed out all but the brightest stars and muted the moonlit panorama of the Earth so it wasn't too hard to ignore them. I could look away from the ports and, seated as we were, almost forget I was in space: except for the fact that I didn't weigh anything.

My stomach felt odd but so far I was keeping it under control. In zero g there was a tendency for my arms to hang limply in the air rather than drop naturally onto the armrests, unless I consciously pushed them down. I was tempted to undo my straps and try some free fall acrobatics, like you see in recordings of pretty much everybody who ever went into space and had the room to play. There were grabrails fitted to the walls, ceiling and chair backs, suggesting crew activity in zero g was planned for. However I resisted. It might look too juvenile and it was also a sure way for me to put my foot through a control panel or something.

I added to my notes for what was absolutely guaranteed to be the most amazing article *The Gazer* would ever run. I fretted over a good title. "Destination Moon" I'd already thought of. "Objective Luna?" A bit clinical. How about an offhand: "My Weekend on the Moon?" We weren't going to be the first on or in the moon so that eliminated HG Wells.

Finally I fell back on Jules Verne, that long dead French writer of *les voyages extraordinaires,* for a working title. In his story of 1865 he fired his imaginary space capsule out of a *columbiad*: a huge iron cannon two hundred and seventy five metres long which was sunk vertically into the ground, propelled by the detonation of over a hundred and eighty tonnes of nitrocellulose! The crew had been two Americans and a Frenchman and the trip had been financed by international subscription. Supposedly Great Britain had rather stuffily decided to have nothing to do with the whole project, which had been pioneered by the Gun Club of Baltimore.

I wondered what old Jules would think of our little venture. Well our launch had been a lot less noisy than his for a start.

* * *

We caught up with dawn about twenty minutes later as we were passing over the Eastern Pacific. Amber alerted me and I had my camera running again to record it.

The thin shell of the atmosphere that had been invisible up until now began to glow. From grey to red to gold the horizon ahead of us brightened, changing sixteen times faster than during a normal sunrise. Then a brilliant sliver of the sun's rim appeared and the window polarizer's dimmed the glory of my first dawn in space.

Putting the drive onto low power, Cavendish turned the *Eclipse* about so that it was nose down with its upper hull square onto the sun, maximising the solar intake. The ship manoeuvred surely and steadily, much to the Professor's evident delight. He'd built himself one hell of a toy. I wondered if he'd ever let anyone else fly her. He set the autopilot to hold that orientation relative to the sun as we continued on over the dayside of Earth. Vance started reading off the battery charge as the levels began to rise.

In bright sunlight we crossed over South America.

The speed of our orbit was the most striking thing. Indistinct features emerged from out of the pale cerulean horizon haze and a minute later were sliding past beneath us, sharp and brilliantly coloured, from sapphire blue waters and emerald forests to dun and orange deserts. If you want to

48

know what we saw in detail there are plenty of pictures of the Earth from orbit taken from Skylab, shuttle and International Space Station crews of far better quality than any I took. We were at a much lower altitude than the ISS, by the way, so there was no danger of an embarrassing encounter with it. What the photos can't show is what it's like seeing it for real through a few centimetres of glass. Sorry for the cliché, but you just had to be there.

Then the land was gone again and we flew out over the Atlantic.

Our low orbit had compressed a day into ninety minutes. Soon the ocean ahead of us dimmed as the shadows of great cloudbanks gathering moisture from the sea lengthened and before we reached Africa the sun had set behind us.

After conferring with Amber and Vance, Cavendish turned to me and I dutifully recorded his announcement. His face shone with pride and eager anticipation.

'The *Eclipse* is functioning perfectly. We can safely proceed on to the moon. I plan to leave orbit in a little under ten minutes. This is not the most economical use of our orbital vector but I don't wish to stay in low orbit longer than absolutely necessary. We'll depart along the line of Earth's shadow and will remain there until we are out of visual observation range before altering course towards the moon.'

'I understand, Professor. And how long will the journey take?'

'Since we'll be travelling in sunlight most of the way and so recharging as we go, I plan to maintain a constant one gravity of acceleration for our comfort and convenience. Allowing additional time for turnover midway and orbital manoeuvring, we should be entering lunar orbit in about four hours.'

Just four hours to the moon? Yes, because constant acceleration adds up at a surprising rate. Assume the Earth-Moon distance is 380,000 kilometres on average and you accelerate at the equivalent of 1 gravity (which gives us our normal weight standing in the surface of the Earth) which is 9.8 meters per second per second, then turnover halfway and decelerate again at the same rate so that you arrive there at more or less the same speed you started out, then it will take around three and a half hours. We could literally go to the Moon and back in a weekend!

'And what will we do when we get to the moon?' I asked.

'We will first enter a two hour equatorial orbit to make a survey and check all is well with the ship. Our journey has been timed to allow us to photograph a portion of the far side under daylight illumination. This will help provide evidence that we have made the journey.'

'And then?'

'Then, if all is well, we shall select from one of a number of possible landing sites: the Sea of Tranquillity, the Fra Mauro highlands, Hadley Rille...'

Those names were familiar. 'You mean the old Apollo Project landing sites.'

'Exactly. Once on the surface, apart from collecting geological samples, we'll bring back parts from the equipment the Apollo crews left there. Unique items! That and this record will furnish indisputable proof we have made the flight. That'll show them!'

I didn't have to ask who the "them" were. I began to understand. Cavendish wanted overwhelming evidence of his brilliance so he could rub a few noses in it. This trip was partly about revenge and the vindication of his reputation. He was getting back at the establishment who had doubted him and the media who had haunted him. And what better way to underline the point than to use a junior reporter from a school newspaper to tell the story to… well, to the world.

Which (Oh My God) would be me!

* * *

Orbital departure was much less eventful than lift off. We accelerated along the cone of Earth's shadow for about a thousand kilometres and then made a long powered turn towards the moon, plunging back out into sunlight. It was just the sort of manoeuvre you see in SF films that no ordinary space rocket ever pulls for real, which emphasised how the *Eclipse* was really living up to its name.

Ahead of us was the brilliant half-moon. At the moment it didn't seem much larger than we saw it from Earth but I knew that would change rapidly. I took a few snaps of it for the record but decided to save my efforts for later when we'd be right on top of it.

Once we were on course Cavendish rotated the ship so that its long axis was positioned at right angles to the direction of thrust, giving us a "down" that ran from ceiling to floor. The ship's orientation didn't matter in airless space, of course, and the drive field seemed to work in any direction. Setting the autopilot, the Professor then unstrapped, got up and stretched his legs. Amber and Vance did the same. The steady acceleration mimicked the force of gravity perfectly so they could move about normally. Apart from the background hum of the drive, if you were not looking out the ports we could have been parked in its hangar back in Fulchester. It was easier on the stomach but still disconcerting. The Apollo craft were only powered for a few minutes and then coasted the rest of the way on their momentum.

'You can get up as well,' Amber told me.

'I know. It's just that constant 1g drive takes a bit of getting used to.'

'Would you want to make long trips in perpetual free fall?' she asked. 'Especially when using the bathroom?'

I knew what she meant. Certain essential biological functions are messy to carry out in weightless conditions. 'Don't get me wrong. I'm not complaining. The ship's fantastic. It just all seems, well, almost too good to be true.'

She looked at me severely. 'You really are a doubting Thomas, aren't you?'

'Yes. Sorry. Guilty as charged.'

'Well I promise you the drive is working fine and the ship's hull is airtight. Is there anything else I can reassure you about?'

'Well, actually... can we have some of Mrs Whittle's Shepherd's Pie now?'

'What? You're thinking of *food* when we're heading for the moon?'

'Yes, since as you've pointed out we're out of free fall and can do things normally now, because it's my stomach that could do with the reassurance. Isn't that also one of the advantages of travelling in a ship as advanced as the *Eclipse*?'

I'd had half an eye on the Professor as I spoke and he picked up my cue nicely.

'You're quite right, young man. I could do with a bite myself and it would be a shame to let it get cold. Then you might try to rest. There'll be no time to sleep or eat in a few hours.'

As I was to learn that was typical of the Professor. He had these flashes of kindly consideration when he seemed quite amiable, but if he was distracted by some big idea he was intent on proving he could be rude, selfish and almost childishly single minded. "Mercurial" was the word for it. Growing up with a father like that probably explained a lot about Amber's temperament.

'I agree with Tom,' Vance added heartily. 'Let's all have something to eat and drink now. I'll get the hot box…'

He went through to the storage compartment and returned a moment later with the picnic box and the smaller carton I'd seen him carry in back in the hangar.

'What's that, Oliver?' Cavendish enquired.

Vance grinned. 'Something else that also needs gravity to enjoy properly. Wait and see…'

He opened up the box and handed out the Shepherd's Pie. Mrs Whittle had thoughtfully packed it in clingfilm-covered plastic bowls with plastic cutlery included. We opened them up and a delicious smell filled the cabin.

With our seats turned to face into the cabin we all tucked in. Amber ate just as enthusiastically as the rest of us, I noticed, although she kept checking her display panel.

'For your information,' she declared, glancing at me, 'two minutes ago we passed through the centre of the inner van Allen belt. The hull radiation detector showed a strong flux of mostly high energy protons. The cabin detector registered no significant change. You might wish to note that for the official record.'

The van Allen radiation belts, named after the scientist who discovered them back in 1958, are a pair of toroidal (that's doughnut-shaped) zones situated one within the other and almost merging, where charged high-speed particles from space get caught up in Earth's magnetic field thousands of kilometres above its surface. They're now included within the general term *magnetosphere* for this strange invisible environment that surrounds the Earth. All the Apollo moonships passed through them. As long as you don't linger the radiation exposure is no worse than a dental x-ray.

'All in good time,' I said with a grin, taking another mouthful.

When we had finished and packed the bowls away, Vance carefully opened his carton and from a nest of foam packing took out four fluted glasses and a small bottle of champagne.

'With your permission, Professor,' he said. 'I thought we should toast the success of the mission. The *Eclipse* has clearly been a personal triumph for you and we must mark the occasion properly with a spot of bubbly. It's not very strong stuff so I think

Tom and Amber can safely have a small glass each without doing them any harm.'

'That's very thoughtful of you, Oliver,' said Cavendish amiably. 'Yes, we must have a toast. Record this, Tom.'

Dutifully I positioned my camera so that it could immortalize the scene. Vance carefully popped the cork and, rather clumsily, poured out four fizzing glasses.

'Another record,' I said for the commentary. 'The first time champagne has ever been poured normally in outer space.'

Everybody laughed.

Cavendish beamed at us as he held up his glass and then suddenly looked uncharacteristically lost. 'Er... is there such a thing as an established in-space toast?'

'Does it matter, Professor?' Vance asked, still holding his glass at the ready.

I said: 'On occasions like this in old SF stories they used to wish each other "Clear Ether" for luck. We can always do with a bit of that.'

'Clear *what*?' Amber said.

'The old "ether" theory,' her father explained. 'The hypothetical transmitting medium of space. Nonsense, of course.'

'So it's a superstitious, antique, fictional and scientifically invalid, toast?' Amber said, mercilessly picking my suggestion to bits.

'I'll still drink to it,' said Vance, raising his glass again.

But Amber, clearly annoyed at my apparent lapse into irrationality, was still making her point. 'Tom, one thing we do know about is the nature of space between Earth and Moon. Now the ship has proven itself in vacuum we don't need "luck" to cross it.'

I don't know if this sounds weird but I was enjoying the attention Amber was paying me even while she was putting me down. She could be so wonderfully pedantic. 'But can you be absolutely certain we know everything?' I persisted, deliberately stoking the fire. 'Space is huge. Less than two dozen people have ever travelled this far before. We've no idea what might be out there.'

She checked her console again. 'Well this bit of it has been very well studied. We're now passing through the outer Van Allen belt right on schedule and, to reassure you, the cabin reading is normal. These are facts so let's have no more talk about…'

Just then the steady hum of the Cavendish drive rose to an angry whine and the instrument displays flickered. The ports lit up with a brilliant bluish flash of light, the drive cut out and the ship suddenly tumbled end over end.

For a frozen instant I saw the expression of disbelief on Amber's face before she was thrown across the cabin while Cavendish seemed to take off from his chair and hit the ceiling. I heard Vance cursing and glass breaking even as I was sent spinning head over heels. Then a corner of one of the grab rails came up and hit me on the side of my head and I fell into blackness…

Chapter 4
We Have a Problem...

The first thing I saw when I opened my eyes was Amber floating over me like a jump-suited angel with an unearthly sparkling halo around her head. For a moment in my confusion I thought I'd gone to my personal version of heaven. Then I realized the drive was off and we were in free fall and the sparkles were floating fluid droplets illuminated by the cabin lights and silvery moonlight flooding in through the forward ports.

I was strapped into my cabin chair once more which had been tilted back in a reclining position. My head was throbbing and I felt seriously sick. Amber was dabbing my temple with a damp cloth that smelt of disinfectant and looked so concerned that it almost made the pain worthwhile.

'Ow... what... happened?' I said unoriginally.

'We don't know yet,' Amber said. She was struggling to stay calm but I could hear the strain in her voice. 'You've only been unconscious a few minutes. 'Father and Oliver are checking the systems now. The drive cut out for some reason, there was a power fluctuation and we went into a spin. Everything else has come back online, but they've got to be sure the drive tubes are undamaged before they reenergize them. If they're out of phase they could tear the ship apart.'

'Tell them to take all the time they like,' I said with feeling.

Amber dabbed my wound with more vigour than an injured man deserved and lowered her head. 'Just don't say you told me so, right?' she hissed.

'Never crossed my mind,' I assured her.

She straightened up and pushed the cloth into my hand. 'Now if you can take care of yourself I've got to clear up. There's still champagne and bits of glass floating about and its going all over the screens.'

'I'll be fine.'

Amber got to work with a towel, clinging to grab rails as she snagged and absorbed the floating drops. Meanwhile Cavendish and Vance were hunched over their controls tapping keys and studying the displays intently. Vance looked very pale. I saw a large damp stain splashed across the rubber floor matting between the chairs where the rest of his spilt champagne had soaked in. Pity. I'd have liked to have drunk that toast. Maybe if we had the ether would have been clear instead of throwing us all over the place.

As my head cleared of this nonsense I could feel the fear rising inside me. A new title for my article loomed in my mind: *Lost in Space!* Before panic could take hold I grabbed the camera, still on its mount, and turned it towards me. I had to have something to do, something to focus on...

'The time is... er... 23.07 GMT and we have a problem,' I said, echoing some famous words from a past moon mission with an unlucky number. 'As we were passing through the outer van Allen belt there was a blue flash from outside, the ship's systems crashed and the drive suddenly cut out...'

Abruptly Cavendish spun round to face me. 'What did you say, young man?'

'Er... there was a blue flash... as we were passing through the Van Allen belt...'

'Ah, of course!' He snatched off his glasses, pulled a cloth from his pocket and began polishing them vigorously. 'The outer belt is comprised mostly of high energy electrons. In some way they must have interacted with the drive field and destabilized it. Ha! Something I did not anticipate.' He slipped his glasses back on and scowled, half talking to himself now. 'Still, if our momentum has carried us clear of the belt we should be able to restart it safely. How far have we travelled?' He consulted the displays. 'Yes, we should be well clear. Amber, take your seat. Oliver, begin the charging sequence.'

They did as they were told. Vance worked his controls. 'Field building...' The familiar hum filled the ship together with a tingle of static discharge. 'Stabilizing... and locked!'

Cavendish cautiously applied power to the drive and I felt the gentle pressure of acceleration push me back into my seat. The remaining floating drops of champagne fell like rain and splattered against the rear cabin bulkhead. We were travelling nose first towards the moon at about half a gravity.

We all breathed an audible sigh of relief. We were no longer helplessly adrift in space.

'Everything seems to be functioning normally,' Cavendish said. 'At least the drive tubes were not damaged. The automatic cutouts protected them. No harm has been done.'

'But how do we get back through the belt?' I asked.

'That's quite elementary. Now we understand the problem we shall change our flight profile to accelerate before reaching the outer belt and then coast through it with the drive inactive. It will only add a few minutes to our overall trip time. Now, I shall recalculate our course and we'll continue on to the moon.'

'Excuse me, Professor,' I said anxiously, 'but we've just had a major breakdown. There might have been damage we don't know about. Shouldn't we go back home and give the ship a thorough overhaul before making another flight?'

The Professor's face darkened ominously while Vance actually looked shocked at the suggestion.

'Young man,' Cavendish said slowly. 'You can have no conception of the personal sacrifices I have made to make this trip a reality. I will not turn back now!'

Apparently I was being too timid for his liking once again.

Amber was looking troubled. Gently she said: 'Father, you know how much I want this trip to succeed as well, but I think Tom might have a point. Perhaps we should go back home now. Treat this as another test flight. We've made a valuable discovery about the Van Allen belt interference with the drive. The moon will still be there next week. Don't you agree, Oliver?'

'No,' Vance said firmly. 'Sorry, Amber, but I'm with your father on this. We know what happened and can avoid it on the return trip. The ship's working fine now. No reason not to go on.

We'll orbit the moon first and run another system check before we attempt a landing.' He glanced at me meaningfully. 'That should satisfy anybody of a nervous disposition.'

I blinked at him in surprise. What had happened to the man who had given me a boost when I'd been down?

'Thank you, Oliver,' Cavendish said. 'That's what we shall do.'

Amber sighed. 'As you wish, Father.'

I pinched my lips and said nothing. The Professor seemed to take this as assent for he got busy recalculating our course. Vance kept his attention on his own console. I could see Amber was unhappy but she said nothing. Perhaps the unfortunate timing of my little game of doubt had shaken her self-confidence. Her brilliance had made life easy for her so far, but now we had taken a step into the unknown, into the territory I'd explored virtually through all those SF stories I'd devoured over the years. In an odd way perhaps I was better prepared for the unexpected than she was... as long as I didn't then screw it up by letting my imagination get the better of me, of course!

'Can I take a look the moon on one of the outside cameras?' I asked Amber. 'I want to get familiar with some place names if we're going to be flying over the top of them in a few hours.'

Amber worked her controls and an image of the half-moon filled one of the screens above her chair. 'Do you want a map as well for reference?' she asked.

'Thanks.'

61

The screen divided and an outline moon map appeared beside the live image with the major seas and craters named. I frowned at it for a moment.

'Which way is the image orientated? I can't match the two up.'

'They should both be lined up normally,' Amber said. The picture flipped. I still could not match it with the map. Amber flipped it back. It was no better. She enlarged the image. We both stared.

The familiar side of the moon that faces Earth shows three main types of features: dark lava plains that were picturesquely and quite inaccurately called "maria" or "seas" by the first astronomers to name them hundreds of years ago, lighter rugged upland mountain chains and ring-like impact craters. I could see plenty of all of these on the camera image but the trouble was they didn't match exactly with anything on the map. In the Moon's north eastern quarter there's an isolated sea called the Mare Crisium that should have shown up clearly, but it appeared now to form one bay of a sea to the south. Then there's a bright crater called Tycho that should have been visible on the terminator line between night and day. It's reckoned to be the result of a relatively asteroid impact which threw pale "rays" of debris halfway across the moon. It's a landmark we can easily see from Earth... but it simply wasn't there.

The moon has no system of continental plates riding a molten mantle to move its landmasses like Earth does, nor has it any weather as we know it. Things don't change there on any scale for thousands or millions of years except for a few new meteor craters. And yet somehow its appearance had been subtly but completely altered.

Amber turned a very pale face towards me. It was unfair that somebody who up until now had always been firmly in charge of her life should get hit twice like this in quick succession. 'That's not our moon, is it?' she said quietly.

'No, I don't think it is,' I agreed.

She took a deep breath and turned to Cavendish. 'Father, you'd better have a look at this…'

It took ten minutes for the Professor and Vance to convince themselves that we were not mistaken. When they finally accepted the truth Vance actually buried his head in his hands while the Prof polished his glasses furiously, his jaw clamped tight. I imagined his brilliant mind was trying frantically to process this impossible new data and make sense of it.

As for me the numbing initial shock had faded and now the fear was starting to bite again. I turned back to the camera and began recording. 'Update: we have another problem. We seem to have lost our moon and found another one in its place…'

'Tom, stop it!' Amber snapped.

But I was in no mood to give way this time. 'No, I'm just doing the job you got me here for! You wanted a record of this great adventure. Well I can't help it if it's not going according to plan but it's a hell of a story and right now playing at being a reporter gives me something to do instead of totally freaking out!'

'Of course he must continue to record everything, Amber,' Cavendish said. 'Whatever has happened we must investigate it fully and detail all the facts.'

Then a terrifying new thought struck me. 'Has anybody looked at the Earth recently?'

After its tumble the *Eclipse* had stabilized with its nose pointing at the moon. Since the drive was cut back in we'd been under low power heading towards it in the same orientation while the Prof recalculated our flight path before resuming our previous 1 g approach configuration with the floor at right angles to the line of thrust. I think he'd let us run on like that because he was impatient to keep going toward his goal. In all this time none of us had taken a look back at the Earth.

The Prof cut the drive and swung the ship around so that blue/green Earthlight filled the forward ports. We all gaped at it. I think Vance gave a little choking moan of despair.

The Earth was where it should be, still huge and filling most of our field of view. Like the moon it was in half phase but with the pattern of illumination reversed. But it was what surrounded the Earth that we stared at.

It was as though the whole planet had been suspended within an ovoid of ghostly blue-green radiance, like a turquoise jewel the skin of which could only just be made out. As we watched slow shimmers passed across it, blurring the stars, like ripples of clear water breaking languidly on a shallow shore. They reminded me a little of pictures I'd seen of the Northern Lights. It was eerily beautiful... and of course utterly wrong.

'It's boundary seems to coincide approximately with the outer Van Allen belt,' the Prof observed. 'What that means I cannot say...'

I dragged my attention from this cocoon of light to the Earth itself. Even though fine details were obscured by the shimmering energy field I could still make out the patterns of oceans and continents under the swirling cloud spirals. They looked normal enough... almost. At this distance we should still have been able to see the lights of big cities on the dark side of the globe. From space night-time Europe is lit up like a Christmas tree, as we'd seen less than an hour ago when we made our first orbit. But the landmasses below us were totally dark.

There was another long silence finally broken by Amber who said solemnly: 'That is not the Earth we left a few hours ago, is it?'

'No,' her father agreed softly.

'But... how?' Vance wondered bleakly.

It was obvious to me but apparently not to them.

'You should read more science fiction,' I said, struggling to keep my voice steady. 'How is easy. When we hit the Van Allen belt and the drive got screwed up it didn't simply tumble the ship, it flipped us right out of our own set of dimensions. The Earth and the Moon haven't changed. We're the ones out of place. That isn't our Earth and this isn't our solar system. We're in an alternate universe: another reality!'

Vance looked dazed while Amber gulped audibly. After another long pause

Cavendish nodded slowly. 'For the time being, unlikely as it seems, that will have to serve as a working hypothesis. The next logical step is to find out everything we can about our new surroundings. Amber, are there any radio transmissions from that world, which I suppose we had better call *Para-Earth*?'

Still looking dazed, Amber turned back to her controls and began searching the radio wavelengths. She turned on a speaker and we heard the mushy hiss of static. Even out here there should have been plenty of signals that could reach us. Earth was the radio equivalent of the audio-visual output of a Saturday night funfair. At least our Earth was, but apparently not this one.

Then we heard it through the background crackle: '...*dah dah deeee dah... dah dah deeee dah...*' repeated over and over. There was something eerily forlorn about the signal, but it had to be artificial. There was intelligent life down there! We were not alone in this new version of the solar system.

But Amber was frowning, her fingers dancing across her keypad as she analysed the signal. 'I've got a rough directional fix... but it's not coming from Para-Earth.'

'Where, then?' her Father demanded.

'It's coming from the Moon!'

Chapter 5
Circumlunar

There are three likely reasons for sending out a signal like the one we could hear. Either it was a navigational beacon, a warning of danger or a distress call. But which category did this fall into?

'Can you get an exact fix on its position?' Cavendish asked Amber. 'If it's on the surface then we should be able to locate it.'

'You don't mean you want to chase after this thing?' I said.

'Of course. We are equipped to make a moon survey and landing and that world, whatever it is, appears similar enough to our moon to be treated as a viable objective. This is a unique opportunity!'

'Or we could try to get back home,' I suggested. 'If we can get back.'

'That will either be perfectly straightforward or virtually impossible,' Cavendish said impatiently. 'If passing through the outer Van Allen belt with the drive on brought us here then it is logical that going back the same way will reverse the process. However the radiation belts are constantly fluctuating both in size and intensity. If the precise energy states at a given moment are crucial to making the transition, then they have already changed and we might never be able to duplicate those circumstances again. That's to say nothing about what influence the energy field we can see occupying its normal position in this reality would have on such an attempt.'

Both Amber and Vance were looking very pale as the Professor calmly announced we might never find our way home. The true realities of our situation were gradually dawning on them.

'Well I'd like to find out one way or another right now, Professor,' I said, 'because I really can't face not knowing. If we can get back home you can always return again later.'

'Think, young man, think!' said Cavendish, jabbing a finger at my forehead. 'Making the attempt to return through the belt now or in a few hours' time will make no difference to our chance of success, whereas we don't know how long the source of that signal will remain there. Furthermore that transmission indicates advanced technology, while there's no sign of it on this Para-Earth below us. We may find knowledge on the moon that will allow us to make a more informed decision as to our next course of action.'

'The Professor's got a point, Tom,' Vance said slowly. He still looked pale but there was fresh determination in his words. 'I know this all seems pretty scary, but we've nothing to lose by checking it out. I mean we're all set up to go to the Moon anyway. I guess there won't be any Apollo relics to find but there might be something even bigger. If we can pinpoint the source of that transmission and it looks safe we'll touch down and take a look. If not we can be back here inside twelve hours and be no worse off.'

I asked a question I really should have thought about much earlier. 'How long can the *Eclipse* stay in space? What's our endurance?'

Amber answered. 'As long as we can recharge our batteries the air plant will run for about three weeks before it needs a major servicing. We can get recycled water from its dehumidifier as well to extend our fresh supply. Our emergency food rations should last for about as long.'

That information made me feel a little better. We were not going to run out of anything vital in the next few hours. 'Do you want to try to find the source of this signal?' I asked Amber.

I could see she was torn both ways. 'I want to know if we can get back home or not as well. But it also makes sense to find out more about this signal. Maybe it's from a spacecraft or a moonbase. If there are people there... well, beings, anyway, they might be able to help us.'

"Beings" was a nice way of saying aliens. If we'd dropped out of our own slice of space and time who knew what we'd find. But if she was willing to face that big unknown I could hardly do anything less.

I shrugged. 'Right. Let's go for it.'

In ten minutes we were on course for the moon once more, travelling at a little over one g to make up for lost time and match up with the original flight profile by turnover.

* * *

I was too excited to rest. Had everything gone as planned I suppose I might have had the cool to get a couple of hours sleep on the way to our familiar old moon, but now there was no chance of that. Even if I'd wanted to there was too much tension in the cabin.

Cavendish and Vance were keeping a far closer watch on their displays than they had intended when the journey had almost seemed routine. Meanwhile Cavendish had assigned Amber the task of plotting a new moon map to overlay the original charts they had on file in the navigation computer, so he had some reference points to relate to when planning our orbit and possible landing sites. She also kept checking the beacon signal. It remained steady. She was getting a closer fix on its location, which seemed so far to be in the middle of the visible disc.

While they all worked I recorded an updated report. Even as I spoke I could hear phrases from old SF stories begging to be given a fresh airing.

'It's been an hour since we found ourselves in these strange new circumstances. How we got here we can only guess at for now. There's something on the moon sending out a signal and we're going to take a look at it if we can. It may help explain what's going on. And then of course we've got to see to the problem of getting back home…'

* * *

Midway turnover was accomplished smoothly. By then we were making better than sixty kilometres per second. Unless we wanted to arrive at the moon with a velocity far too high to make an orbit it was necessary to start killing some of that speed now. There was a few seconds of weightlessness while the Professor flipped the ship through a hundred and eighty degrees and then the drive was cut back in, restoring a sense of "down" once more. Now we were decelerating with the moon almost below our feet, visible through the lower ports and on the monitor screens.

You could see the moon growing larger almost by the minute: a world of jumbled craters, craggy mountains and dark dead seas that had never known a drop of water. At least that was what our moon had been like. This one might have hidden secrets.

But even as I stared the halfway familiar face of it was slipping away towards the east, along with a shrinking crescent of sunlit surface as our course took us swinging around its western limb and entry into the equatorial orbit Professor Cavendish had originally planned.

'Father, I'm losing the beacon signal,' Amber said.

'Has it stopped sending?' Cavendish asked.

'No, it's fading gradually, as though it's being blocked. I think it's just that the body of the moon is getting in the way.'

'Have you a fix on it?'

'Somewhere very close to the centre of the nearside… it's gone now.'

I had half imagined the Prof would make a sudden course change and race off after it, but it seemed he did occasionally know when to be cautious. 'We'll find it again after we make our initial survey orbit.'

The *Eclipse* began manoeuvring, making small course corrections as we headed for an imaginary orbital insertion "window" above the dark limb of the moon. We entered the cone of the moon's shadow and sunlight flashed off the last mountain peaks. Amber cut in night vision enhancement on the monitor screens, making the lunar surface seem to glow an eerie blue-green, lit now only by starlight and reflected light from the Earth's sunlit hemisphere, which was many times brighter than full moonlight. We were getting very low, far lower than we could have made a stable orbit about the Earth, but then here there was no atmosphere to worry about.

The Earth with its surrounding jewel-like energy field dropped behind the limb of the moon and I felt a shiver. Even though it was not our world its disappearance emphasised how far we were from home.

Apparently this version of the moon was close enough to our own in mass and diameter for the orbital calculations to work out. We slid smoothly into the planned orbit at a hundred and twenty-five kilometres altitude travelling at fifty eight hundred kilometres an hour, which would take us right around the moon in about two hours. The Professor cut the drive and we were in weightlessness once again.

From this height we could see across some forty degrees of the moon surface which meant a swathe of land a bit over twelve hundred kilometres wide. Because we did not need to travel so fast to maintain our orbit due to the moon's lesser gravity, we made a stately progress with time to take in the sights. An object appearing on the horizon ahead of us took a little under seven minutes to pass directly below.

Peering at the starlit landscape on the screens and out of the ports it seemed to me that it was like our moon only more so.

The far side of our moon has no significant seas and is mostly craters and highland topography. This appeared much the same, except that the mountain peaks seemed even sharper and the craters deeper and more dramatic. It had a brooding desolate grandeur about it. Or of course it could just have been my imagination stimulated by the dim light and our isolation.

After twenty minutes of this the sun rose without warning over the moon's horizon and we were travelling back into daylight. Gradually the jumble of craters and rugged mountain chains gave way to the first of the lunar seas and we crossed the boundary line from the far side of the Moon to the nearside. Once again we saw the blue-white hemisphere of the Para-Earth bathed in its ghostly halo rising over the limb of the moon. Even if it was not our home world it was an unforgettable sight and very welcome.

'What's that?' Amber said, pointing to the screen showing the moonscape directly below us. We all looked. At first glance seem to be just another crater amongst hundreds. It was hard to see much detail as the sun was shining down on it almost from the zenith, so there were few shadows to help delineate its contours. But then I realized there was something strange about it. It must have been about 10 kilometres in diameter with a narrow distinct ring wall which seemed to have a series of regular spaced mounds along its circumference. Also the crater floor, apart from a few pale blemishes, was unusually smooth. In the very centre was a symmetrical peak surrounded by a slim black sharp ring, like a second inner crater. Yet how could it be that dark when there were almost no shadows around it? The main crater was also surrounded by dozens of what looked like bright rough-edged craterlets, cutting into the surrounding smaller craters, hummocks and ridges, at all angles, which suggested fresh meteor impacts.

'That doesn't look normal,' Vance observed uneasily.

I turned the camera onto the screen and said for the record: 'We've just passed over a crater that looks as though it might have some artificial structures in it. We don't know what to make of them just yet.'

Vance chewed his lip while Cavendish frowned but made no comment.

My mind inevitably made an SF connection. Would HG Wells' Selenites build structures like that? We had taken a leap into the unknown. Anything was possible.

The strange crater slowly fell away behind us as we continued on our orbit back over the nearside of the moon. The sun swung round behind us and gradually the shadows cast across the dead lava seas by the craters and promontories below lengthened, stretching away ahead of us. It was a magnificent panorama which we none of us were able to appreciate fully knowing that we did not belong here.

'I'm starting to pick up the beacon signal again,' Amber announced.

'What's its bearing?' her father asked.

'Almost directly ahead of us. It should be on the horizon now…'

We all stared out of the ports or at the screens. A dark sea was rolling past beneath us. On our moon it would have been the southern shores of the Sea of Tranquillity where the first moon landing was made back in 1969. Then came several ranges of hills and chains of craters. This time I was sure they were sharper and more rugged than the corresponding formations back on our moon. In our reality lunar peaks tended to be rounded and softened whereas these seemed to have teeth and cast jagged shadows. Beyond them the landscape smoothed out again, curving away into darkness. It was almost featureless except for the walls of a lone crater. It was just this side of the terminator and could not long have been in sunlight.

'That's it,' Amber said. 'That's where the signal is coming from!'

I tried to place it on the image we'd taken of this new moon before we passed around to the far side. Exactly in the middle, it seemed to be: pretty well zero latitude, zero longitude. Something clicked in my mind.

'That odd crater we saw over the eastern limb, would that have been about on the ninety degree meridian?' I asked Amber.

'Yes, about that I should think. Why?'

'Because I think this is another one of the same set.'

'You mean a pair of structures spaced ninety degrees apart on the equator?'

'Maybe more than a pair. There might have been a couple we missed on the dark side.'

'A series of artificial craters going right round the equator of the whole moon? But what would they be for?'

'No idea... I suppose that's what we're going to find out.'

Amber looked pale. I think she was inherently braver than I was but she was used to anticipating problems. A potentially inhabited moon had not been on the schedule. Well, none of this had been...

Now we could see the regularly spaced mounds about the beacon crater rim and the slender summit of its oddly symmetrical central peak rising over its ramparts. It was certainly not natural. There also seemed to be more of the small bright impact scars around it, like we had seen about the crater on the eastern limb. I had no idea what that signified.

'Strap in and prepare for deceleration,' Cavendish said decisively. 'We're going down. I shall follow our planned lunar descent flight profile. Tom, you will record everything that happens. This is an historic occasion...'

We may have been lost in another universe, but Cavendish was still determined that the touchdown of his brainchild on another world would be properly documented for posterity.

The pressure built up as the Professor gradually killed our forward velocity and we began to descend, dropping out of orbit and down towards the moon's surface. It was a smooth ride. The Prof was a good pilot and the *Eclipse's* wonder drive could deliver precise increments of power as he needed them. Vance began calling out the battery charge level while Amber relayed our height above the moon's surface. Below ten kilometres she began calling it out in metres.

At two thousand metres Cavendish swung the ship round into a circular course that skirted the outer ramparts of the crater at a respectful distance. Now for the first time we could observe it properly.

In places the crater walls, which must have been about three hundred metres high, were cracked and pockmarked and had slumped down but there was no doubt it had been artificially formed, though whether it was a natural crater that had been modified or it had all been built from the ground up was impossible to say. The eight mounds growing out of the crest of the crater wall resolved themselves into structures like beehive domes, taller than they were wide, with external bands of vertical and horizontal ribs.

'They look a little like the turrets in the outer wall of an old castle or walled city,' Amber said.

'With big guns,' I pointed out.

We could now see there were metallic rod-like objects mounted on blisters in the dome sides. It was hard to judge their exact size but they must they must be big to be visible at this distance.

'You can't be sure they're guns,' Amber challenged me.

'You were the one who mentioned castles,' I reminded her. 'They sort of go together. And if these are defensive turrets then the big tower in the middle is like a mediaeval keep.'

'Actually... I think I can see devices of the same kind pointing out through its sides as well,' Vance said.

'Perhaps this whole place is some kind of huge fortress,' I suggested. 'And those little craters and scars all around it are battle damage. Hits from weapons that didn't reach their target...'

The level of tension inside the *Eclipse*, already high, raised another notch or two. Amber glared at me as though resenting my suggestion, but it wasn't my fault. I only called as I saw it.

'Amber, tune the air traffic radio to the frequency of the beacon,' Cavendish said, pulling on an earphone and mic headset which for obvious reasons had so far hung unused from a clip on the side of his chair. She did so. Cavendish said in clear steady tones: 'This is Professor James Cavendish commanding the Earth spaceship *Eclipse*. We are a peaceful exploration vessel. I request approach and landing instructions for your base...'

But there was no change to the steady beep of the beacon.

Of course if he had got a reply then it would have been wildly unlikely that it would have been in any recognisable language, but he had formally alerted any occupants of the fortress, if that was what it was, to our presence. Perhaps he hoped his tone would at least convey the sense that we were friendly and open.

'It must be operating automatically,' Amber said. 'I don't think anybody's hearing you, Father.'

'Very well,' Cavendish said determinedly. 'I'm going to take us into the crater and set down near the central keep, or whatever it might be.'

I eyed the huge gun barrels, if that was what they were, jutting out from the turrets. 'Can you please fly us in an unthreatening way, Professor?' I asked.

With a grim smile on his face Cavendish turned the *Eclipse* and sent it gliding over the rampart walls and into the crater.

The still low sun threw long dark shadows from its outer walls far across the crater floor, while the eerie Earthlight glow from directly above filled them with faint blue tinged highlights. The floor must have been artificially levelled and was even smoother than one of the lunar seas. It was virtually featureless, apart from minor blast scars and rock fragments, with the keep at its centre. Then I saw there was one other object on the plain almost between it and us that spoiled the sterile symmetry: an indistinct almost formless mass that glittered metallically.

'What's that?' Amber said.

The Professor altered course slightly, losing altitude, and we headed towards it.

The thing lay almost exactly halfway between the crater walls and the central keep. As we came up to it the Professor flew the *Eclipse* in a slow circle about it so we could take in the details while I swung the camera round so I could film it directly through the viewports.

It was the remains of some vessel, presumably a spacecraft. It was hard to tell exactly what its original form had been, except that it must have been as large as a medium sized ocean liner. Now it lay crumpled and twisted and apparently half melted. We could see where streams of green and coppery metal had flowed out from its gashed sides onto the crater floor and solidified in great pools. It didn't look like the kind of crash anybody would walk away from.

'We've found what looks like the remains of an alien spacecraft,' I said for the record. 'It must have been brought down by the fortress's weapons. But who, or what, crewed it? And why were they attacking the fort?'

Nobody had anything to add to my observations so we flew on towards central keep, if you could call it that, with the sun throwing the distorted disk of our shadow far ahead of us across the crater floor. Nothing stirred. If anybody in there was aware of our presence there weren't showing it.

Cavendish flew us in another wide slow circuit about the keep. It was a massive structure that rose sheer from the depths of what appeared to be a circular dry moat before at ground level its walls began to curve inwards. The outer lip of the moat was chamfered and it was surrounded by a skirting of material that differed from the rest of the dusty crater floor, looking more like fused bare rock or dull grey metal plating. Because of the shadows cast by the low sun we could not tell how deep the moat was. The softly shimmering turquoise Earthlight did not seem to penetrate to its bottom. The keep was another beehive dome but even larger than the wall turrets. The image crossed my mind of it as a huge egg resting point upward with the moat its oversized cup. It had eight equidistantly spaced massive vertical ribs running down its sides. These were cut across by four courses of horizontal ribbing between ground level and its summit. The topmost surrounding the apex of the dome and supported a cluster of eight tapering masts or pinnacles, rather like a vast coronet, linked by a pair of tubular rings. The lower ribbing bands divide up the segments of the dome visible above ground between the vertical ribs into three panels of decreasing size in each tapering segment. Within these panels were embedded spherical blister turrets carrying huge barrels wound with massive coils and rings and supported by buttress-like pylons.

What they fired I have no idea but I could bet it was nothing as simple as bullets or shells.

'This thing is huge,' I said, keeping up my commentary. 'It isn't easy to judge dimensions in this light and without atmosphere to give a sense of depth but I guess from the crater floor level up it's as tall as the London Shard and wide enough to block the Thames. And there's still more of it going down into the bottom of the moat. From its actual base up it's probably taller than any building on our Earth.'

Halfway round this symmetry was broken. Below the blister of one of the lowest guns a small cowl-like canopy jutted out over the middle of the horizontal panel rib that lay at ground level. Under it could be just be seen a small ledge. From this a slender spidery bridge extended out across the moat to where what looked like a freestanding rectangular arch stood on its outer rim.

'We may have found the front door,' I said.

There were no other visible windows or ports of any sort in the keep. But then any openings would have been weak points and this thing was clearly built to withstand almost any external force. Even so its surface was heavily scarred and pitted and several of the gun muzzle arrays were clearly damaged.

'There must have been an incredible battle here once,' I said. 'But just when there's no way of telling.'

Inspired by my suggestion, Cavendish asked Amber: 'What's the radiation reading in the crater?'

'Normal background level, Father,' she reported. 'I don't detect any fallout. Maybe it's decayed.'

'I don't think they ever used anything as crude as our atomic bombs,' I said.

'What did they use, then?' Amber challenged me. I think this incredible scene right out of an SF fantasy was offending her sense of how a well-ordered universe should run.

'No idea. Maybe we'll find out if we get inside the fort.'

The *Eclipse* completed its circuit and came to a stop, hovering a hundred metres above the ground close to the outer edge of the apron surrounding the moat and opposite the bridge archway.

'I think we've seen all we can from up here,' Cavendish said. 'I now propose we land and continue our exploration on foot.'

There was nothing else to say really. If we wanted to learn more there was no choice. We all nodded in agreement.

With a whine and clunk the landing legs were extended and locked into place. The *Eclipse* descended smoothly. There came the slightest of shudders and then a soft grating sound. Cavendish cut the drive and the background hum of the engines faded away.

'It is 05.06 GMT Saturday morning and the *Eclipse* has just landed on the moon,' I said for the

82

sake of the recording and with as much solemnity as I could muster. I wished I had a breathless ground crew and half a world hanging on my words and then I could have borrowed from the first moon landing and said: 'Earth, this is Fortress Base here. The *Eclipse* has landed...'

But the truth was we were lost and alone and might never get home to tell anybody what we had just done.

Chapter 6
The Bridge

'Perhaps one of us should stay with the *Eclipse*, in case something unexpected happens, Professor,' Oliver suggested as we unbuckled our seat straps and stood up cautiously in the low lunar gravity.

'No, I don't think we should separate the party,' Cavendish said. 'We must all stay together until we understand exactly what the situation here is. This is not our moon, after all.'

'As you wish, Professor,' Oliver conceded.

I had seen Amber opening her mouth ready to protest, clearly thinking Oliver was going to suggest that she stayed on board. This of course erased any ignoble impulse I might, briefly, have felt to volunteer for the task. Anyway I was done with letting my imagination get the better of me, wasn't I?

We all took turns using the toilet to remove the messy necessity of having to pee in a spacesuit, and then we took the suits and life support packs out of the locker and put them on in the cabin. I was grateful for the room that gave us because as I discovered there is a lot of wriggling about involved getting into a space suit, even though Cavendish's suits were certainly a lot less cumbersome than the things the Apollo astronauts had worn on the moon. Apart from there being new materials available since then he had applied all of his considerable genius to making them as unobtrusive and simple to wear as was possible: in other words simple enough for somebody like me to use without prior training.

This is quite a challenge when you consider they had to maintain our fragile human bodies at the correct pressure and temperature while warding off such unfriendly dangers as micro meteorites travelling faster than bullets and cosmic radiation.

We took off out jumpsuits and sneakers leaving us in our close fitting base layers which at last made sense. They would form a close-fitting comfort underlayer to the moon suits. Amber helped me put mine on, explaining its functions as she went. She made me feel like a child who needed help with dressing. Maybe she thought I was too dumb to work it for myself, but oddly I did not mind her neat sure hands giving my suit a tug here and there.

'It has an outer non-pressurized jointed hard shell hung on a mesh underlayer which serves as passive thermal control, radiation, impact and micrometeorite protection,' she said. 'It has side pockets for samples and additional tools. The inner layer is a thinner, actively thermal-controlled pressure suit, using solid-state micro thermocouples for heating and cooling through the Peltier effect.'

I nodded sagely as though I understood all this. All I knew was that it felt spongy and rather lose against my thin form-fitting underwear. 'It doesn't seem like much of a fit,' I said.

'It will when we get it powered up,' she assured me.

She helped me strap on and connect up my life support pack which held my oxygen, radio and temperature control systems. Its functions were monitored on a flip up display panel mounted on the chest of my suit.

'All the parameters are monitored and adjusted automatically,' Amber explained. 'You shouldn't need to do anything.'

'How much air does it hold?' I asked anxiously, thinking of all the SF stories I'd read about space explorers running short of oxygen

'It's got a rebreather unit so it works as long as you've got power for it. Say about a day. Don't worry, we don't plan on being outside that long.'

'You mean you didn't plan on an EVA that long when this was simply a trip to our own friendly moon,' I pointed out.

Amber pinched her lips. 'No,' she admitted.

She activated the backpack and it seemed as though the suit came to life about me. Gently but firmly the inner layer was tightening about my body.

'Wow... that's a bit weird,' I said.

'You'll get used to it,' Amber said briskly. 'It's a derivative of the technique that activates the shadowmask elements. It has integral sensors that adjust it dynamically to your movements and maintains your body at full cabin pressure so there's no need to decompress.'

The pressure was oddly comforting yet as I took a few steps and waggled my arms about the joints remained flexible, or at least they adjusted as I bent them to give that illusion. It was very nearly the ideal one-size fits all spacesuit.

'The suit also generates a static charge to repel the dust,' Amber added. 'There's a precipitation unit built into the outer hatch floor grating as well to keep it out of the airlock.'

On a microscopic scale moon dust is jagged and abrasive and is also electro- statically charged by the solar wind. This all makes it act as though its "sticky". The Apollo astronauts came back from their EVA's with their suits covered in it. Exposed to oxygen and moisture it then briefly becomes quite chemically reactive, meaning it's not the kind of stuff you wanted to get in your lungs.

A padded flight cap went over my head. It carried integral earphones and a mic which linked with the backpack transmitter. Finally a transparent polycarbonate goldfish bowl style helmet was locked into the neckring of my suit. It was encased in an external opaque hard shell outer cap, rather like a crash helmet, which carried a gold anodized glare visor for regular conditions plus an extra dark sun visor that could flip down over the top of this. It also had forward facing LED flashlights clamped to its sides. As mission reporter I also carried the camera with me now encased in its protective cover.

When we were all helmeted we tested our radios. The circuit would remain open and four-way all the time we were outside. Then we crowded into the airlock and closed up the inner door. Unless it was properly sealed the outer door would not open.

The Prof worked the controls set in the lock compartment that pumped out the remaining air. Through the porthole set in the outer airlock door I saw the unpressurized rear hatchback open up and the ramp folding down. As the pressure dropped I felt the suit automatically compensating, remaining flexible about its joints. All external sound faded away, leaving me shut in with my own breathing, the creaks of the external suit joints and the slight hiss and crackle of the radio channel.

'Comfortable?' Amber asked over the radio.

'Fine,' I lied, trying to keep my breathing under control. I'm just going to step out in a hard vacuum in a new type of spacesuit but I'm not going to die, I told myself.

When the air was exhausted Cavendish opened the outer door and stepped through it out onto the ramp. For a moment he stood there, surveying the stark scene outside. This was what he'd dreamed about for so long, I thought. It was just a pity his triumph had become so complicated. Then he strode on down the ramp, moving with light, bouncing steps. We followed after him.

I was the last to step off the ramp onto the floor of the crater. Moon dust and grit crunched under my feet. There were sparkles and glitters in it. The desiccated soil was thick with jagged shards, splinters and shiny blobs of melted and re-solidified metal. For a moment I could not work out what they were and then I realized they were battle debris. At some time they must have rained down out of a war-torn sky. The low sun cast my elongated shadow across the ground, highlighting every pit and hollow in the dust. Some of those blurred marks might be footprints of the people who had once manned the fortress. Now I was making my own footprints beside them.

The elation I should have felt was confused by the weird circumstances. Stepping out onto an alien world and into this battle-scarred fortress at the same time was almost too much to take in. If this had been our own moon as planned I would have felt a thrill knowing I had just joined an elite comprising only a dozen other people. But this place was no virgin satellite but an old battle ground, tramped across by who knew how many beings before me. I was following on after too many other footsteps to feel like a pioneer. We had become archaeologists, trying to unravel the secrets of some abandoned alien war zone.

Before my imagination could go into overdrive I swung the camera around in a long pan to take in the bleak crater floor, the distant ramparts of its rim, the tangled mass of the wrecked ship out across the plain, the great pit of the moat and the looming bulk of the central fort building that towered over us.

The others had walked out onto the hardened apron surrounding the outer rim of the moat. I followed them. Nobody was saying much. I think we were all too awed by our surroundings, even the Professor.

This apron was perhaps twenty metres wide and was, I now saw, made of slabs of fused rock which had a slight metallic lustre. It was only lightly scattered with blast debris.

The moat itself was a perfect ring about a hundred metres wide and over five hundred in diameter. The outer rim was chamfered back for perhaps ten metres at an angle of forty-five degrees, sloping down to join its vertical outer wall. This was presumably to give no shelter to any ground attackers. There also seemed to be a series of vertical slots groped in pairs running down the sheer curve of its outer wall. The sides of the central tower opposite us ran down into the moat but with the sun low I could not make out any details of its depths, indistinctly lit by the bluish Earthlight from overhead. It was all hugely impressive but also odd.

'A moat seems kind of old fashioned when you're fighting spacecraft,' I said.

'Perhaps not,' the Professor replied. 'If there were heavy weapon impacts close by it would help isolate the main structure from ground shock waves.'

We moved along its rim, keeping well back from the lip of the moat, until we came to the arch at the end of the slender bridge that spanned it.

The arch was made of heavy rectangular slabs of grey metal with a brushed satiny finish, abraded and pockmarked by the impact of micro-meteorites. How many years had it been standing here, I wondered? It was about three metres deep and high and wide enough for an elephant to pass through. The outward faces of the uprights had symbols etched into them. Each showed what appeared to be a standing stylized human figure within an hourglass shape formed by two interlocked S-curved lines with arrowhead, or maybe snake heads, on each end. Jutting out sideways from the waist of the hourglass on either side of the figure were two large arrowheads pointing in opposite directions. Below these etchings were deep recesses set at about head height and backed by what looked like black glass panels.

But is seemed that somebody was not pleased with the symbols because they had used some hard edged tool to scratch several deep score marks across each of them.

I filmed the arch and the defaced symbols. We had no idea what they meant but it was our first clue that the fortress builders might superficially resemble us. I think we were all relieved.

'Humanoid in general outline at least,' Cavendish said.

Set in the ground between the piers of the arch was a metal grille, while the inner faces of the piers and the underside of the lintel were etched with a complex array of swirling grooves that seemed to shimmer like a piece of kinetic artwork. After a minute they began to give me a headache. What their function was I had no idea. Maybe it was a piece of alien art.

We stepped through the arch and examined the bridge beyond which stretched across the dark chasm of the moat to the great battle-scarred gun tower. It was not elegant but then I don't think it had ever been intended to be. Its sheer bulk alone was intimidating and awe inspiring and this close to it we had to tip our shoulders back to see its summit properly. It appeared to be a massive multiple gun turret ringed by firepower, designed purely for one purpose: dealing out destruction. It had probably brought down that huge spacecraft out on the plain, by comparison with which the *Eclipse* was a mere rowing boat.

'It is clearly some form of military installation,' the Professor said. 'If it was occupied then continuous watches would be maintained as a matter of elementary security and they could not have failed to see us land. As we have not been challenged and nobody is coming out to greet us, we can infer that it is unoccupied. Therefore we must take the initiative and see if we can find a way in...'

And the bridge that would allow us to try the handle of the front door, if there was one, lay before us, both unnerving and inviting.

It was a single long slab of grey metal less than a metre wide with no handrail, sloping upward by a few degrees to where its far end rested on a ledge built onto the upper edge of the ground level rib. To our terrestrial eyes it appeared ridiculously slender, but on the moon no doubt it was strong enough to take its weight and our own. And yet we all hesitated because it looked so narrow and flimsy!

'Sorry, Professor, but I get bad vertigo in situations like this,' Oliver admitted sheepishly. 'Didn't want to say so before. I'm not sure if I can cross that. Maybe it would be better if I just waited out here.'

Was it wrong of me to feel a flush of schadenfreude at this admission? Whether Oliver really had a problem with heights, thought the bridge would fail or was simply afraid of what we might find at the other end did not matter. Only a few hours ago he had been the one who had implied I had a nervous disposition. The desire to pay him back a little was irresistible.

'I'm sure it's safe, Oliver,' I said loudly, stepping onto the bridge. 'There's nothing to be frightened of...'

I just meant to stamp on the end of the bridge to test it, but as it seemed firm I took another step, bragging: 'You see. Nothing to it...'

And then another. Then before I knew what I was doing I was out beyond the chamfer of the moat rim with a terrible sheer-sided black canyon underneath me and it was too late to turn around because I knew I would either fall or not have the courage to step out on it again.

At least Oliver had been brave enough to admit his fear.

So I simply had to keep going: striding on as though I was out for a walk in a park, trying not to bounce too high with each step and flip myself off, with my eyes fixed on the far side and not looking down; ignoring the terrible sucking attraction of the void under me that had nothing to do with gravity and all to do with my own fear. Every second I expected it to start swaying. And even on the moon a fall from this height would be fatal.

Over the radio I heard Amber and the Professor being ridiculously solicitous to Oliver. 'You see, Tom's fine. It's perfectly safe. We'll steady you... come on.'

And so they helped him across in my lying, boastful footsteps.

A massive gun barrel jutted out like a crazily leaning cathedral spire above me. Beneath it was the outthrust hood-like canopy that covered the end of the bridge, which I now saw was a half shell a metre thick. Under this was the level sill or ledge that had been built up from the sloping upper side of the horizontal structural rib that encircled the tower at ground level. Only now did I fully realize the massive size of the ribs. They were at least ten metres deep and perhaps twice that wide. Were they purely there for structural reasons or did they also act as blast deflectors, helping protect the weapons mounted around them from flying debris?

Whatever their function they were reassuringly solid underfoot and I stepped off the end of the bridge onto the sill this one supported with my teeth clenched. The bridge had remained absolutely rigid during my crossing but my heart was thudding and I was in a cold sweat.

The sill was as deep as the rib and maybe five metres wide, with thick walls at each side rising up into the canopy. Half way in from the lip of the sill another wall ran across it between the side walls, but with gaps between its ends and them that were large enough for a person to pass around. It must have been built like that to provide protection from blast debris or flash radiation. Presumably the entrance proper was on the other side.

I took a deep breath, turned and waved at the others who were halfway across the bridge by now. 'Solid as a rock,' I said. 'No trouble at all.' But I did not have the heart to taunt Oliver any further. Instead as he got closer I held out my hand to help him onto the ledge.

'Thanks,' he said, rather bitterly I thought.

We cautiously made our way round the ends of the blast wall, switching on our helmet lights as we lost the illumination given by the sunlight reflected off the crater floor. Behind the wall was a massive recessed metal sliding door. Set in it was a plate bearing a deep slot in the shape of a hand with five spread fingers. It was an obvious invitation.

Tentatively the Professor pushed his hand into the cutaway. It went in almost elbow deep. 'I can feel a lever...' he reported. 'I'm going to turn it...'

The lever released the plate which swung open to reveal a recessed polished spoked wheel like the wheel of a ship. Vance and Professor began to a turn it and the door slowly rolled aside into a slot in the wall. Behind it was a slab that filled the mouth of whatever passage might lay beyond. Weirdly it had a hole in it like a life-sized gingerbread man: a human figure with its arms lifted away from its body and feet spread. The slab was a metre deep, but the man-shaped hole cut through it would just be large enough for us to shuffle through in our space suits.

'Is this some crude way of filtering out any visitors unless they're human shaped?' Amber wondered.

'That is one possibility,' her father agreed. 'Or it's a warning that only humanoid shaped beings are welcome.'

'So what shape are the things they're trying to keep out?' I asked.

Nobody answered.

One by one we squeezed through the strange aperture to find ourselves in a chamber with a massive hinged door like that of a bank vault in front of us. It was dimly lit by cool pale green glowing strips on the walls, which were completely washed out by the glare of our helmet lights. The Professor examined one of the strips. 'Possibly some kind of radioactive phosphor-powered emergency lighting system,' he speculated.

Whatever energised them they were they were feeble and ghostly. How long had they been illuminating this place, fading a little each year as their atoms decayed?

There were fittings that might have been power links to the bolts that secured the door but it also had a manual operating wheel in plain sight. We turned this, withdrawing the bolts, and swung the great door inwards. I expected to hear a creaking of hinges but of course there was none in the vacuum. Beyond lay a small chamber and a second apparently identical door.

'If all this is contained within the outer wall of the tower then it must be incredibly thick,' Amber observed.

'Maybe because these people took whatever war they were fighting incredibly seriously,' I suggested.

The Professor had been examining the rim of the huge door. 'From the seals on the inside and the direction it operates, I think this is part of an airlock,' he said. 'We might find pressure further within the structure.'

The inner door would not open until the outer door had been swung shut and locked once more, which was a sensible safety feature. The inner door swung open to reveal yet a third door. They were not taking chances with the integrity of their base.

'If this is an airlock, Professor, shouldn't we be feeling air filling it by now?' I asked.

'The pumps may not be working,' Amber pointed out.

'In which case we won't be able to open up the final door against the internal pressure,' I said. 'Unless there's some manual valve to equalize it.'

'Suddenly you're an expert in the mechanics of airlocks?' Amber said.

'You pick these things up when you read enough SF.'

She sniffed. I don't think she thought that counted.

'It's possible all the air in the fortress has bled away,' the Professor said.

How long would that take, I wondered? How dead was this place?

There was no manual valve to be seen but the third door opened easily enough and we stepped into a large chamber, dimly illuminated by more of the glowing green strips. I was tensed against the possibility of something alien leaping out at us, but there was no sign of life.

We must be inside the fort interior by now but there was still no trace of air about us. The chamber was at the head of a series of ramps with ribbed treads that descended downwards as they wound about a cluster of half a dozen transparent vertical tubes over a metre across, which continued up into the roof. They had panels set in their fronts large enough for a person to step through into metal mesh capsules, but they were all sealed tight.

'Some kind of elevator system,' Cavendish speculated. 'But I presume there is no power to operate it…'

There were a number of small black glass panels mounted beside the elevator tubes where you might have expected to see call buttons. Tentatively the Professor pressed them but nothing happened.

Amber said: 'Look at this.'

There was a large panel mounted on the wall bearing several lines of bold symbols that had to be a written text. It did not resemble any kind of script I'd ever seen before.

'An alien language,' Amber said with wonder in her voice.

I took a still image of it with the camera. Maybe we could puzzle it out later.

There were three other smaller doors leading off from the chamber but they were all locked and had no visible means of opening them manually. This left us with only one way to go.

'We'll use the ramps,' the Professor declared.

And so we headed downward into the shadowy unknown depths of the fortress.

Chapter 7
Nerve Centre

At each sub level there were doors opening off the landings but they were all locked, so there was no choice but to continue on down the ramps.

'Does anybody get the feeling we're being directed this way?' I said.

'I think that's obvious,' the Professor said.

So we carried on. There were bold symbols on the walls by the head of each new ramp that changed on succeeding levels.

'They must be floor numbers,' Amber said. 'Maybe we can learn a something about how they counted from them.'

I estimated each level was a good five metres deep. In our heavy suits and life support packs we'd soon have got tired if it was not for the low gravity. As it was my calves were beginning to protest from the odd strain being put on them by the sloping ramps when we finally reached the tenth level, over fifty metres below the crater floor, and came to a landing deeper than any of the previous ones. This one had an open door at the end of a broad, ghostly green lit corridor that led deep into the heart of the tower.

'This looks promising,' Cavendish said.

I could not help thinking that in all the SF films I'd seen, people exploring spooky abandoned alien spaceships or cities sooner or later had a nasty surprise and my imagination was populating the shadows with all kinds of monstrosities. But I said nothing and followed after the others. I had no choice. The only other member of our party to show any apprehension had been Oliver. Amber and her father seemed quite fearless.

The long hall was made of buttressed slabs of fused rock with many large open sliding doors leading off it on both sides revealing empty side rooms whose function we could only guess at. There were more of the black glass pads by the sides of the doors which had to be switches and there were long strips set in the ceilings which could have been lighting fixtures. But they were all completely inactive. How long was it since they had last worked? I had the feeling everything should be thick with dust and hung with spiderwebs but of course that was silly. But it still felt long abandoned.

Then we came to a big side chamber that was not empty.

There were rows of floor to ceiling posts supporting between them wire mesh and sheet metal panels fitted on both sides with racks and clips of different size, very like an Earthly changing room. They were almost all empty except for a handful that held some lengths of webbing and a few items of what looked like military kits of grey body armour, with helmets, boots and gloves connected by loose mesh coveralls with belts of empty loops and clips. We examined them curiously. Whatever material they were made of they seemed undamaged by exposure to vacuum and the straps and mesh were still pliant. The helmets had protective transparent visors but they were otherwise open. They were combat suits, perhaps, but not spacesuits.

'These were certainly designed to fit people of about our size,' the Prof said, holding up a chestplate.

'If they left these behind then why not some spacesuits as well?' Amber wondered. 'They must have had them. They couldn't stay inside all the time. These would be no use in a vacuum.'

'Maybe their space suits are stored up near the airlock,' I suggested. 'Behind one of those doors we couldn't open.'

Even as I said it I felt there was something wrong with that assumption, but I could not quite see it. We were surrounded by so many wonders and mysteries that there was no time to think on it further.

Along one wall of the harness room was a long dark glass panel with a row of slots in its base. What was dispensed from them we had no idea. A side door led to what was clearly a washroom with basins and toilet stalls, all fashioned out of some antiseptic-looking polished metal, which even formed the panel of mirrors over the basin. It could almost have been a minimalist, ultra-hygienic facility in some Earthly public building.

'Well it looks like they sat down to poop like we do,' I said.

I tried one of the basin faucets, but of course it was dry

'Any water in the system must have boiled away or frozen long ago,' Amber said.

'How cold is it in here?' I wondered.

'There's a thermometer display on your suit readout,' Amber said.

I checked. Plus three degrees. It had not frozen through the long lunar night so it might not boil when the sun was right overhead. Deep underground it must be insulated from the extremes on the surface. At noon the crater floor above would literally be as hot as an oven.

The next room along contained, for no obvious reason, a freestanding arch apparently identical to the one at the head of the bridge, except that the etched symbols on this had not been defaced. There was an angled panel of what looked like black glass or plastic mounted on a pedestal in front of it and larger panels of the same material hung on the walls.

'Do you think that these function like touch sensitive screens?' Amber wondered, running a gloved hand over the slab on the pedestal and leaving a trail in the thin layer of dust that lay over it.

'Perhaps,' her father said. 'But without power we'll never know.'

We moved on. Opposite this room on the other side of the big hallway was what seemed to be an identical arch room: an exact duplicate of the one we'd just left.

'Why would they need two of them?' I wondered aloud.

'Either they must be very important or they were used so much they needed two,' Amber suggested.

There were signs on the walls by both rooms which might have helped explain but of course we could not read them.

The end of the corridor was closed off by double blast doors with more of the bold signage in the alien script written across them. They were probably motor driven when the power was on but they also had manual operating wheels which turned easily when we tried them, withdrawing the locking bolts and rolling the doors apart. We stepped into a chamber barely illuminated by the ghostly green wall patch radiance, swinging our helmet lights about.

'This is it!' I said with a catch in my voice.

It was a huge circular chamber with a high domed roof braced by massive arches. Three arcs of control panels and chairs faced walls hung with dozens of big black glass screens. At the back of the room looking over the consoles was a raised dais on which stood what must be the command chair: looking a little like a heavy grey armchair but on a fixed swivel mount and with screen pads built into its broad arms. There was some unidentifiable device behind it and a low metal pillar set in the floor to one side of it with a slot in its top.

This had to be the nerve centre: the central control room of the fortress.

We wandered along the silent dead ranks of control boards that ringed half the room. In front of them were swivel chairs bolted to the floor that you might have seen in any commercial office equipment catalogue and not blinked at. Again it suggested that the base had been used by beings like ourselves. But where were they now?

'I think we should return to the ship,' Oliver suddenly said. 'This place is clearly dead and abandoned. There's certainly nobody here who can tell us anything about what happened to the Earth.'

He seemed to be getting cold feet. Maybe the atmosphere of the place was getting to him. I could sympathise. I wouldn't like to explore this place alone.

'I think we can stay a little longer,' Cavendish said. 'There seems no immediate danger and this is a unique opportunity: a chance to examine the relics of an alien race.'

'And there might be records in computers or physical files of some kind, Oliver,' Amber pointed out.

'Locked up in some data system with no power to access it and written in a language we can't read,' Oliver countered.

'I want to find out if we can get back home or not as much as anybody,' I said honestly. 'But now we're here we might as well look around properly.'

As he was clearly in a minority we all carried on.

There were three smaller doors leading off the chamber, which, keeping close together, we cautiously investigated.

One door opened onto another tube lift lobby which must serve the core of the tower. The other doors led to a suite of what might have been office rooms, chambers with pallets jutting out of the walls that we decided were probably sleeping quarters, a big room with fixed tables that might have been a mess hall and several more rest rooms.

I recorded everything we saw but there was nothing her to tell us more about the people who had built the base. There were no physical files,

104

clothes or even small items like penholders or desktop pictures of the family. The place seemed to have been cleaned out of everything movable apart from built-in furniture. Finally we returned to the control room and gathered by the command chair. The Professor addressed us solemnly as though he was delivering a lecture, summing up what we had discovered.

'I think this facility was abandoned some time ago but it was done methodically and without panic. Although there has undoubtedly been conflict here there are no bodies or waste material of any kind. They had the time to take everything of value with them and leave the rest clean and orderly. Even the console chairs have been left neatly facing the same way. But without power I don't see that we can learn much more here. Presumably there are generators of some kind down on the lower levels. Whether it would be possible to reactivate them or not, I can't say. That might take more time than we can spare.'

I could sense the struggle he was having with himself. He would no doubt have loved to spend a month in this place teasing out its secrets. But even his self-absorption had its limits, apparently. We were here due to an accident and if this fortress could not help us get back home safely then we would have to take the risk and do it for ourselves.

'There must be some power to keep the beacon sending,' Amber pointed out.

'Probably some isolated circuit somewhere connected to a dedicated power source,' her father said. 'That won't be enough to reactivate this entire facility, even if we could find it.'

'So why were we guided down here?' I wondered.

'I don't know,' the Professor admitted. 'But they seem to have left us no other clues to follow. We are dealing with an alien mentality so perhaps we shall never understand their logic.'

'Maybe this whole place is like some kind of memorial or living museum?' Amber said.

That was an idea. It might explain a lot of things. Except: 'So where are the tour guides?' I asked.

'Maybe it's their day off?' Amber suggested.

'That could literally be true,' her father admitted, with a dry regretful chuckle. 'We may never know.'

'So we'll be going back to the ship now?' Oliver said impatiently.

'Can we wait just one moment?' I asked, 'there's something I've really got to do…'

We had glanced over the big chair on the dais but its function was so obvious there hadn't seemed the need to examine it closer. This was where the base commander had sat: the one clearly personal and unique space in the whole fortress. Perhaps that was why we had not intruded upon it. Maybe the equivalent of a Wellington or a Nelson, or in SF terms a Port Admiral Haynes, Kirk or Pickard, had once sat here? Well it was not cordoned off like some gilded chair in a stately home, so there was nothing to stop me…

I stepped up to it, turned and carefully sat down. The fabric it was covered with resembled the mesh of the combat suits we had seen down the hall. At least for a minute I could imagine what it had

106

been like to be in this room when it was full of activity. What battle had been fought with that huge ship lying smashed out of the crater floor? Who were the enemy and who were defenders? And where they gone?

'How very juvenile,' Amber said.

'Oh come on, lighten up!' I protested. 'I'll never have another chance like this...'

And then I realized that on the arm of the big chair was something different. Besides the small black glass display/control panels there was a small protective hinged hood. It was transparent but it had been dulled and misted by dust. Curiously I flipped it back. Underneath was a large raised yellow button. It was the only control of that type we had seen so far. Everywhere else there were just the smooth black switch pads.

It was irresistible... so I pressed it.

For a moment nothing happened. And then the strip lights in the ceiling glowed softly and shone out, bathing the chamber with cool sky-blue radiance. These illuminated thin sparkling puffs of dust that blew out of vents set around the walls. I could feel a faint throbbing hum through the floor and then a growing rushing sound which seemed to be coming from all around us. Air was flooding back into the fortress!

'Oh Tom... what have you done?' Amber snapped, as though talking to a naughty child.

I sprang guiltily out of the chair, bouncing in the low gravity. 'I think I've found the "on" switch...'

Then everything seemed to come alive at once and there was almost too much to take in.

Coloured operating lights flickered in waves across the arcs of the control panels as small screens and keyboards lit up. At the same moment the huge black glass wall screens glowed and resolved into a panorama of images showing us the interior of crater, the *Eclipse* and the distant wreck, all viewed from high angles. The fortress must be ringed with external cameras. There was movement out on the lip of the moat as a series of slabs set into the hard apron rose smoothly upwards, revealing they were the tops of more of the big arches, apparently identical to the one we had passed through onto the bridge and in the duplicate rooms down the corridor. There were eight of them in all.

Other screens were coming to life displaying schematic diagrams of different kinds. The tower was shown in cross-section from topmost pinnacle to the base of its moat. We could see every level delineated with the massive gun emplacements and a central silo occupying its upper levels and then the midsection including crew quarters and the command room we were in and below that floors of service machinery with what must have been hangars and storage spaces set at the bottom. Below that buried half a kilometre deeper still was a thick-walled sphere that had to be its main power plant. Another screen showed a plan view of the gun tower and crater with a short web of lines linking it to the ring of arches around the moat. They flashed blue for a moment and then all but the one at the end of the bridge became solid green. Beyond that the eight rampart turrets were illuminated in amber, with little taglines in the alien script beside them. A web of flashing blue lines appeared, linking the keep to them. One by one five of them turned a solid green.

A screen showing a globe of the whole moon came in to being, marked out with a complex web of gridlines and bearings. Our fortress showed up as a green point in the middle of nearside. Three other points lay equidistant from it around the equator, ninety degrees apart, and there was also one at each pole. I had been right: there were more of the forts. But they were all marked in amber, with lines of script beside them that presumably imparted important information about their status. A web of flashing blue lines came into being linking our fortress with the others. Only the one connecting it to the North Pole turned a solid green.

There was both a live picture of the Earth as it must appear vertically above the crater and a schematic showing its landmasses in outline and also a flowing pattern of lines about it like weather map isobars, presumably delineating the strange energy field in which it was enveloped. More blocks of script and what might have been columns of numbers floated around the edges of the screen.

Another screen showed a symbolic diagram of the solar system set out as though it was an orrery display with all the planets and moons spaced out in a halo about the sun in the centre in their correct relative positions in their orbits, each named in the unreadable script. The moon in orbit around the Earth could be seen quite clearly and from it was slowly spreading out in all directions like questing tendrils a flashing blue web of lines.

But there was something strange about the order of worlds.

'A fifth planet!' the Professor exclaimed. 'This system has a fifth planet!'

It was true. In the space between Mars and Jupiter where in our system there are only a band of thousands of chunks of rock of different sizes that make up the asteroid belt, here there was just a single globe showing.

'And the second planet, where we have Venus, has got a pair of satellites,' Amber pointed out.

In our solar system Venus is moonless.

As we blinked in amazement at this sudden onslaught of imagery I realized that the rushing of the air through the ducts had faded away to a steady whisper. My suit felt less tight about me. I checked the thermometer display on my chest panel. It now read plus seven degrees. A pressure display also read normal to within a few points.

'There's enough pressure now to take our helmets off,' I said.

'Even if there is we don't know if this air is safe to breathe,' Amber said sharply. 'And we haven't any way of testing it. We never imagined we'd need to bring atmosphere analysis kits.'

'But we have to find out,' the Professor said. 'Now it seems this place is not as inactive as we imagined obviously we have to examine it further and it would be much simpler to work without our helmets on to extend our endurance. I think it's reasonable to assume this place is biologically inert. It's just a matter of the atmospheric composition. I don't think brief exposure will do much harm, even if it's not suitable for us...'

Whatever his other faults, Cavendish was no coward. Even as he spoke he was unlatching the neck ring of his helmet and lifting it a crack to let some of the external air in. We saw him sniffing it cautiously, ready to reseal his helmet again if need be.

'Is it all right, Father?' Amber asked anxiously.

'I think so,' he declared. He raised helmet further and took a couple of deep breaths. Then he smiled. 'It's rather flat and lifeless. Presumably it's been stored somewhere for a long time. But it doesn't seem to be doing me any harm. I don't feel dizzy at all so it must have sufficient oxygen. In fact...' He removed his helmet entirely and looked about him with satisfaction, breathing normally.

'It's all right,' he said, 'I think you can all take your helmets off. This will certainly make exploring the base a lot simpler.'

I unlatched my own helmet and lifted it off. The air was cool and dry and it had a faint metallic tang to it. It certainly seemed as fresh as the recycled air I'd been breathing in my suit, perhaps even a little better.

Oliver and Amber had cautiously removed their helmets. Oliver looked about him with his mouth hanging open, apparently dumbstruck. Amber said: 'This must mean the people who built this place were very much like us. Perhaps they came here from Para-Earth. Presumably it evolved along the same lines as ours so it has a similar atmosphere.'

'That's very possible,' Cavendish agreed. 'We might discover more about them now that the control systems are operating. There must be general data bases here, the equivalent of reference books, dictionaries and encyclopaedia's. We've just got to find them…'

But then something happened that interrupted the Professor's planned investigations. A bright beam of light shone down from a device in the ceiling directly over the command chair, making it appear to shimmer. And then an image materialised out of the radiance and formed itself into a ghostly human figure seated just as I had been only moments earlier.

Chapter 8
A Warning from the Past

The image was of a woman, perhaps in her forties with a strong but careworn face and short cropped blonde hair and blonde eyebrows, which contrasted oddly with her skin which was coffee brown. She was immaculately dressed in what looked like a dark blue military uniform. She wore a peaked cap with a badge pinned to its crown and what might have been symbolic lightning bolts and stars on its sides. Her jacket had silver bands and insignia on the shoulders, and cuffs and she wore another badge and medal ribbons on her chest. There was some kind of holstered sidearm slung from her belt. On her feet were her high black glossy boots.

I heard the sharp intake of Amber's breath. 'She's human!'

She was. She also seemed incredibly weary as she looked straight ahead from her chair, not making eye contact with any of us. I think we all realized almost immediately that this was a recording: a holographic projection of some kind. If you looked closely you could see the real chair showing through her body.

Then she spoke a few words in a fluid but unintelligible language. We heard them quite clearly and they seemed to come from her lips. I had no idea how that trick was done but it made it feel as though she was actually in the room with us. Then she appeared to wait for a response.

'What do we do now?' Amber said, looking at me as though I should have all the answers.

'Well I don't know what she said,' I protested. 'You were the one who was so interested in learning the language. Now's your chance.' I was a bit annoyed that Amber hadn't yet congratulated me on discovering that the base was not as dead and deserted as we imagined. Perhaps she would have been happier if it really had been a museum piece.

The woman in the chair repeated her words and paused once again. Then she appeared to get up from her holographic chair and take a few steps forward, making all of us skip aside as nimbly as our suits permitted. Her arm actually passed through Oliver who was a little slow to get out of the way, without causing any harm. She was quite intangible. Then she turned and held a hand out towards the chair as though inviting one of us to sit in it. Then the image froze as though the playback had been put on pause. At the same moment the top of the cabinet at the back of the chair opened up. What looked like a metal mesh helmet on a hinged arm emerged and flipped itself over the back of the chair so that it hung there invitingly like an empty crown. Hundreds of fine wires snaked across the surface of the mesh.

'Apparently she wants us to put it on,' Cavendish said.

'No, Father,' Amber said firmly. 'You took a chance with the air but this thing looks like it's designed to interface with the mind in some way. You've no idea what it's meant to do. It's too much of a risk.'

'Well I'm not going to put that thing on,' Oliver said firmly. 'It might be a trap.'

'No, I think I know what it is,' I said slowly.

'What is it then?' Amber demanded.

'Well it's obvious, isn't it? The fortress was designed to be reactivated after a long interval so they can't assume whoever found it would still speak the same language as the original occupants. Remember the Middle English glossary we had to keep checking when we did Chaucer's Canterbury Tales? About every tenth word needed explaining. And imagine trying to make sense of it spoken in a local dialect. And that was only from the fourteenth century in our own country. This place might get visitors from different worlds. So this has got to be a mechanical educator of some kind that can imprint their language on our brains.'

The reasoning had sounded perfectly rational in my mind, but saying it out loud made me realize it could have come from some creaky old SF film. We couldn't make such a device, but allowing for the fact that the fortress builders must have had a technology far ahead of ours, it did make sense.

'That is reasonable,' the Professor agreed. 'But it would still be a tremendous risk. Even if you're correct about its function we can't be certain its creators' minds were structured exactly as our own are, despite their obvious external similarities.'

'And after all this time how do we know it's even working properly?' Amber added.

'Well as Tom has shown he's the expert in these matters, he can have the honour of demonstrating its safe,' Oliver said with a barely concealed sneer of contempt on his lips.

And so I had no choice, of course. There was no way I was going to be a coward again in front of his eyes… or Amber's. I took a deep breath and sat down on the chair.

'No, Tom, you can't!' Amber exclaimed with a look of deep concern on her face.

It was almost worth the risk just to see that look. I pulled my flight cap off and handed it to her. 'Look after that for me, will you' I said, trying to sound offhand even as my stomach was knotting up in fear. I took hold of the mesh cap. 'Wish me luck…' and I pulled it down over my head before I could change my mind.

For a moment I felt nothing. Did it need to be switched on somewhere? Maybe it was sensing the structure of my brain and recalibrating to suit. I realized what an absurd amount of faith I was putting in this unknown machine. But then I was living the SF dream and I had to believe.

And then a buzzing itch began in my ears and little flashes of light began streaking in front of my eyes, clouding my view of Amber's intent troubled face. I screwed my eyes up but the lights did not go away. Instead the feel of my suit and the chair and everything around me went away until I was alone: just a mind floating in nothing. I could not speak or move. The itch became a throb that seemed to burrow deep into my brain. I could hear a thousand voices in my head all talking at once while shapes and symbols flickered in front of my eyes. I was being force fed a whole dictionary in a torrent of sight and sound, compressing what would normally take years into moments. I'd been right! Yippee! Then it began to seriously hurt. It was too much too fast. I couldn't take it! My mind was going to burst…

116

And then I was sitting slumped in the chair with the educator cap lifting itself off my head. Amber was peering at me anxiously. 'Tom, can you hear me? Are you all right?'

'Oww....' I said with feeling. 'Has anybody got an aspirin?'

The projection said: 'If there are any more who need to take the linguagram then say: "Pause and Repeat." When you are ready to hear what I have to tell you about the past and the Great War and the evil that may still live on, say: "Resume full playback."'

'Pause and repeat,' I said to it.

'What did you just say?' Amber asked.

'Didn't you hear me?'

'It sounded as though you were speaking in the same language she was.'

'Was I? I thought she was speaking in English. She said she's got some message for us about the past and a Great War and something evil that might still be hanging around...'

'What do you mean evil?' Oliver asked, looking about the control room anxiously.

But I didn't answer. My splitting headache was fading and I was suddenly feeling ridiculously elated. 'Wow... it really worked! Do you get that, Madam Dupont?' I called out, thinking of our French teacher at Stapleforth. 'Forget your past participles and having to remember what sex the French think a table is. This is how you learn a language in sixty seconds!'

'You were in the chair for nearly ten minutes,' Amber said.

'Was I? Well it only felt like one. But you timed me. Thank you... that's so... so kind. You are, you know... really amazing!'

'He sounds drunk,' Amber said with distaste.

'I think it's a reaction to the process,' the Prof said. 'Perhaps the mind's natural inhibitions have to be temporarily suppressed to accept the input of so much new knowledge. No doubt it will wear off shortly...'

They pulled me off the chair while I was still burbling merrily. Once he was sure I could stand unaided the Professor took my place. 'The sooner we all become familiar with this language the better we can find out what's going on here,' he said. 'And perhaps what happened to the Earth.' He pulled the cap down over his head.

While Amber anxiously watched over her father as he got his language lesson, I amused myself by waving my hands through the ghostly frozen projection of our military host standing by the chair until Amber chased me away. So I stumbled around the room a few times, occasionally bumping into the furniture. Oh, this was all so neat! Thank you, ancient ascended ones of Science Fiction! Positronically Yours, Blessed Isaac, I grok you Noble Bob, Serendipity Rocks, Wise Arthur.

I almost ran into Oliver, who was staring at me in bewilderment, and I gave him a Vulcan salute. 'Everything is totally cool,' I assured him.

I looked up at the huge display screens and to my delight I realized I could now read the text on them as easily as if they'd been written in English.

The names of the planets now made sense. I could read *Mercury, Venus, Mars and Jupiter...*

118

The words they used felt like they had ancient mystic associations and our familiar godly names for the major worlds seemed correct. Local versions of the same things? Had we got a true parallel universe here? Possibly.

However there were some differences. The Earth here was listed as *Terra* which was an ancient Roman name for the Earth goddess, from which we get *terrain* and *terrestrial.* In SF stories humans were sometimes called *Terranians* by aliens. It sounds a little cooler than plain old *Earthmen...*

Then I came to the planet we had no counterpart for, but I could still read it: *Janus.* The name of the fifth planet was "Janus", after some ancient Roman God, and in our system it had been given to a moon of Saturn. Here it rated a whole planet. I told Oliver about this amazing discovery but he did not seem impressed.

No doubt due to the superior power of his brain, Professor Cavendish did not behave as dopily as I had after taking the linguagram. He simply pinched the bridge of his nose and took a few deep breaths. Resolutely Amber took his place.

As I came down from my high state of happy befuddlement I found myself hoping that Amber might also loosen up after she had her mind filled with this new language. But she only sat still for a few minutes with her head in her hands saying she felt sick. Spoilsport!

So there was only Oliver left.

By now he appeared agitated and indecisive, looking between the main doors and the chair as though he was contemplating leaving. I could not understand what he was so unhappy about. We'd proved the thing was safe (thanks to my pioneering efforts) so he might as well get the benefit.

'Do you want to be the only one not in the know?' I chided him gently. 'It doesn't hurt... much.'

Reluctantly he took his place on the chair. I was pleased to see Amber flash him a look that was very close to being contempt. He had certainly blown a lot of his stock of goodwill with her in the last few hours. Still if the market interest in shares of Vance Ordinaries was in decline I dared to hope that Mallory Preferred might be in the ascendant.

While Oliver was getting the treatment the Prof was eagerly examining the wealth of data now accessible to him on the screens, especially the one showing the energy field around the Earth. I could now see a lot of figures detailing magnetic flux and charged particle flows which seemed to be interesting him.

But the most active big screen was the one showing the schematic of the solar system. Links of some kind were being established between the moon and other worlds. The blue lines that had reached out across the inner solar system were now all solid green, linking the moon with Mercury, Venus and Mars, but flashing blue tendrils were still heading out from the moon towards the outer planets.

'Why are they taking so long?' I wondered aloud.

'The speed of light, of course,' Amber said, joining us. She looked pale but she was clearly fully in control once more.

120

Of course, I should have worked that out for myself. Light travels at close to three hundred thousand kilometres a second, which is fine for most Earthly purposes but looks like a crawl when you get out into space and start measuring distances in millions or billions of kilometres.

'It must be a communications net of some kind,' the Professor said. 'What we are seeing are representations of signals being sent out to test the functionality of stations scattered across the entire solar system.'

'To more fortresses like this?' Amber asked.

'Perhaps.'

It would take time to get data back from the moons of the giant planets. As for distant Pluto, getting a return from it might take half a day.

There were now notes displayed by some of the solid connections. *Mercury: 1 transweb terminal. Status: Fully Functional. Access locked from lunar terminal. Links to other terminals: 0.*

I had no idea what a "transweb terminal" was but it seemed Venus by contrast had three of them functional with two links to other terminals while Mars had five running with three secondary links.

'I can see more differences between this system and ours,' Amber said. 'If those other figures by the planets show axial rotation then Mercury is turning in 88 days and is locked with one face to the sun, while Venus seems to have a 36 hour day.'

'A twilight zone on Mercury!' I said. 'Just like the old astronomers used to believe. Classic! Things really are different here...'

Two worlds had no transweb lines linking them to the moon at all: Terra and Janus. Terra we could see might be a special case, but what was different about Janus, apart from the fact that in our version of the solar system it did not exist?

A groan announced Oliver had finished his language lesson and we heard the projection asking again if we wanted to hear her message. I told her to pause but not repeat.

We clustered round Oliver in case he needed a hand getting over his treatment. He pushed the teaching cap off his head and clutched his temples, cursing and mumbling: '... I had to... there was no other way...'

'What are you talking about, Oliver?' the Professor asked

Oliver lifted a very pale face. 'Nothing... I really don't feel well... dizzy... just give me a minute... leave me alone!'

He heaved himself off the chair and stumbled away into a corner, looking as though he might be physically sick. Amber scowled after him in deep disapproval and did not attempt to follow.

The Vance Investments bubble had really burst, I thought. He wasn't even an amusing pseudo-drunk as I had been.

The Professor waited impatiently while Oliver recovered. Clearly he was anxious to hear the rest of the playback. So was I. Looking into the frozen but determined features of the mystery woman in that immaculate uniform, you knew for certain that she would never have gone to this trouble over anything trivial. What I could now read on one of the screens confirmed that.

The moon globe listed the names of the six structures spaced evenly about it. This one in the centre of the nearside hemisphere of the moon always facing Terra which we were in was called "Fort Adamant". The farside fort was named "Endurance"; the North Pole fort was "Resolution", the South "Defiance", East was "Indomitable" and West was "Guardian".

You don't choose names like that for fun destinations. They were for inspiring warriors.

Amber had been reading the same list. 'They were fighting an interplanetary war,' she said grimly.

'I think so,' I agreed.

At last Oliver came back, looking a little more human. 'Sorry about that,' he said. 'That really shook me up... but I'm feeling better now. Let's hear what she has to say.'

I took a deep breath: 'Resume full playback,' I said.

The projection resumed her seat on the command chair. We gathered in front of her as she stared through us. Even though there was no eye contact I could feel the intensity of her gaze.

'I am General Romally Skane, Commander of Fort Adamant and senior officer of the Lunar Defence Garrison. I do not know how long it has been for you since I recorded this message or what you know of the past history of the Great System War. By now I may have been dead many centuries. I am recording this on System Year nine four eight, seventy-three years after the Dark Mind came from the depths of space and took control of the Janus colony. What his origins were we never knew, only his terrible lust for power and conquest. He became known as Janus the Destroyer, and tried to enslave the rest of the system with its war machines and vile biomechanical agents.

'Worlds were laid to ruin and billions died before we achieved a victory of sorts. But now both our people and resources are exhausted. Communications are failing and I fear the capacity to maintain what is left of our spacefleet or the transweb will be lost. If that happens worlds will become isolated and a dark age will fall across the system. Therefore I'm taking what actions I can to preserve its core knowledge. We do not have enough personnel left to properly garrison the moon, so Adamant has been left as a beacon and warning to future generations and a memorial to all those who fell. But it may be over time that memories of the Great War will be confused and pass into myth and legend. How long this age of ignorance will last I do not know. If you are here watching this then perhaps it has passed. But future generations must not forget the terrible danger. So I tell you that Janus is no myth. He was caged but might still live even now, within sight of this Fortress. Because his cage was Terra itself!'

We all started at that and glanced at the screen showing Terra. That light show was a vast prison?

Skane continued: 'Even after it had been devastated by decades of war, Janus still wanted Terra, the jewel of the system, so we laid a trap him. Terra's remaining human population and all the higher animals possible were evacuated. The fleets were arrayed as though to protect it and Janus's forces were lured in for a final battle. I ensured events were properly archived, both as a document of a vital engagement in the struggle and a memorial to those brave soldiers who died so that you might live free. As you witness what happened when the trap was sprung, remember them with honour…'

More projection beams suddenly shone down from all over the ceiling and the whole room seemed to fill with sound and movement.

The big wall screens no longer showed the still crater with its long shadows but fast changing images and displays of frantic activity, while the arcs of control consoles were now manned by a hundred men and woman in dark blue uniforms. Warning beeps and trills filled the air, along with the clipped urgent words of the soldiers as they made their reports and gave orders. General Skane was still seated in the command chair but now she was hatless, hunched forward, checking the displays on its arm screens and rapping out orders to junior officers who stood beside her. We flinched as their projections hurried off and passed through us as though we were ghosts.

In a way we were ghosts, but ghosts from the future looking back into the past to witness the fortress's final battle…

Chapter 9
The Terracage

On a big screen showing Terra-Luna space clusters of coloured lights were moving rapidly while others formed defensive lines. Another screen showed Terra itself, almost full, blazing above the dark fortress crater without its jewel-like cocoon.

'Alpha fleet are engaging the enemy prime fleet!' an operator called out.

There were sparkles in the void about Terra: the flashes of explosions thousands of kilometres out in space.

'Enemy sub fleet has broken off. Lunar Vector confirmed!'

'Fire first interceptor salvo!' Skane commanded.

A screen showed segmented doors opening in the apex of Fort Adamant between its pinnacles. Missiles flashed away into space at monstrous acceleration, trailing nothing more than pale blue glows behind them.

'Salvo away!' an operator reported.

'Endurance reports coming under attack from long range missiles... all but one intercepted... minor damage to ringwall turret!'

'Resolution also under fire... sustaining heavy damage...'

There were more blossoms of fire out in deep space.

'Our missiles have encountered the sub fleet... heavy damage inflicted... five ships still active. Still on approach vector! Closing fast... '

'Main batteries fire at will!' Skane commanded

Adamant's great upper guns swung about and then the interior of the crater lit up as they crackled and flashed electric fire, sending brilliant balls and streamers of lambent flame up into the sky.

'Ringwall towers on automatic,' Skane commanded. 'Prepare for low level attack prior to ground landing.'

On the screen the eight sub-towers ringed about the crater wall swung their guns about, seeking targets.

'Beta and Gamma fleets are now fully engaged with the enemy,' an operative said. 'Heavy losses on both sides...'

The ringwall turrets began spitting fire out across the dark lunar sea. In response great orange fireballs of molten rock and incandescent dust filled the sky beyond the outer ramparts of the crater.

'Indomitable has taken heavy damage... Enemy forces inside ringwall...but primary transmitter and keylink are still good.'

Adamant's guns were now spitting fire continuously, raking the heavens about them although nothing was visible to the naked eye. Then a lance of blue flame stabbed down out of the night and burst on the crater floor. The second bolt blew a hole in the crater wall. There came an impression of a huge dark shape flashing across the sky over the fort, occulting the stars. But Adamant's guns caught in their beams and it exploded.

'Gorgon Class cruiser destroyed!' an operator reported.

As its blazing mass tumbled away into the night beyond the distant ringwall, debris rained down in a shower of glowing fragments across the crater floor.

'Landings confirmed to the south. Enemy ground forces are approaching…'

'Ready all mobile units in crater,' Skane ordered. 'Prepare for close order combat…'

Platforms rose up out of the depths of the moat, climbing the slots we had seen in its sides, carrying with them six-wheeled tank-like vehicles with multiple turret guns and spiked rams. They radiated out to form a defensive ring about the fortress.

'Main fleets falling back according to plan… the remains of the enemy fleet is approaching Terra….'

Skane pulled something hung on a lanyard out of the front of her jacket. It was a sliver of clear plastic perhaps fifteen centimetres long by five wide and one deep within which was embedded a complex pattern of silver wires. She pushed one end into the slot in top of the pillar mounted beside her chair and held it ready.

'Confirm key link with all forts,' she said. 'Ready for activation.'

The response came back: 'Keylink confirmed. All commanders awaiting order to activate.'

There was a series of explosions around the ramparts, throwing chunks of rock impossibly high into the darkness. The turret guns were blazing wildly out into the cold lunar night, blasting new craters into the ancient rock. From out of the darkness their fire was returned. Parts of the rampart walls began to crumble.

'Turrets three and seven are out of action. Outer wall breached. Enemy ground forces are entering the crater!'

'Redirect light batteries to crater floor. Advance mobile units...'

The lowest ring of guns about the tower depressed their barrels and began blazing away at the base of the distant rampart walls. Now we could see there were things swarming through a hole blasted in it: metallic bronze and green things with many legs. On their backs were guns that flashed electric fire. A squadron of the fortress's tanks raced away across the crater floor to intercept them, spraying moondust in waves from their churning wheels.

'Fleets have retreated to position Amber,' an operator reported.

Skane pushed the key strip deeper into the slot. 'Send to all forts: begin charging Terracage transmitters!'

Out across the crater the fortress's tanks smashed into the front rank of the enemy walking machines. Guns blazed at close quarters, spiked prows and blades cut into hulls and tanks and walkers disintegrated in flares of fire and spinning shards of metal.

'Enemy ground forces being held in South East quadrant!'

A handful of walking machines evaded the tanks and scrambled on across the crater floor like a swarm of metal centipedes. Adamant's light guns depressed their barrels still further and began blasting away at them. More were blown apart or melted into slag but a few still struggled on.

'Ready infantry!' Skane ordered.

'General: a single vessel has detached from the enemy Prime fleet....' an operator reported. On the screen a red flashing point of light separated from one of the enemy formations and headed towards Earth. 'It registers as a Kraken class ship...' her voice caught '...it must be Janus!'

'Confirm identification!' Skane snapped.

'Energy pattern is confirmed! Kraken class. It is Janus!'

'Incoming!' another operator shouted. 'Hydra class carrier... it's heading right at us!'

'Not now!' Skane rasped, half to herself. Then: 'Maximum fire! Don't let it through!'

All the fortress's guns on one side swung about and concentrated their fire up into the void where a dark shape was hurtling out of the stars, spitting darts of fire that flashed down and struck the fort itself, gouging pits in its massive walls. The control room shivered and swayed, making the operators clutch at their consoles for support. Then the carrier began to glow under the impact of multiple bolts and rods of energy boring into its sides. Its hull split and spouted fire, disintegrating even as it hurtled onwards, growing larger and larger. At the last moment the blasts from within deflected it from its collision course. Veering sideways it impacted on the crater floor, tearing a deep gouge across it and spewing debris.

Yet incredibly, hardly had the crumpled twisted ship come to rest, than more of the many-legged metal things burst out of its sides and swarmed on towards the fort.

'Melt it down! Don't let any of more of them out!' Skane commanded.

The fort's guns held their beams on the shattered vessel, pouring energy into is twisted hull until it flared and then sagged and melted into shining streams of liquid metal, throwing up a silvery haze of incandescent metal vapour.

Now there were tiny human figures out on the plain, radiating out from the fort. They advanced in great leaps and bounds firing hand weapons at the approaching enemy machines, blowing their legs out from under them. They threw grenades that stuck to their sides and flared with intense light, melting their body shells. The machines struck back with what looked like sprays of glowing hailstones that cut into the troops. Their advance faltered but still ground relentlessly on.

'The fleet has reached position green!'

'Janus is now within the magnetosphere! Approaching critical altitude… critical attitude has been passed. Still heading for Terra!'

'Send command: Initiate Terracage on my mark!' Skane said. 'Three, two, one… Now!' And she twisted the key in the slot.

The lights in the fortress dimmed and the ground trembled as though some vast store of energy had released. A screen showed jagged fingers of lightning running up and down the sides of the fort's topmost pinnacles.

For a moment despite the carnage out on the plain and in deep space everyone in the command room seemed to hold their breath. They were all watching the live image of the Terra. Then with a shimmer a cocoon of swirling blue-green radiance came into being around it.

'It worked!' a young operator sobbed. 'We did it!'

'Not yet, son,' Skane said, her voice rigid. 'It's still got to contain him…'

A lighting storm seemed to erupt within the shimmering jewel of energy. Searing jagged white forks of fire clawed at the inside of the barrier, seeking some weak point. The storm swirled about and then darted away toward the poles. The camera's followed it, zooming in tighter.

Meanwhile out on the plain the attacking machines wavered and lost their footing and collapsed, twitching uncontrollably and then lying still. On the screens the tight formations of lights marking the positions of the enemy space fleets began to break up as they drifted apart on random trajectories.

Across the face of the Terra and out into space as far as the lower limits of the impalpable cage, the storm flared and swirled but it could not break free.

And then, just for a moment, we saw it!

The flaring storm shaped itself into the caricature of a vast face the size of a continent that howled and snarled, its hollow eyes flashing with lightning glaring balefully out at the puny creatures that had trapped it.

It was the face of Janus!

A terrible thunderous roar of rage and frustration burst from every speaker in the room, wailing and shrieking in hate and burning malevolence. The operators clamped their hands over their ears and turned their heads aside.

Only Skane faced the screen squarely, her jaw clamped hard and defiant.

And in that moment we understood the true horror of the thing these people had been fighting against. I can't explain it any better. You had to feel it for yourself. But if pure evil had a face and voice then that was it.

Then gradually the howling faded, the face dissolved and melted from sight.

A trembling white-faced operator checked her readouts and then announced: 'The Terracage is secure and holding...'

And then command room erupted into cheers of wild jubilation.

Skane sagged in her chair, for a moment burying her face in her hands and whispering something inaudible to herself. Then she straightened up with her back ramrod stiff once more and said: 'Send to the Admiral of the fleet: "Janus has been successfully contained within the Terracage..."

Their sense of elation was so powerful it seemed to bridge the gap across the centuries and for a few seconds we felt it as well. Then the cheering ghosts gradually faded away as the ceiling projectors dimmed...

* * *

Once more the screens showed the silent crater with the melted remains of what had been the enemy Hydra class carrier lying still and dead out across the plain. We were alone again in the empty control room with only the projection of Skane seated in her chair. I shivered and saw the same look of dazed wonder on the faces of the others. For a short while we had experienced something of the fear and joy of all those long dead warriors in their moment of triumph.

'I do not understand exactly how the Terracage field worked,' Skane continued. 'I'm just a solider. It was a creation of our finest surviving scientists and engineers. It was a field of energy that followed Terra's magnetosphere, the most powerful of all the inner planets, and it is energised and sustained by solar radiation. This energy was opaque to the frequencies that comprised Janus's mind. He was trapped within its annulus. And without his guiding intelligence his machines failed all across the system. But our forces were also decimated and only a handful of spaceworthy ships remained. Without the resources of Terra I'm not sure we can ever recover. Therefore I'm ordering the remaining personnel to abandon the moon and relocate to whatever habitable worlds remain.'

She pointed to the pillar by chair which had the empty keyslot in it. 'That controls the activator buried deep below this fortress, as its duplicates are located beneath the other lunar forts. They are all still functional, even though the forts above them were damaged. The activators are still in resonance with the Terracage field and the only way to deactivate it is to use all six keys together. Any attempt to bypass them or penetrate the field will trigger an overload that will scorch the face of Terra and may, possibly, destroy Janus. We could not risk it failing, however, because we knew we would only get this one chance, which was why imprisonment was the only safe option.'

'In case any of Janus's machines or biomechanicals remain active somewhere out in the depths of the system we will take the keys with us and will keep them safe until they are needed again. We have also protected Adamant from intrusion as best we can. Since we do not know who may visit it in the future, for safety the main batteries have been code locked from the manual control boards. Unless the very worst happens I hope they never have to be fired again. But a detector field is operating which will activate them and automatically target any of Janus's machines should any still survive and attempt to approach. It will remain operational even when the rest of the fort is shut down. The tramsweb is also inactivated and protected and we have put filters on the manual entry port. If you are watching this then you have been passed as human and uncontaminated. Perhaps you are even my distant ancestors...'

Then her face seemed to darken. 'However there is a chance you may be human but in your hearts still follow the cult of Janus. They were the worst of traitors, who worshipped his power without being converted and secretly aided his conquests. If you are one of them then I say that you may hunt for the keys on every planet and moon in this system but they will not bring you what you desire. If you are untouched by Janus's evil you must follow in the path of those who fought him, even as they sat in this room and believed in the values of the badges I wear, that stood for justice, honesty and freedom. If the monster awakens again they will be your true keys to unlocking the means to destroy him.'

'I do not know if it will ever be safe to open the Terracage. You may know better. But if you do choose to use them, you must be certain beyond doubt that the mind of Janus is dead first. Without material resources and human minds to use as his tools he will be weakened and even he cannot live forever. It would be a great thing to reclaim Terra for humanity and look on its green forests and blue seas once more, but not at the price of letting loose that abomination on the system again. But that will not be my responsibility. Whatever you decide, remember us and what we fought and died for. And know that we did our duty to the end...'

She stood and saluted. Then her image faded away.

There was a stunned silence as we tried to get our minds around these incredible revelations. Then Cavendish crossed to one of the control consoles and checked a display.

'There is a calendar readout here I noticed earlier. It reads SY (system year, I assume) 1953. If this uses terrestrial year as standard, which is likely, and counting from the date General Skane gave, 948, then all this occurred over a thousand years ago.'

I shivered again. All this futuristic hardware was weirdly also ancient history.

'And this place has been waiting all this time for somebody to visit it.' Amber said. 'Skane was worrying about a technological collapse, but all this seems so well preserved. Everything's working.'

'That is very different from being unable to maintain or replace the systems and devices sustaining a technological society in everyday use,'

136

the Professor pointed out. 'This base has been mothballed in vacuum at an equitable temperature without being used, except for a small amount of power to maintain the beacon, detector field and a central data core, ready to reactivate the systems when required. The exterior was certainly built to last and there seem to be no moving parts in any of these devices or the fort itself, except for massive ones. In such circumstances it could very well last that long.'

'Do you think there are still people out there, Professor?' I asked. 'Descendants of people we saw on the recording. Living on bases on Mars or Venus or the satellites of the gas giants?'

'That's a question for another day, Tom. As it stands our discovery of this alternate world and its remarkable past alone will rock the disciplines of both science and history to their foundations, when we take news of it back home.'

I could see the Professor was already staring into the future, perhaps imagining more photographs for his display in the hall of Continuum House, possibly showing him receiving the Nobel Prize both in physics and archaeology. Would they have to invent an entirely new category: astro-archaeology?

'If we can get back, Professor,' Oliver said bitterly.

'Don't look so glum, Oliver,' the Prof said with a sudden chuckle. 'After what we've just learned I'm far more confident that flying into the energy field we can see around this Earth with the drive on will transport us back to our own world.'

As you can imagine we all pricked up our ears at that. 'Why, Father?' Amber said.

'Because I now know that our arrival here was not the result of some chance fluctuating natural phenomenon as we first thought. What happened to us must in some way be linked to this *Terracage* they created, via some interdimensional energy transfer into the magnetosphere of our world. Very probably the people who created it had no idea this was occurring. It was only the interference with the drive field of the *Eclipse* that opened up a physical portal through which we passed. And now I can see from these displays that the barrier is being maintained within quite narrow parameters, no doubt because it might cease to serve its purpose otherwise. As long as we take suitable precautions to ensure the drive is not damaged during the transition we should be able to return quite simply.'

By then we were all looking a lot more cheerful.

'Well then let's get going,' I said, getting ready to put my helmet back on.

'Be patient, Tom. First we must collect samples to take back with us. After all, this is going to seem to most people an even more unbelievable journey than the one we planned to our moon.'

'We've got the camera records,' I said.

'We need irrefutable physical evidence,' the Prof said. 'I will not risk being accused of perpetrating some elaborate deception. I was going to bring back samples of Apollo era technology as proof of that expedition. Now we will gather samples of machinery or materials from this fort that if possible embodies physical principles unknown to our world. For a start one of these console display screens. They seem far in advance of our LED or plasma screens...' He blinked at us impatiently through his spectacles, his eyes gleaming. 'Well come on, then, let's get going!'

We could see he was determined and there was no arguing with him, but I did have a reservation.

'We shouldn't trash the place just for a few specimens, Professor,' I said. 'I mean not after what the people who fought here went through. I think they deserve our respect.'

Amber was nodding in agreement. 'Tom's right, Father. We don't want to act like looters.'

Cavendish sighed. 'I assure you we'll select our samples with care. I don't wish to cause any unnecessary damage either. After all, within a month there might be a team of researchers from Earth here, probing the secrets of this place. Think what they'll learn and the advances we will make! This fortress has been a frozen monument to its makers long enough. Now it must play a part in our future,' he declared grandly.

Oliver spoke up. 'Well, if we're going to be working in this place for the next few hours, Professor, perhaps we can do it comfortably? It's getting warmer in here now so we don't need our full suits. Maybe we can take our life support packs and hard shells off and store them in the harness room with our helmets.'

'Yes, that'll make things a lot easier,' Cavendish agreed.

So we made our way back along the main corridor, now brightly lit like the control room, to the harness room. The sign over it which we could now read showed we had been correct at least in part about its function: *Combat Harness and TW Ration Dispensary*. The panel on the wall was also active now, with text and symbols showing and the rims of the slots along its base were illuminated. Now we could read system text maybe we could find out what it did.

We hung our helmets and packs on the hooks by the webbing combat harnesses. Then we stripped off the suits' jointed outer hard shells, leaving us in the inner pressure skins, which now they were inactive were rather like wearing loose-fitting wet suits.

It was only then that I realized that although Oliver had been fumbling about and ducking down on the other side of the panel I was hanging my gear on, from what I could see through it he had not actually removed his suit.

'Is there anything wrong?' I asked.

'Yes…' he said slowly. He came round the end of the row of panels, still fully suited with his helmet hung off the back of his pack. His eyes were now shining with a strange desperate determination. In one hand he held a length of webbing taken from one of the harnesses. In the other he was holding an automatic pistol which trembled slightly as he pointed it at us. '…you are wrong, Tom! I said you shouldn't have come. And now you won't be going back home. None of you will. You'll all be staying here. For ever!'

Chapter 10
Traitor!

I'd never had a real gun pointed at me before. If you haven't either let me give you a head's up: it isn't nice. You can't believe it for a few seconds until you look right down the black mouth of the muzzle and realize that might be the last thing you'll ever see. If he pulled the trigger would I even have time to register the muzzle flash before the bullet hit? Even the fact that Oliver's hand was shaking slightly as he held it didn't give me any comfort.

While we three gaped in disbelief at him Oliver said almost apologetically, twitching the gun slightly: 'I never wanted to do it this way.' He jabbed it at the Professor. 'I kept trying to find an excuse to stay behind but you insisted we all had to stick together! Now I can't wait any longer. There are people expecting me and I'm already late. Get away from your suits and go out into the hall. We're going back to the control room. And don't try anything stupid. I don't want to shoot you but I will if I have to. The hard shells might have stopped a bullet but not the undersuits...' he gave a strange little manic chuckle at his own cleverness. '...that's why I had to get you to take them off. Now move!'

In the films your typical hero manages to turn the tables on people waving guns at him by creating some distraction or else doing an agile martial arts manoeuvre involving some convenient stage prop. I was too shocked to work out anything that clever.

The three of us marched ahead of Oliver back out into the hall towards the control room. He didn't make the mistake of getting so close that we could turn round suddenly and jump him.

By then the Professor had recovered his wits enough to say: 'This is insane, Oliver! What are you doing this for?

'For money of course, what do you think?' Oliver said with contempt. 'Or rather for the money I'll be paid for delivering the Cavendish drive to certain people. Do you realize how much its worth? Its military and commercial potential?'

Amber, still looking stunned, asked: 'How long have you been planning this?'

'From the start. I arranged all those failed public demonstrations that convinced your father to work on his wonder craft in secret.'

'You sabotaged my work!' Cavendish growled.

'Yes. Don't look so angry, Professor. Maybe it motivated you. Unfortunately it also made you more paranoid and secretive. I would have taken the prototype unit as soon as you got it working but you kept it and the plans under such tight watch that in the end I realized it would be easier to steal the whole ship. I think I deserve it for putting up with your tantrums all this time when nobody else would. Now you'll stay here while I take the *Eclipse* back to Earth.'

We had reached the big sliding doors of the control room. Oliver waved us through but he stayed on the other side. While he held the gun on us with one hand through the gap between the doors he began looping the webbing around one of the manual door wheels with the other.

142

'Who did you sell out to?' I asked. I had a compulsion to keep the conversation going because when he left that was it. And perhaps Oliver was willing to answer because in a weird way he wanted to justify his actions. He was clearly an amateur criminal and not some professional assassin. If he had been we'd all be dead by now. Instead he was going to keep his hands clean of actual blood by marooning us.

Oliver gave a kind of twisted smile. 'You know I'm not exactly sure. The black ops division of a multinational company, maybe, or government agents for some rogue state... or not so rogue, perhaps. Maybe people much closer to home. Take your pick. They're the kind of people who don't encourage curiosity. Serious players. But whoever they are they wanted you out of the way. My original plan was to drug you with that celebratory champagne after we left Earth orbit and then take over the ship, but the van Allan transition messed up that idea.' He glared at me. 'You held us up with that ridiculous toast business just too long. And after I'd put you down as a coward who wouldn't be giving me any trouble!'

I felt sick. That was why he'd given me the thumbs up after my panic during launch. Because he believed I was too wimpy to spoil his plans!

'A pity,' Oliver continued. 'The champagne would have been kinder. You'd have just gone to sleep and not woken up. The gun was a backup but I couldn't risk using it in flight, especially after we ended up in another universe. I mean what the hell, Professor, you don't make it easy for a man to steal your secrets, do you? And then we found this place.

143

I was curious as well and you kept making these incredible discoveries… but I had to draw the line somewhere and get back to my original timetable. Now you've said the ship should be able to return to our version of Earth safely, that's where I'm going.'

'Listen, Oliver, it's not too late,' the Professor said, desperately trying to sound reasonable. 'Why can't we all go home? We've made an amazing discovery that you can share in. If you do then we'll say no more about this… aberration. Wouldn't honest fame and reward be better than profiting by a criminal act?'

I was nodding in agreement perhaps a little too eagerly. Amber was still glaring daggers at Oliver.

But then a terrible expression of anguish spread across Oliver's face and for a moment I thought he was actually going to cry. 'No… it's too late for me! There's no home to go back to! Like they say, I had to burn my boats… literally.'

I felt a sudden shiver. The Prof said: 'What do you mean?'

'I left a couple of fire bombs behind to destroy the house and workshop,' Oliver said. 'They were timed to go off at one o'clock. That left me leeway to disarm them if the launch failed or we had to abort our Earth orbit and return early. But after that I was committed. If we'd turned back after things started going wrong we'd have met them going off. So we had to carry on to the moon until the deadline passed. That was hours ago now…'

'But… Mrs Whittle…' the Professor choked, sounding almost childlike in his disbelief, while Amber sank to her knees and buried her face in her hands.

'Don't you think I know what I did?' Oliver grated, and I saw his eyes fill with self-loathing. 'But my backers insisted. They want the exclusive rights to the drive without its inventor being around to accuse them of stealing it. By then I was in too deep. You don't say no to people like that! I had to do it! But I put some sleeping tablets in her cocoa jar, and you know she always has a mug before she goes to bed. By the time the bombs went off she wouldn't have known anything about it. Now all the evidence of the drive will be gone along with the house and you'll never be found. People will think you've had another "accident" out flying, though they'll never know what in or how high you went.'

Amber looked up at Oliver. Her eyes were red and wet with tears and burning with hate. 'You killed her, you unspeakable, revolting, filthy...' and she added some words that seemed wrong coming out of her lips but with which I totally agreed.

Oliver gritted his teeth and began cranking the doors closed one-handed.

'You might be able to get this open again but by then I'll have made sure you can't follow me outside,' he said. 'I'm going to take the only functioning Cavendish drive ship in existence back to Earth and you can't stop me. Sorry... there really is no other way...'

Then his face and the gun vanished as the two halves of the door clanged together. There was a faint scrabbling from the other side as he wrapped the webbing across the other wheel and then there was nothing.

Amber was still crying softly, looking more lost that I'd ever seen her. The Professor was standing glaring at the doors with his hands and teeth clenched. As for me I was in a numbed kind of daze. Part of that was shock at what had happened to Mrs Whittle, who I'd liked a lot even though I'd only known her for a couple of hours, but most of it was the thought of what my parents would think when I never came back. Did they know about the fire already? If they found no remains would they go on hoping? They'd never know the truth...

'I will not give just up!' the Prof said suddenly. 'There may still be a chance...'

He ran to the door and put his ear to it, listening for any indication that Oliver was still on the other side. Then he moved to the door frame and pressed the opening symbol glowing in its black switch panel that had come to life along with the rest of the base. Oliver, too busy covering us, hadn't thought of using it.

Maybe there was an electronic dead-locking code for the door but we didn't know it. That was why Oliver had to improvise. A motor hummed, locking bolts retracted and the doors parted and then stuck with just a couple of centimetres gap between them.

'Tom, help me...'

Together we twisted the manual wheels on our side of the doors, adding our muscle to the door motors. Grudgingly they opened a little wider. Through the narrow gap we could see the webbing stretched across between the wheels on the other side.

'Ease off a bit… give some slack…' Cavendish said. 'Amber, there's just room for you to slide your arm through. Try to unwind the webbing on the right side. Oliver was winding it about that wheel one-handed while he held the gun. He could not have tied a proper knot…'

Amber crouched down and reached between the doors, twisting her arm round to feel for the wheel. She winced as she tugged blindly at the webbing. 'It's wound tight… I can't feel the end…'

Then came the sound of three shots fired in rapid succession from a distance and bullets spanged into the doors. Amber gasped and pulled her arm back through hastily and we shrank away from the gap. We heard distant footsteps and there came a heavy clang. Amber snatched a glance through the gap.

'The doors at the end of the corridor are closed now,' she reported. 'Oliver must have gone through them…'

'Try again…' the Professor said.

Amber squirmed her arm through the gap once more, biting her lip as she ground her shoulder against the side of the door. 'I can't feel the end… wait… I think I've got it… yes… now try…'

We heaved on the wheels and the webbing unwound and suddenly the doors parted.

Unencumbered by our hard suits and packs we bounded down the corridor in huge low gravity strides, past the harness room entrance and almost collided with the doors opening onto the ramp and lift tube shaft. But heave as we might we could not open them. Oliver had the time to tie these properly on the other side with more webbing from the harness room.

'If everything's working now we might be able to use the lift tubes from the lobby on the other side of the control room,' Amber said. 'There must be a cross corridor at the crater floor level to connect with the bridge entrance. Maybe Oliver forgot about them!'

'Unless he's already using the tubes in the main stairwell,' I said.

The Prof clutched at this slim chance. 'Either way he'll still reach the airlocks first. He's got too much head start. But even if he gets to the ship it will take him a few minutes to prepare it for launch. We might still be able to catch him before he lifts off…we'll need our suits…'

We bounded back to the Harness Room only to stop dead.

Our life support packs and hard suits were still hanging on the racks but our helmets were gone. That was why Oliver had wanted us shut up in the control room, to buy him time enough to make a bundle of them and take them with him. They were too tough to smash easily and a handgun bullet might not have been powerful enough to punch a hole through their heavy face plates. This was simpler. He could drop them off the bridge as he crossed it and that was that.

The Professor pulled off his glasses and pinched his brow, his eyes closed. Amber bit her lip and shook her head, fighting back more tears. Without helmets our suits were virtually useless.

In the famous movie *2001: A Space Odyssey* an astronaut dramatically enters a spaceship from an

148

EVA pod without a helmet, enduring a few seconds exposure to hard vacuum before he can close the airlock and fill it with air. It's been estimated in real life that a person could remain conscious and active for maybe ten or fifteen seconds in such circumstances. It would not be fun but those seconds might make the difference between life and death.

But a few seconds was not enough for us!

Even now I could picture Oliver running up the ramps in the low gravity and then entering the massive triple outer locks. He would not want to hang about. But once he was through them he knew we could not follow without our helmets. Even if we took the chance it would take too long to pass through the locks from air to vacuum, let alone tackle him outside. He could then stroll across the bridge and through the arch to the ship knowing that airless space was his protection. In ten minutes he would be gone...

Wait... what had I just thought? I looked around the harness room. What was it about this setup that still did not feel right? Something I'd half wondered earlier about spacesuits and soldiers that did not make sense. But I'd seen them in action on the holographic recording...

And then suddenly it all made sense.

Oh wow! Just maybe it worked like that, allowing for one mega-big assumption! But if I was wrong? Well I had nothing to lose. How long could we survive here without food and water? Dithering was not a luxury I could afford: it was as they say time to do or die...

Frantically I began stripping off my useless inner pressure suit layer. The Prof and Amber looked at me in a daze, maybe wondering if I'd gone mad.

'Tom, what are you doing?' Amber said.

'No time to explain,' I said, tearing the clinging leggings off me. 'I might be able to stop Oliver, but it's a long shot. Don't get in the way…'

By then I was down to my long grey one piece underwear. I snatched up the nearest harness set and began to pull it on, fumbling with the sliding buckles to adjust it to fit. A little dust came off it but it flexed easily, like it might have been hung up yesterday. It must have been woven of some incredibly stable and tough synthetic, as shown by how the webbing had held the control room doors shut.

I tightened the straps that held its chest-plates on front and back, and then adjusted the shoulder, elbow and knee pads. The belt had loops in it, presumably for more kit of some kind, maybe weapons. I wished I had one now. Oliver still had his gun. Then I pulled on the boots. They were thickly padded inside and fitted reasonably well. It was the same with the helmet and gloves, which had knuckle guards. I didn't know if all this was necessary to make things work the way I hoped but it might be and either way it would give me some protection against bullets.

'Tom, that's not a spacesuit,' Amber said.

'I know it isn't. Just let me do this my way…' I was frightened that if I had to explain it would waste time we had not got and seem too far-fetched… and also that I would lose my nerve.

150

I ran from the harness room out into the corridor with the Prof and Amber trailing after me. I could now read the sign by the next door along which was one of the arch rooms: *Lunar Transweb Terminal.* The sign on the matching arch room opposite read: *System Transweb Terminal.*

Yes, just maybe…

Inside the wall panel, pedestal and arch screens were now powered up like everything else on the base. The wall screens seemed to duplicate some of the displays in the main control room, showing the web of lines connecting the fort to the arches around the moat and rampart towers and the whole moon with the grid linking the individual forts. The recessed panels on the front of the arch were glowing amber while the mouth of the arch was outlined by a bright red stripe.

I went to the pedestal screen which showed the same displays on a reduced scale, together with an array of other symbols and wordage. I told myself again that it should be simple, robust, quick to operate and, hopefully, fool proof. It was designed to be used in combat situations by warriors not scientists. That the technology I suspected it controlled was way beyond my understanding did not matter. All I had to do was press the right buttons.

The display appeared to show there was plenty of power in the system and nothing seemed to be flashing a warning. But then everything had been preserved in vacuum all these years with nothing to wear out. There were several rows of symbols to the sides of the screen I did not have time to decipher. I concentrated on the diagrammatic centre section of the display. It showed the fort at the middle ringed by eight radiating arch symbols, all softly green except for the one linked by the bridge. Yes, even that made sense now.

I touched the arc symbol one around from the bridge arch. It doubled in brightness at the same time as other symbols came to life next to it, some of which seemed a little odd. Apart from the interlocked arrows by themselves and the arrows superimposed on a figure, which I thought I understood now, there was what looked like an open eye and an ear. A text block appeared: Transform Processor Ready.

I touched the eye symbol.

The end of the arc in the chamber in front of us blurred and then filled with a one to one scale image of the surface outside as would have appeared if you had been standing looking out through it. Okay, I got that now...

'It's some kind of remote viewing system,' the Prof exclaimed.

'Not just viewing,' I said.

I pressed the ear symbol. A soft mushy static sound came from the panel. I was not sure what that meant in context, but at least it was doing something.

I pressed the interlocked arrows symbol next to the arch I had selected.

The interior of the arch frame and its floor lit up with an antiseptic blue glow while the amber panels set in its front faces turned green, showing the arrow crossed figure. Everything still seemed to be functioning. I took a deep breath, possibly my last, and I pressed the figure and crossed arrow symbol combined.

Strings of arrowhead lights began flickering in succession below the figures on the arch panel screens, all appearing to be racing inwards. At the same time the red outline around the mouth of the arch turned green.

Go, go, go it all screamed at me!

I ran past Amber and the Prof and through the arch before my nerve failed. Sudden pressure on my back helped push me onwards. There was a moment of twisting nausea combined with a tingle like an electric shock that seemed to course through my whole body.

And then I was stumbling out of a matching arch on the lip of the fortress moat onto the arid, dead and airless crater floor.

Chapter 11
Pantropy

I should have passed out within a few seconds and died soon after that. But I didn't. I was alive and breathing vacuum!

Well I was alive but I was not breathing. And weirdly somehow not feeling the desire to either.

That's not to say I was feeling normal. My skin and throat were thick and tight, my eyes felt odd and my ears seemed to be full of an odd soft hissing, sizzling sound. But although the low sun was shining full on me it did not feel particularly hot on the exposed skin of my face, nor was it burning my retinas out. Something radical had changed inside me but my lungs were not boiling dry and my eardrums were not rupturing and my eyes were not bulging out of their sockets or any of the other gruesome things that came with sudden exposure to hard vacuum, so on balance I was not complaining.

But then what had happened to me?

I pulled off a glove. The skin of my hand was a smooth, even silver, looking as though it had been sprayed with a clinging film of metallic rubber. Was I like that all over? Presumably. I tried not to be sick even as I marvelled at it.

There are three ways to live on an alien word. You can either carry a tiny piece of your native environment with you in a space suit or pressurized domes, or you can reengineer the whole world, which is call terraforming, or you can radically adapt the human body to fit the environment. An

SF term was coined for this last option in the 1950's by a writer called James Blish: pantropy, which roughly translated means *changing everything.*

Of course his method supposedly took years of genetic manipulation in test tubes to produce a new adapted race whereas my transformation had been slightly faster. Still I felt as though I'd just been pantropied... pantrified... whatever. It had worked!

And weirdly I could still hear something beyond the shuffling of my feet on the ground carried up through my body as vibrations. There was that distant whispering, fizzing sound that rose and fell as I turned my head about. Overlain on it was a faint regular note, almost like a birdcall... *twit, twit, twoo, twit...*

Were they the radio emissions of the sun and Adamant's beacon?

Could I hear radio waves?

I turned and looked back through the arch into the control room at Amber and her father's incredulous faces seeming only a few paces away from me instead of the few hundred metres I knew they really were.

'I'm fine,' I called out instinctively, before I realized there was no air coming out of my mouth to make a sound and no atmosphere to carry it even if there had been.

There was no time for anything more, even to see if the process was automatically reversed (as I desperately hoped it would be) if I went back through the arch. I had a job to do...

I was forty-five degrees round the moat rim from the bridge arch which put me about two hundred metres away from the *Eclipse* where it rested a little in front of it.

And there was Oliver!

He was trudging over the spindly bridge. He had not seen me appear as I had been sheltered by the arch. Now I had to stop him taking the ship and leaving us stranded. But he was armed and I wasn't. If only I had a weapon of some kind!

I looked about me at the hard moat apron and churned grey soil beyond. There was something with a straight edge lying half buried amid the shattered fragments of rock and metal beads.

I bounced over to it and pulled it out of the dust. It was a twisted spar of metal about half a metre long with a melted lumpy end, which would make a pretty good improvised club.

I began to run towards the *Eclipse* in great bounding strides, kicking up splashes and spurts of dust as I went. Away from the transweb arch there was no cover so my only hope was speed. Without a spacesuit weighing me down and hampering my stride I knew I could move much faster than Oliver.

I was dressed in grey against a grey background but in the low light I cast a long and rapidly moving shadow. If he looked up…

He did. I saw the gold tinted bowl of his faceplate turn towards me.

Shock must have paralysed him for a few seconds. He could not have recognised who I was from that distance with me clad in the combat gear. Maybe he thought I was some ghost of a fortress warrior or an avenging angel conjured up out of his guilty conscience, which I hoped by now was giving him hell. Maybe he did not believe his eyes, unsure if I was real or not.

Then he began to run as well.

He almost fell off the ramp before he reached the arch. By then I was ahead of him. I would reach the ship first. If I could keep him away from that for long enough for Amber and the Professor to join me we were safe!

But Oliver bounded out of the other side of the arch with his right arm raised. He was pointing his gun at me. Would it work in a vacuum? Unfortunately yes…

There were three soundless flashes in quick succession. The first two bullets missed but the third hit my chestplate.

It felt like I had been kicked in the side. The impact knocked me off my feet and I tumbled over into the dust. For a moment I lay there with my ribs aching, terrified that I had been wounded, scrabbling at the chestplate of the body armour with my thick gloves. There was a dent but no hole. Whoever had made this stuff a thousand years ago had done a good job.

I scrambled to my feet snarling silently in rage and leaped onwards.

But the delay had given Oliver a chance to reach the ship's ramp where it still lay extended. He paused to fire another couple of quick shots at me but I dodged to one side and then threw my club at him. It spun end over end and struck him on the side of his helmet. He staggered and almost fell and then clawed his way into the ship.

I reached the ramp a couple of seconds later and bounded up it only to crash into the outer airlock door. Through its thick armoured glass viewport I saw Oliver holding on to the inside actuating lever with one hand while he worked the lock control panel with the other. His sun visor, with a scrape across it where my club had hit his helmet, was now up so I could see his face. His nose was bleeding. The impact must have shaken him enough to bang his head on the inside. Our eyes met and he looked terrified. Good!

I heaved on the outer door lever but it would not budge. Oliver was braced against it, holding it shut. I picked up my club where it had fallen after hitting Oliver and jammed one end into the handle recess, trying to lever it over. Then inside the lock the control panel lights flashed to show the lock was full. Oliver suddenly jammed his gun right up against the hatch as though he was going to try to shoot through it into my face. I flinched backwards. In that moment he lunged for the inner hatch and wrenched it open.

Now the outer door was automatically locked because the inner one was open. And Oliver deliberately left it open as he staggered through the forward hatch at the end of the service corridor and into the main cabin. Furiously I pounded on the outer hatch with my club but it was no use. In two minutes he would take off. How long could I cling to the ramp before I fell or he shook me off?

Then I remembered that the rear hatch was not the only way into the ship.

I dropped off the ramp onto the ground. Standing on its landing legs the top of the ship's hull was almost four metres high. On Earth I could not have reached far enough up its curving hull to get to the top. But this was the moon.

I took a short run up and jumped.

It was an amazing feeling as I soared up over the ship and landed on top of it. And there was the circular emergency escape hatch that led down into the corridor beyond the airlock. Escape hatches should be made for easy access in both directions, or so I hoped. Oliver had run straight through to the control cabin so he had no time to lock it off or jam it.

There was a panel set in the thick hatch cover that opened up to reveal a quick acting central latch wheel actuating bolts all round the hatch rim and an emergency air bleed valve, all clearly labelled with big letters and bold arrows. The hatch opened inward against internal air pressure so there was no way I could have forced it against that. As shown I twisted and popped the bleed valve open. A fountain of air rushed out soundlessly past my head, boiling away into the vacuum. That should shake Oliver up. Would he have wasted time taking off his helmet or would he be too busy prepping the ship for takeoff? If he had removed it he would only have a few seconds to get it back on again.

The blast of air died away. I twisted the handle and the hatch swung downwards, extending the folding ceiling ladder. Just as I started down it the ship wallowed, tilted backwards and then lifted off.

I tumbled the rest of the way down the ladder. Fortunately my body armour cushioned my landing. I struggled onto my feet against the pressure of acceleration. The door to the control room had swung to but it was not locked. As though climbing up a sloping floor I charged through it waving my club and yelling soundlessly.

Oliver was sitting in the command chair with his helmet still on. As I burst in he twisted round pointing his gun and fired at me once again. The shot glanced off my helmet, making my head ring, but I had too much momentum to be stopped. With one swing of my club I knocked the gun out of his hand and with the next I landed a solid smack on his helmet, scarring its faceplate and making his head rattle about inside. His helmet was tough and would not simply shatter but I could certainly give him a bad headache as I put the fear of what the next blow might do into him.

Unfortunately he did not simply cave in. Maybe he was getting over his initial shock or he was driven by desperation, but he fought back.

He blocked my next blow with his arm and lunged out of his chair at me. We grappled, rolling about the floor. Oliver was bigger and stronger than me but he was hampered by his bulky suit, which, however, also worked quite like body armour. My combat gear was just as protective, though and it was also lighter and I think I was madder.

With nobody at the controls the ship spun crazily. One moment the stars, sun and Earth were tumbling past the viewports and the next it was the fort and crater floor. But neither of us dared let go of the other. Oliver had raised the stakes to the kill or be killed level. In fact he was already a murderer after what he had done to Mrs Whittle and an attempted murderer after what he had tried to do to us. It was the knowledge of that which kept me slugging away at him, leaving little room for

160

rational thought. At that moment I think I'd rather crash the ship than let him get away with it.

Then he landed a punch on the chin guard of my helmet that made my head ring and left me groggy. He tore himself free of my limp grasp, staggered to his feet and clawed his way back to the command chair. He took hold of the controls and fought to level the ship out.

Shaking my head to clear it I dragged myself to my feet and looked around for my club. And then I saw it was too late.

Filling the forward ports was the pitted grey crater floor and we were heading straight for it!

Fighting with the controls, Oliver just levelled off the *Eclipse* enough to avoid the hull boring straight into the ground, but the undercarriage, which he had not had time to retract when I had messed up his escape, gouged long furrows in the dry earth, sending up sprays of dust and rock. There was a groan and screech from its tortured shock absorbers that I could feel through the floor and the ship bounced crazily several metres upward. Then drive cut out completely and we were falling freely. Oliver and I were flung up against the cabin roof and then smashed back down as the ship pancaked into the dust, almost collapsing the landing gear for a second time. Then the *Eclipse* bounded freely along on its big mesh wheels, tossing us about from side to side of the cabin like dice in a shaker.

A wall of melted green and bronze metal loomed up in front of us.

With kilometres of open level crater floor to land on, we had come down on a collision course

with the wreck of Janus's Hydra class carrier!
Oliver threw up his arms as we hit it. There was a
tearing impact and everything went black. The
cockpit burst inwards and I was thrown forward
against the backs of the control chairs.

Chapter 12
Things in the Dark

Everything went black... but not because I was knocked out again like I had been when we hit the van Allen belt. It was black outside because we were somewhere out of the sunlight. The only illumination came from the control panel lights. When everything stopped rocking and rolling I found I was lying on my back behind the arc of control chairs dazed and shaken, but thanks to the combat armour I had suffered only a few extra bruises and I don't think I passed out.

The *Eclipse* was resting with its nose tilted upward by about twenty degrees but the hull seemed to be intact, except for the cockpit canopy itself. A jagged horizontal spar of bronze-coloured metal had punched a hole right through it, crumpling up the multi-laminated panel which had been torn out of its frame and now lay in a twisted glittering heap at the back of the cabin.

Flimsy shreds of bronze and green metallic foil seemed to have come in through this hole and bits of it were lying all over the place while more of the stuff was draped over the outside view ports. For a moment I could not work out what it was. Then I realized it was the remains of the solid looking wall of the wreck that we had hit. In fact it had only been as substantial as cardboard with some clear space beyond it into which we had run on until we hit the spar and whatever the ship's keel was resting on. And a good thing too otherwise right now the ship would have been a shattered wreck itself and me along with it.

But though I'd survived the crash landing I wasn't feeling right, even by the standards of my recent dramatic session of pantropy. Hunger was gnawing away at my stomach and I was feeling weak and drained as though I had not eaten for days. Had I injured myself? But then why would I feel so hungry?

And then a more immediate worry penetrated my addled brain: what about Oliver?

Ignoring my hunger pangs I scrambled to my feet.

Oliver was lying on the other side of the control chairs in the footspace between them and the forward rim of the hull. As I reached for him he stirred and then suddenly jerked round, throwing up his arm. He was holding his gun again and he jabbed it into my face. There was more blood on the inside of his helmet and his eyes were wild. I sprang backwards, looking for my club. Oliver hauled himself to his feet, keeping the gun pointed at my face. I could see his lips moving but of course I could not hear his words.

He grinned manically, enjoying his moment of triumph. I'd have to risk jumping him and hope he would miss or hit my body armour again. Third time unlucky? Then, even as I crouched down, I thought I saw a flicker of motion in the blackness beyond the viewports...

Suddenly I could hear Oliver's words inside my head, as though I'd just tuned into the suit radio channel. '... I don't know what you did to yourself but it's not good enough...'

'Don't count on it,' I said automatically, clenching my fists.

He started. He'd heard me! Somehow the movement of my vocal chords was being translated into radio waves of the same frequency my ears were tuned into and had been transmitted to him. I would have appreciated the neatness of it more if I had not been so preoccupied with the muzzle of his gun.

'How the hell did you do that?' Oliver asked, for a moment giving in to genuine amazement.

'Alien tec,' I said simply. 'If you hadn't been a double crossing murderer you'd have been there when I worked it out.'

'Alright, so I underestimated you, Tom. But it's the last time I do...' he took careful aim at my face.

I looked over his shoulder. 'Oliver... there's something moving out there.'

'Don't try that old trick on me...'

And then a huge green metal insect-like arm reached in through the shattered cockpit and closed its big triple pronged claw crushingly hard about Oliver's shoulder.

He cursed and yelped in horror as the claw arm dragged him struggling and kicking wildly back out of the shattered cockpit and he vanished into the darkness. But I could still hear his sobs and screams with my radio ears. There were muzzle flashes from the gun as he fired at something I could not see. Then his screams cut off abruptly in a burst of static and he was gone.

Right then I just wanted to run from that horror in the darkness surrounding me! Maybe I could break out of the rear hatch and sprint for the daylight and leave it far behind? No, I had to save the ship if I could, for all our sakes.

I saw my fallen club, snatched it up and then scrambled into the pilot's chair.

I could drive a car. Ever since my legs had been long enough for my feet to reach the control pedals, my father had been giving me lesions on private roads and fields and it had been made clear to me that the son of a driving school owner was expected, when the time came, to pass his driving test first time. So driving did not scare me. But as I gaped at the controls on the panel in front of me I struggled to remember what the Prof had done to get the *Eclipse* rolling out of the hanger. He'd used the joystick to steer but the main drive had not yet been powered up. How did he link it to the wheels… assuming the wheel motors still had power and would turn?

Another claw arm, or the same one without Oliver in its grasp, came groping in through the gaping hole in the canopy in front of me. One handed I beat at it with my club and it jerked back, snapping at me.

Then I saw the button: *Undercarriage Drive Select.* I punched it and pulled back on the joystick. Nothing happened. Desperately I pulled on the lever by the joystick and power flowed into the wheel motors.

There was a grinding, screeching vibration and the *Eclipse* lurched backwards, pulling itself off the spar on which it was impaled. It slid back out through the windshield, taking the claw arm with it. The loose foil draped across the ship fell away.

166

I twisted the joystick hard over, sending the *Eclipse* round in a circle until I saw the raged rent in the flimsy foil wall the *Eclipse* had torn when it had crashed into the wreck. I drove the ship towards it at top speed, grinding and bounding along. Whippy metal tentacles and grasping claws lunged out of the shadows and rattled and scraped at the side ports, but I kept on going, knocking them aside. Something crunched beneath the wheels.

The *Eclipse* erupted out of the crumpled side of the wreck back onto the sunlight crater floor. I swung it round and headed towards the distant bulk of the fortress, looking fearfully at the display screen that showed a view from a rearward pointing camera, expecting to see a hoard of those things pouring out of the wreck after me. But nothing moved. Apart from the hole the ship had made in its side it looked just as it had when we had first landed.

If I had been breathing I would have sighed in relief.

And then far ahead I saw a figure running in long low-g bounding strides across the crater floor towards me from the direction of Fort Adamant.

Faintly I heard a voice calling in my head: 'Tom! Is that you?'

It was Amber. But how was she talking to me?

'Yes,' I called back. 'Don't get any closer to the wreck. It's dangerous.'

'What do you mean?'

'Just stay there and I'll come to you...'

Amber stopped and I drove as fast as I could, which was only about fifteen or twenty kph, to meet her, dust spurting up from the wheels. As I drew

167

closer I saw she was also wearing a combat gear set over her ship suit. Where her face showed under her helmet it was bright silver.

'I don't know if the rear hatch is still working,' I said. 'Come in through the top... it's open... the whole ship's depressurised.'

'So I guessed,' she said, looking at me through the missing cockpit canopy panel.

She jumped nimbly up onto the top of the hull and a moment later she was clambering down into the back of the ship. I got up as she came into the cabin. She pulled off her helmet and I saw her hair was silver as well. And her eyeballs looked like ball bearings, only slightly less reflective than the rest of her skin. Of course they had to let in some light for us to see. No wonder Oliver had been shocked at my appearance.

'Do I look like that?' I said stupidly.

'Well obviously...'

'So... you thought you'd try the same look?'

'It seemed the best thing to do...'

And then, just for a moment, she hugged me. With us both wearing combat armour it wasn't as much fun as it sounded, but it was the thought that counted. Then she was her old super-composed self again, moving me aside and taking over the pilot's chair. I took her old chair and we were off again, wallowing slightly as we ploughed through the dust.

'What have you done to the *Eclipse*... and where's Oliver?' she asked.

'We had a mid-air fight... mid space fight... and the *Eclipse* crashed into the wreck. Oliver's still there.'

'Is he...dead?'

'I don't know. He survived the crash but something took him...'

'What?'

'The things we saw on the recording of the final battle. Janus's machines. I think there are still some alive in there... working, anyway. They took him. They would have grabbed me as well if I hadn't got out quickly... there was nothing I could do...'

Just then the Professor's voice rang out inside my head, sounding clear but distant, like he was talking through a loudspeaker from a long way off.

'Hallo... Amber... Tom... can you hear me?'

'Yes, Father,' Amber replied. 'Tom's with me and we're bringing the ship back. Oliver is... gone... we'll explain when we get back.'

The Prof didn't ask for any more details right then. Clearly he had a new set of priorities. 'I can see you on a monitor screen. I'm in the main control room now. I think almost all the main functions of the base can be directed from here. It's just a matter of working out the symbology they use on their instruments. Is the ship damaged?'

'She's got some superficial damage, she lost a cockpit panel and she's depressurized but otherwise she seems intact.'

'Good. I'll see if I can do something about the rest. Keep going...' and he faded out.

'How did you work out this radio head business?' I asked.

'When you ran out through the arch... which was a very stupid thing to do, by the way... we heard you calling back to us over a speaker on the arch control panel. We realized it communicated

169

with you somehow. I thought that you might need help. So I put on another combat suit and came through the archway after you.'

'And your father let you?'

'I can dodge faster than he can,' she said simply. 'Anyway it made sense for him to stay behind and try to work out the controls. He thought we should be able to communicate both ways. Obviously you can send and receive radio signals through selected arches to adjusted people, and, apparently, we can also communicate between ourselves. I suppose our vocal cords have somehow been modified into organic transmitters. I don't think we're very sensitive though.'

'But we are adaptable. Somehow I tuned into Oliver's suit radio. We exchanged a few insults… before he got snatched.'

'Oh… we must be subconsciously scanning the frequencies, like searching for a particular person's voice amongst a babble of others at a party and then tuning out the rest.'

'Can you hear the sun's radio output and Adamant's beacon as well?'

'Of course, that was what it was!' she exclaimed. 'I was a little too… preoccupied chasing after you to work it out.'

She'd been preoccupied coming after me!

I pulled off a glove and held up my silver hand. 'Pretty weird isn't it?'

'Quite. I was nearly sick after I went through.'

'Me too,' I said, showing solidarity. 'Are you feeling hungry?'

'Yes, very. You as well?'

'Yes. Not sure why.'

'Well, we're not breathing…'

'I noticed that.'

'So we've got to be getting energy from somewhere else. We must be breaking down whatever food we had in us when we were transformed…'

'Pantromorphed,' I suggested

'If you insist. Anyway we're breaking it down at a tremendous rate which increases with the energy we expend. I've been running and you've been fighting so we've both used a lot and we're starting to feel it. When we get back to normal I'm going to eat a huge meal.'

'I'll join you. I wish there was some of Ms Whittle's shepherd's pie left…'

I saw Amber's silver lips pinch tight. I should not have said that. 'Sorry. I only knew her for a short time but she seemed very nice.'

'It's all right,' she said stiffly. 'It's not your fault. And she was wonderful. But we must get through all this first. I'll remember her properly later…'

Can you cry when your body had been morphed for surviving in a vacuum? Tears would just boil off so probably not. But Amber looked like she wanted to.

I didn't say any more until we reached the fort. By then the Prof had clearly been busy. 'Drive up to the edge of the moat on the clockwise side of the arch you passed through,' he told us. 'I've found a means of external access to the fort's maintenance and hanger levels, as we saw on the recording. I'll meet you down there…'

171

A platform about fifteen metres square rose up from the depths of the moat supported by a gantry running up the slotted tracks in its outer face, and then slid outward, so that it bridged the chamfered lip and its top was level with the hard apron. It was like the platforms we had seen the tanks riding on when they had been deployed to fight Janus's invading war machines.

Amber drove us onto it. The platform pulled back from the edge and then dropped smoothly downward, carrying us into the depths.

The sheer sides of the moat rolled up past us, framing an arc of stars and Terra in its jewelled cage above our heads. It must have been at least two hundred metres deep. We were already far below the level of the control room.

We almost reached the bottom when we saw heavy double doors opening in the base of the tower between two of its massive ribs. Beyond it was what looked like a huge airlock, the largest of a ring of doors about the base of the tower. Of course it made sense to have access to the interior of the fort down here in the shelter of the moat. The cradle arm the platform was mounted on began to slide smoothly inwards towards the doorway as we continued down, keeping the platform level, until it butted up against the outer rim of the lock floor. Amber drove the *Eclipse* off it into the lock. The big doors rolled shut behind us and we were back inside the fort. Having its massive walls between us and whatever still lurked in wreck felt reassuring.

The inner doors opened and we drove forward into the hanger proper. It was a big space with several secondary bays opening off from the

172

entrance zone, divided by heavy partitions with big transparent windows let into them and large sliding doors. Built into the partitions were both standard looking man-sized airlocks and more of the transweb arches, but built on a more door-sized scale than the big ones upstairs or the array around the moat. The high ceiling was fitted with tracks supporting a suspended mobile crane with grab jaws large enough to have picked the *Eclipse* up in one go. At the head of the chamber was a large elevated control booth with access to glassed-in stairways and gantries that led to the different bays. At its back was a cluster of lift tubes and standing at its control console was the figure of the Professor who waved at us through the glass.

'Go to the open repair bay at the back left,' he said over the radio head circuit. 'It's the only one still fully equipped.'

Amber drove the *Eclipse* towards the sub bay at the back of the hangar that had its door open and turned into it. Its door slid shut behind us.

'I think you should get out now and pass through the arch next to you before I pressurise the bay,' the Prof said. 'I'm not sure what effect exposure to an atmosphere will have on you in your... er, transformed states. If I have interpreted the symbols correctly, they should just transmute you back to normal without sending you anywhere.'

I hoped so too.

'We'll be out as soon as I can release the rear hatch,' Amber said.

Amber worked on the controls of the airlock for a minute and managed to get the outer door released, so we were able to leave the ship down the ramp, the lower edge of which was now a little battered. It had never been retracted during our brief flight and crash landing.

I looked at the impressive equipment racks, machine tools and control panels built into the back of the bay. Some items like hammers and screwdrivers were so basic they looked familiar while others I did not recognize. Presumably they had been used to maintain the fortress's vehicles. Glancing through the dividing partitions I saw all the other bays had been stripped bare. Good of them to leave one set behind. Could we use them to repair the *Eclipse*?

We crossed to the nearest arch which connected to an enclosed corridor that ran between the bays. The arch was a smaller version of the big ones we had already seen in height and width, but it was just as deep making it look like a truncated corridor. I saw what the Prof had said about the symbols. The arrow crossed figure engraved onto it did not have the double headed arrows behind it. Its front edges were rimmed in welcoming green, as was the screen icon which also shone green and the inner arch with its complex engraved patterns was a shimmering, eye-watering blue.

'Let's hope it knows how to change us back,' I said.

'Should we go through one at a time?' Amber wondered.

'It's wide enough for two of us. I think there would be a sign if it wasn't safe to double up.'

We had to lean forward as we stepped into the arch together. At the other end was the fully pressurised air of the fortress interior, which must have been held back from rushing out into the unpressurised bay by some kind of diffuse force curtain. We were fighting its resistance as we came in out of the vacuum. It was spread out because if it had come as a single sharp transition from nothing to full pressure we could never have forced our way through it. Half way along I felt the tingling churning, twisting sensation I had experienced briefly as I had run through the Transweb Room arch. Beside me Amber was clutching her stomach. We pushed on another couple of steps feeling sick even as our insides were reorganized. With my head down I saw a haze about my feet and legs. Moondust was somehow being pulled off our clothes and drawn down into the grille under out feet. So that was what it was for...

Suddenly I had to take in a huge lungful of air, feeling as though I would suffocate if I did not breath. Sounds seemed to beat on my eardrums: all those little atmospheric whispers that define your surroundings that you don't notice until they were missing. Then we were stumbling out of the other end of the archway, gasping and twitching, looking at each other fearfully. Amber's face was its usual pinkish-brown again and her eyes did not resemble silver marbles. Hopefully mine were back to normal as well.

'Looks like it worked,' I said, once again using sound waves and not radio to speak. It felt weird.

Amber nodded, while looking as though she was trying not to throw up.

I could also smell things again. Outside I hadn't realized I'd lost that sense. Well there had been a few more important things on my mind.

Now it was back I was amazed how powerful it was, even if what I smelt was mostly me in need of a shower.

There was a single transparent pressure door, presumably as a safety backup, between us and the corridor. We went through it. Behind us air began hissing into the bay holding the *Eclipse*. There were displays by the airlock and arch which showed the pressure rising. But then something else caught our attention.

In the corridor next to the arch door was a black panel on the wall with a single slot at its base, a little like a cutdown version of the one in the harness room. It was illuminated and of course now I could read its display lettering.

RATION BAR DISPENSER.

There were two options illuminated: *Type 1* and *Type 2 bars.*

Type 1 read: *Standard service ration bars.*

And it seemed there were a range of flavours on offer, although the names meant nothing to me. What was *Orajino* or *Plarm*? Possibly they were trade names that had no other translatable meaning. But it was the Type 2 display that really grabbed my attention.

TYPE 2 TW RATION BARS.

Suitable for mid temperature range hard vacuum metaforms: Venus orbit, Terra-Luna interspace, Luna surface, Mars orbit and satellites.

Only to be consumed in transformed state.

Provides all fluid, protein and metabolic oxygen requirements.

No more than eight bars to be consumed in one Terran day

'I think we know what to eat to stop us getting hungry next time we go outside,' I said.

I pressed the button by the slot and a block the size of a chunky chocolate bar wrapped in heavy metal foil dropped out. It was marked Type 2 ration bar and carried the same warnings as the display. Cautiously I broke it open. Inside was an unappetising grey slab with the texture of moist dense cake with flecks of green and black in it. I realized the bar fitted the empty pouch pockets in our harness belts.

'No need for life support packs. Carry all your, food, water and oxygen with you in one bar,' I said. 'Neat.'

'These can't have been stored here for a thousand years,' Amber pointed out.

'They'd definitely be past their sell-by date if they had,' I agreed. 'They must have been freshly synthesised out of basic compounds that are storable.'

'Maybe, but you've no idea what they might do to you if you ate them. Don't risk it.'

'Says the girl who took a run across the moon without a space suit.'

'That was different,' she said stiffly.

Amber was saved from explaining why by the Professor who had descended from the control booth and who now rounded the end of the corridor.

His face lit up as he saw Amber and then abruptly stiffened. 'You should not have gone out like that Amber,' he said sternly. 'Tom did not need your help. It was very… unwise of you.'

'No, Father,' she agreed.

Then suddenly, and very awkwardly, he hugged her to him.

He was a brilliant man who could design a revolutionary spaceship to fly to the moon, but who did not know how to handle elementary emotions.

'I miss her so much,' Amber said in a whisper, and I knew who she meant. And now I saw the tears she could not have shed outside.

'So do I,' he said, patting her back clumsily.

Both broke off the brief embrace looking relieved but slightly embarrassed, doing their best to wipe away all traces of this brief show of emotion. Solemnly Cavendish held out his hand and shook mine.

'That was really quite resourceful of you, Tom. I must admit I had my doubts about you at one point... but you have shown considerable promise.'

From him that probably counted as high praise.

'Thank you, Professor,' I said, trying to match his gravitas.

'Now I must inspect the *Eclipse* and ascertain what damage she has suffered.' His lips pinched. 'And you must tell me what happened to Oliver.'

'Can we eat as we go, father?' Amber said. 'We're both starving. I think it was only our last meal that's kept us going...'

We showed him the ration bar machine and explained how we thought it worked.

'Yes, that makes sense,' he said. 'A remarkable system. I must try it myself as soon as possible. But the ship must come first...'

He made his way to the airlock opening into the now pressurised bay.

'Come on, Tom,' Amber said. 'There's food in the ship.'

'I am going try some of these Type 1 bars,' I said, punching the buttons for a plarm and an orajino.

'Now you're just playing again,' Amber said despairingly.

Back in the ship, which had filled with air as the hanger bay had been pressurized, Amber and I removed our combat armour and put our crewsuits and sneakers back on. The Prof changed out of his pressure suit back into his jumpsuit as well. Then we sat on our chairs in the main cabin eating while the Prof inspected the crash damage. Amber ate from a sealed sandwich pack from the ship stores while I had my fortress ration bars. For your information plarm tastes like a spicy onion chickenburger while orajino tastes like marzipan flavoured fishcakes. I guess it's an acquired taste, but pride made me keep forcing it down. At least it filled my stomach.

In between chewing I told Amber and the Prof about my fight with Oliver inside the *Eclipse* and what had happened when we crashed through the wall of the wrecked carrier.

The Professor looked grave when I described how those insect-like metal arms grabbed Oliver while Amber actually went pale. She really did not like science fictional nightmares come to life around her. In her well-ordered universe such things should not happen. Of course we were no longer in her universe…

When I was finished, Amber asked: 'Could some of those machines we saw on the recording still be functioning after a thousand years?'

'Well this base is still operational,' I pointed out, 'so I suppose there's no reason why they should not have lasted as well. A dozen at least, from the number of arms that tried to grab the ship as I left. Our crashing in like that must have caught them by surprise. I suppose they took us for fortress soldiers and did what they had been programmed to do.'

'But after the battle the fort soldiers must have checked the wreck out for survivors.'

'It's a big ship. Maybe a few machines managed to hide out somewhere in its core. Perhaps they assumed that with Janus locked away inside the Terracage any remaining machines would just run down of their own accord. But I think they've been busy in there. What looked like a solid wall of melted metal had being hollowed out from behind until it was hardly more than paper thin. Maybe they were cannibalizing the wreck from the inside, drawing energy from sunlight to keep themselves operating, going into standby mode during the night.'

'But if they were still functioning then why have they not attacked the fort?' Amber wondered.

'They may not realize it's been abandoned.'

Her father interjected. 'Whether they know that or not, they would still hesitate to attack. Remember what General Skane said on the recording. The automated monitor systems are still on and sensitive to Janus's devices. Presumably they are attuned to some particular energy or spectrographic characteristics unique to them combined with motion sensors, otherwise they would have fired on us when we first arrived. If the surviving machines had shown themselves outside the shelter of the wreck they would have been destroyed. The only alternative would be to stay put and wait for some change in their situation. Even for a thousand years...'

'And those are the things that took Oliver,' Amber said, looking slightly sick.

'He made his choices,' Professor said coldly. 'If he hadn't betrayed and abandoned us he wouldn't be where he is now.'

We were all silent for a bit after that, brooding over Oliver's fate. Then Amber took a deep breath. 'Now I think Tom had better explain how he worked out how the arch transformation system functioned. I'm sure he's dying to tell us...'

Was there a touch of sarcasm in her words? Nevertheless I did not refuse the opportunity because I didn't often have two such smart people ready to admire my thought processes.

'There were lots clues, it was just a matter of putting them together,' I admitted. 'For a start there was something wrong about that big triple airlock at surface level we first came in through. It was useless if you wanted to get troops deployed quickly. That bridge was probably only a kind of side door and never the main entrance. All the doors opening off it at the head of the ramps and tube lifts were too small for large numbers of soldiers to use even if there had been spacesuits stored behind them, which would have been the logical place if it was a main access point. I think it was just for maintenance use.'

181

'Then we found what looked like a space suit store down at the control room level, except that there seemed to be no suits there. Even if there had been, why would they then get soldiers to climb all those levels fully suited just to get outside? Even if they used the lift tubes it just didn't make sense.'

'Once we were able to read what the displays said they showed this "trans-web" network. That could just have meant regular communications but then Skane mentioned evacuating Terra to turn it into a trap for Janus. I can't imagine any ordinary space fleet being able to do that, even if there were far fewer people on Terra than our Earth, and they did not have any ships to spare. But if there was some way of sending people between worlds directly and more or less instantaneously then that might be possible, especially if they could live on their surfaces without artificial protection or massive terraforming. The signs outside the arch rooms confirmed that, once I could read them.'

'You're suggesting the web system we see on the screens could be used to transport people from here all over the solar system,' Cavendish put in. 'Intriguing.'

'Maybe, Professor, if it's still working. Then I was just worried about getting out of the fort as fast as possible to stop Oliver. On the recording of the battle, we saw from a distance what looked like men in spacesuits out on the crater floor fighting the machines, but with all the excitement I didn't notice how they got out there so quickly. Of course it made sense if they went out through the ring of archways.'

'In fact all the clues were on the first archway we saw at the end of the bridge. The symbols engraved into it had been scratched out. The people at the base didn't want anybody used to using things like that thinking it was still functional when it was only left elevated to mark one end of the bridge. The symbol said it all. A figure with arrows on either side of it, suggesting travel or movement, crossed over with those two interlocking "S" curves, which could be interpreted as...'

Amber said quickly: 'Of course! They're meant to symbolize the double DNA helix, aren't they? The blueprint of our bodies! And with arrows at each end they suggest it being changed or rewritten! I should have seen that myself...'

'I'm sure you would have done if you'd read enough SF,' I said generously. 'This is kind of my speciality. Anyway I put all these things together when I thought I had nothing to lose. The harness room was right next to a chamber with an arch in it that seemed identical to the ones around the rim of the moat. It made sense if they could somehow get out of the fortress directly through the archway *and didn't need any other kind of protection!* I wasn't sure if I needed to put the combat armour on as well, but I did because for all I knew it might somehow trigger the transition. And I was going up against Oliver and his gun so I thought I'd need all the protection I could get. But there was no time to explain all that to you and anyway...' I took a deep breath '... I was worried I'd chicken out. You see I wanted to make up for losing my nerve when we took off.'

'Oh, Tom,' Amber said despairingly. 'You can be very silly sometimes.'

I really hope she meant that in an affectionate way.

'Well, whatever the inspiration it seems your reasoning was sound and it has saved us from being marooned here,' Cavendish conceded.

'How badly is the ship damaged?' Amber asked.

'As far as I can tell the drive tubes themselves are functional, but some of the power circuits need to be repaired before they can be energised. At the moment the *Eclipse* cannot fly. There is also considerable damage to the outer hull and we must repair or replace the lost cockpit panel. We can't travel from here back to our own Earth and re-enter its atmosphere without a properly sealed cabin. Hopefully we can make use of the tools in this bay to help repair it. It may take some time to learn how to operate them of course...'

'But what about the wreck?' Amber wondered. 'I mean if there are still machines inside and they know we're here now, what are they going to do next?'

'As long as the fortress's defences are still active then any assault on their part it will lead to their destruction,' Cavendish said. 'They must realize that or else they would have made some move long ago. For our part we have no weapons or means of attacking them so we can make no pre-emptive strike. The only thing we can do is leave them alone and hope they do the same.'

'What about the fort's weapons?' I asked. 'We saw how powerful they were. Maybe we could use

184

them to blast the wreck.' I thought of those grasping, snapping claws and tentacles being blown to pieces. It felt good.

'We don't actually know that Oliver is dead,' Amber pointed out. 'He might still be alive in there.'

Why did she have to make things so complicated? 'You still care about him after what he's done?' I asked.

Amber gritted her teeth. 'Just because I hate what he's done doesn't mean I'd sink to his level. We might have to leave him because we haven't got the power to do anything else, but I wouldn't like to think we had actually killed him in cold blood.' She added meaningfully, staring straight at me: 'Not like some trigger-happy boy given a big ray gun to play with…'

Ouch, that hurt.

'If you recall we don't have that option,' Cavendish reminded me. 'As General Skane said the weapons are on an automatic trigger linked to some kind of detector field and locked off from manual control. I examined the consoles while I was waiting for you to return and found the weapon control board and confirmed her statement. It would require the correct code key to unlock them, which would hardly have been left lying around for anybody to find. Whatever actions we take we cannot count on using the fortress's main weapons to assist us.'

Amber looked relieved. It made sense of course. You wouldn't want just anybody who turned up at the fortress controlling such firepower. We were lucky so many devices in the fort had worked for us as it was. Still it would have been reassuring to have the option.

'Then what do we do next, Professor?' I asked.

'Obviously monitor the wreck while applying all our efforts to repairing the *Eclipse*.' Then he scowled as though making an unwilling admission. 'But for that we must be fully alert and I admit that I am badly in need of some rest. We have just had a day and a very long night that have been both wonderful and terrible and now we must allow ourselves time to recover our strength.'

I glanced at my watch. The Prof was right. It was, back home on our own version of Earth, nearly ten o'clock GMT on Saturday morning. We had been on the moon for almost five incredibly eventful hours, which meant, barring a short period of unconsciousness, that I had been awake for over twenty-four hours straight. I never had got that planned nap on the way to the moon and since then I'd been sustained by excitement and fear-induced adrenalin jolts. But now it all began to catch up on me. Even by traditional teenage standards, the prospect of sleep had never seemed so appealing.

Amber was also looking tired but she still raised a possible objection. 'I don't think we should all sleep at the same time, Father. We should take turns keeping watch.'

'That will mean we'll all be less alert than we could be,' her father said. 'We'll lock ourselves into the ship and trust to the strength of the fort's walls and its automatic defences. They can probably keep a better watch over the crater and the wreck than we can. After all, they've been doing so for a thousand years. If those machines that took

186

Oliver emerge they'd be destroyed, and judging by the recording of the battle we saw, if the weapons were activated we would soon know it.'

'It would make quite an alarm call,' I agreed.

Ten minutes later all three of us had reclined the couches and settled back to rest. One sixth gravity made them feel unbelievably comfortable, far better than airline seats. Exhaustion overcame my confused thoughts and fears and in moments I was sound asleep.

Chapter 13
The Signal

A green metal claw was snapping in my face... shaking me... No, it was Amber.

'Bleagh... stop that... gotta to sleep...' I said groggily.

'You have slept for eight hours.' Amber said briskly. I squinted about the cabin through crusted eyelids. Cavendish's chair was empty and Amber looked insultingly bright and fresh. 'Up you get, we've got work to do...'

I didn't feel as though I'd slept at all. I had to check my watch before I believed a whole eight hours had passed. It really was three-thirty five Saturday afternoon.

Suddenly I felt a cold hand squeeze my heart and my stomach knotted. What were my parents doing? They must have heard about the fire at Continuum House by now. They'd have tried ringing my phone and got no response. They could hardly have imagined how out far out of range I was. Were they standing behind some police cordon looking at a pile of smoking ruins and wondering if what was left me was still in there? If only I could tell them I was all right!

Amber was frowning at me. Presumably I let my feelings show. I took a deep breath.

'Sorry, just thinking about my parents. Wondering how they're coping with what they imagine has happened to me.'

Amber frowned. 'Are you sorry I talked you into coming?'

'Oh My God, no! I mean this is the most amazing thing I've ever done. But I just wish some things had worked out differently... you know.'

She must be struggling to keep her feelings about Mrs Whittle under control, but she was not letting it show. 'I know, but we can't think about that now. If you want to see your parents as soon as possible, get up and make yourself useful...'

I had a quick wash and a sandwich and then I joined Amber and her father who were already out in the workshop bay. He was standing at the control panel of a large wall unit with several transparent panels built into it, ranging from book size to desk top. One of the smaller panels was illuminated with a red glow. The Prof's hair was tousled and his eyes were bright behind his glasses, making him look like an overgrown kid playing with a new toy.

As I came up to him a chime sounded and the glow behind the panel faded. He opened it up and took out a fist sized cube of clear glass or plastic which he examined for a moment and then put down on the floor with a pile of other cubes of identical size but different colours and textures. Next to them was an assortment of small items: a universal joint, an angle brace, a length of pipe and so on, all looking fresh and shiny.

Tentatively I asked him: 'What's this, Professor?'

He beamed. 'It's an automated fabrication unit that appears to be capable of synthesising almost any element or simple compound and form them into components of any shape and composition. It has a library of basic components and materials that can be combined as required and a scanning unit that can replicate original shapes. Like one of our 3-D printers but much faster and far more sophisticated.'

'It looks like you've got it up and running already.'

'There are many built in help and advice modules in the system. As we saw with the transweb arch controls they also make extensive use of simplifying symbols to represent the functions of the different devices. It may be because by the end of a decades-long war that had spread across the entire solar system, they were running short of personnel and time to train them properly. So they made the systems as simple to operate as possible.'

That made a lot of sense. It must have been hell for them but it made our work a little easier. 'Right, Professor, what you want me to do?'

'Amber and I will work on repairing the ship because we know her best. You go to the main control room and keep watch on the crater and especially the wreck. While there you can also try to access as many of the Fort's operating systems as possible to see if you can find out anything else that might be of use to us concerning the operations of the base...'

* * *

A lift tube from the terminal at the back of hanger control room carried me smoothly and rapidly up to the main command level, bypassing, about thirty floors of ramps, inside a capsule that could have carried about four people packed close together. I'm not sure how the system worked and I could not see any obvious cables or rails for it to ride along, but like everything else the controls were simple enough to puzzle out and operate.

In the central control room the screens were still active as we'd left them, showing the great bowl of the crater, still illuminated by the fierce blazing disc of the low sun. Even though it had been over eight hours since I had been outside the sun had only climbed about four degrees in the black sky, unlike back home where the sun moves fifteen degrees in a single hour. And there was the crumpled bulk of the Hydra carrier. Nothing moved. It seemed as dead as it had been when we had landed. Of course it might contain one human life now: Oliver's. Perhaps Amber's compassion had got to me, but I did not like the thought that he might somehow still be alive in there, waiting for his suit systems to fail.

I knew he was a murdering traitor, but should I have tried to go after him when I had the chance? No, that would have been taking heroism too far. He'd been armed and hadn't been able to stop that claw carrying him off while I'd only had a club. If I'd hesitated a moment longer I don't think I'd have been able to crash my way out past those things that had tried to claw the hull plates off the *Eclipse*. Oliver was probably already dead by then anyway: perhaps like Cavor, HG Wells's naïve and ill-fated explorer of the moon, fighting the insect-like Selenites as he was finally forced *"into that silence that has no end..."*

I shivered and began examining the consoles, reading their displays and trying to get an idea of what they all did. I was letting my imagination get the better of me again and only succeeding in depressing myself. We had enough problems of our own without worrying about things beyond our control. I had a job to do...

The Prof was also right about the systems having a lot of inbuilt help and advice in the form of how-to drop downs and animations. It was rather like mastering the background for an unusually detailed computer game using the biggest console ever made. Over the next couple of hours I learned how to work some of the fortress's basic systems.

I began with the monitor cameras ringed about the outside of the fort. Apart from adjusting their orientation they had telephoto lenses which could change their field of view. I lined one up on the wreck at full magnification and kept its image on one of the main screens. If anything happened there I wanted to know about it. But it seemed exactly the same as when I had driven the *Eclipse* out of it.

The fort also had an internal security camera and intercom system. After a little practice I managed to connect with the hangar repair bay and saw Amber and Professor working on the *Eclipse*. They seemed to be running oddly shaped hand-held tools over the damaged parts of the hull.

I opened up a two way voice circuit to them to go with the visual image and updated them on my progress.

'How's it going down there?' I asked.

'Quite well,' Amber said. 'We're using these re-shaping tools to repair the damaged hull sections. Then we're going to scan-in the dimensions of one of the undamaged cockpit panels so the fabricator can make a new one. If it works we should be able to have a replacement ready in a few hours.'

'That's great,' I said.

I left one of the screens on the repair bay so I could keep an eye on my fellow travellers. It was reassuring to know I was not alone in this huge building. The fact that I could also watch Amber working anytime I chose to was purely incidental...

I toured the fort through the monitor cameras, looking at floors we had not yet explored. The place was vast. I saw rooms full of machinery that maintained the environmental systems and some great hulking thing that according to the details on the screen was the deeply buried main power core, though how it worked it did not say. I found another fabricator unit in a room a few levels down, which must have been for general maintenance use. I was tempted to go down and try it out myself. I mean what a toy! But nobly I resisted and continued my virtual tour.

Mostly there were just empty rooms and corridors, which were rather eerie. This place had once been filled with people and now there was just the three of us. What had the survivors of the garrison taken with them back to the other worlds? I must admit I was wishing they had left at least a few handguns of some sort. Amber might scorn ray guns but she hadn't fought off an alien metal claw, big enough to bite her in half, with an improvised club. I was hoping to find an armoury, but if there was one it eluded me.

I did link in to the cameras in the upper levels that showed the gun mounts and the machinery that actuated and energised them. There were massive power cables and networks of pipes fed from tanks of, presumably, coolant to refrigerate them as they discharged their bolts and beams of energy. Beside these the gantries and ladders to allow access by maintenance engineers seemed puny by comparison.

The more I saw the more I realized what incredible installations these things were. If they thought that a network of just six fortresses was enough to protect the whole moon and the space about it then they must have ranges of thousands of kilometres. We'd seen them firing on enemy vessels far out in space. And yet now, ironically, when we knew there were enemy machines just a few kilometres away across the crater floor, there was no way to use these weapons against them unless they made the first move.

I found the weapon control boards and examined them myself. But, as the Prof had said, they were locked in automatic mode. When I tried a few buttons they flashed up a sign saying *MANUAL OVERRIDE CODE REQUIRED*. The stations that remotely controlled the operation of the gun towers situated in the crater wall were also locked on automatic.

It felt weird to be in the middle of a fort that probably contained more firepower than all the armies of Earth combined, and not be able to access it. Of course we were safe in here if the sensors connected to the weapon system worked. But had they even been fired in a thousand years? I could see no way of testing them.

Still I could at least make the base as secure as possible. I found out how to lock off the bridge airlock from its external controls, so nothing could get in that way. Then I lowered the ring of moat transweb arches and left them retracted. I was not sure if the machines could override the arches and come in through them but I felt better with them out of sight. We could always deploy them quickly enough if needed.

While I'd been working I had noticed that the web of transweb link lines now filled the schematic diagram of the solar system right out to lonely Pluto and seemed complete. Each contact point was marked with a readout on the status of the terminal it had connected with. Some also showed there were connections between that terminal and others but most were single links. There were no terminals shown on the surfaces of any of the giant outer planets of course but their extensive families of satellites, some bigger than Mercury, were well served.

I went down the corridor to the system transweb room to check that the same display showed on its screen. It did. I stared at the operating console. If I set the controls correctly I could simply step through the arch to Mars or one of the moons of Jupiter.

Were there people living on them even now, either under protective domes or adapted to their surface conditions as Amber and I had been to the moon? Did they still remember the Great System War against Janus, or, like Skane had feared, had they forgotten their past and had sunk into a more primitive level of existence?

Well that was a problem for another time. Right now our priority was getting back to our own Earth safely.

Back in the main control room I sat down for a moment in Skane's chair and looked about me at the arcs of brightly lit consoles and the great bank of screens filling half the wall. I found the images on the main screens could also be called up on the chair's small wing screens. I was the temporary commander, if only a stand in/amateur one, of a genuine super scientific fortress base. What a setting for a space opera...

Unfortunately it was at that moment that Amber came in carrying a sandwich pack from the *Eclipse's* stores. I saw a look of disappointment cross her face as she walked up to me. 'I thought you might be hungry... but I see you're playing spacemen again,' she said with a despairing sigh.

'I was just sitting down for a minute and it's the most comfortable chair in the room,' I protested. 'And, let's not forget my so called "playing" earlier only powered up this whole base for us.'

'That was just luck.'

'I pressed the button.'

'Anybody could do that.'

'You didn't, nor did your Father. You had to be in the chair to see it was there.'

'Why can't you just admit that you have these silly fantasies?'

'What does it matter to you what I'm imagining?'

'Because it's embarrassing to watch. This is serious. You must act your age.'

'You mean act like you do.'

'And what's wrong with that?'

'Well at least I still know how to have fun. And I don't make people imagine things that aren't true...' I winced even as the words came out. I should not have said that but it was too late now.

'And what's that supposed to mean?' Amber said stiffly. 'Is there something you want to say to me, Tom?'

There was something that had been bugging me since before we took off, but so many things had happened I had not had the chance to raise it, and also I'd been worried about spoiling whatever relationship we had been forming, however tenuous. But as we were in hard truth mode anyway...

'In the Gazer office... did you deliberately sit on my desk... swinging your knees that way... so I'd agree to cover this story?'

Amber's lips pinched. 'Maybe... all right: yes. I couldn't tell you the truth then and I had to get somebody to keep Father happy. And I knew you'd been watching me...'

I blushed. 'Oh... you knew that.'

'Of course, I'm not blind. Anyway I wanted to be sure you'd agree. Not everybody would give up their weekend at short notice for a school paper story.'

They wouldn't? Not even when Amber asked them? Was it only me?

Amber frowned. 'Did you think it was a serious come on?'

'No... um... probably not... only, you know, it might have been...'

'Well it wasn't. And I'm sorry if I misled you. It was just... insurance.'

I'd never heard it called that before, but maybe Amber believed it. 'I understand. Er... is it sexist if I said they were very nice knees?'

'Yes.'

'Good thing I wasn't going to then.'

Amber said nothing and I wondered for a moment if I'd really offended her. Then I saw she was struggling to contain her laughter. And suddenly she looked amazing. I mean she always looked hot but now she was opening up, letting me to glimpse the more human Amber underneath her cool, super intelligent self-composure. The Cavendish Shield had slipped a little...

And so I laughed back and then we were both laughing together. There hadn't been much to laugh about the last day and it felt good. Of course it couldn't last but while it did, I wanted to enjoy every second.

And then the idea came into my mind, since Amber was being so friendly, was this the right moment to risk a kiss? Just a comradely one, I mean. Not on the lips, of course, but the cheek, maybe? That was all right, wasn't it? I mean we'd already been through a lot together. I could just say I was being mature and honest and not thinking about spacemen at all...

With my heart thudding I leaned forward...

Suddenly a screen on the external communications console began to flash lights and buzz urgently.

I pulled back guiltily and began punching at the chair controls. The screens displayed the message: *Unidentified incoming signaller requesting two way audio-visual communications.*

I looked at Amber and she looked back at me, our jaws dropping. We were not alone! Somebody from out in space wanted to communicate with the fort.

'Maybe someone's been alerted to our powering up of the base by the activation of the transweb net?' Amber suggested.

'Some descendant of General Skane might have been keeping an eye on it,' I said, thrilling at the possibilities.

The screen kept flashing and beeping.

'Well, are you going to answer it before they give up?' Amber asked impatiently. 'You are the man in the big power chair.'

Which of course made me feel totally inadequate. And this was kind of a first contact situation. In SF stories they often went bad...

'Better get your father up here,' I said, trying to sound calm. 'The fort intercom console's over there. Call button bottom right....'

Amber ran to the console, opened the line to the hangar and said: 'Father, you'd better come up to the control room right away...'

Meanwhile I ran my fingers through my hair and brushed down the front of my ship suit. Then I took a deep breath and pressed the contact on the chair arm to accept the call.

A live image came up on the main screen.

For a moment I thought it was the head and shoulders of a man sculpted slightly impressionistically in greenish tinted metal. The protruding arcs of several thin coppery disks encircled its smooth head from front to back, cutting through an almost vertical disk crossing its crown and joining the bulges where its ears should be. More copper disks rose from its shoulders and the outsides of its upper arms, looking like blades and making me think of a suit of armour. A continuous copper brow-ridge ran across above its eyes...

Eyes which suddenly flashed open; eyeballs glowing red, in which seemed to float totally black irises. Its copper lips parted...

'Hello Tom, Hallo Amber,' Oliver Vance said.

Chapter 14
The Cyborg Evangelist

There are a number of things you can say to somebody apparently freshly back from the dead, but possibly the most foolish is: 'So... you didn't die then?'

I said it anyway, even as I was thinking: *Oh freaking hell, look at what they have done to him!* But it did give my lips something to do and bought me time to shift mental gears. Oliver was not dead and all my pity had been wasted... or had it?

Oliver's face distorted into what might have been intended as a smile. 'No, I didn't die, Tom. There were a few moments when I thought the machines were going to kill me, and I wished they would get it over with, but I did not die. In fact you might say I've been reborn. You see they had a better purpose in mind for me. You should have stayed and they would have done the same for you, then you'd understand what this feels like...' He held up green and copper hands. His right hand still appeared vaguely human but his left looked more like a metal lobster claw. 'You aren't the only one that can undergo a transformation, but unlike yours, mine is permanent and more than skin deep.'

I gulped, trying not to be sick. 'And... now you're a better person and you called up just to say sorry?'

'I am sorry I tried to kill you, Tom,' Oliver said. 'I realize now that was being very short sighted of me. Wanting to take the *Eclipse* for my own petty private gain was also very selfish. In fact

I regret almost everything I ever did. But that's all in the past. I still want the ship but I've got a better, finer purpose for it now than selling its secrets for money.'

By now Amber had recovered her composure sufficiently to ask: 'And what's that?'

'I'm going to use it to free the mighty Janus from his prison, of course. Then he can continue with his great work. One system and one mind in control. Order out of chaos. It was good of Skane to tell us what they had done to activate the Terracage... and how it can be deactivated. Now I'll need the use of the base and the *Eclipse* to recover the keys.'

'I don't think that's going to happen,' I said. 'You didn't exactly make our top ten most favourite people list by trying to steal it the first time, so we're certainly not going to let you have it now to let an alien mega-killer lose.'

'Now that's very unfortunate, Tom. Because I really do need the *Eclipse*. It can't be chance that we came here. It was meant to be...'

'You're saying our journey was predestined for the purposes of freeing some freakish megalomaniac mind thing that wants to make everybody in this solar system his slaves, is that it?'

'Janus is a God, Tom, don't speak of him like that,' Oliver admonished.

'No, I think you're the one getting mixed up here. Janus was some ancient Roman god who they just happen to name a planet after in this reality. Whatever you're working for now isn't a God!'

'That depends on your definition of a God. The name is unimportant. The being that is known as

202

Janus is timeless and ancient and his power and wisdom are beyond our comprehension. He is the rightful ruler of us all!'

Amber neatly punctured this messianic rant. 'If he was so superior how did he get himself trapped in the Terracage them?' she asked scathingly.

Oliver's shiny face contorted into an angry scowl. 'Do not question his ways, Amber!' he warned.

Just then the Professor dashed into the control room. He came up short as he saw Oliver's grotesque new face on the big screen. For once he looked totally at a loss for words.

'Hallo Professor,' Oliver said, regaining his composure. 'I was just explaining to Tom and Amber that I will be requiring the use of the *Eclipse* and the fortress very soon. I hope the ship was not too badly damaged in the crash. That was not my intention. You know I have the greatest admiration for your creation.'

'Apparently Oliver's had a major makeover and a change of heart courtesy of the machines in the wreck and wants to free Janus from the Terracage,' I explained. 'He'd like us to hand over the *Eclipse* to help. Oh yes, and he also wants to transform us into more cyber-disciples to keep him company.'

The Professor's lips pinched as he struggled to control his reaction to Oliver's new body. 'You brought this upon yourself, Oliver.'

'But I'm not complaining,' Oliver said. 'I welcome what has happened to me. I can see everything so much more clearly now. I promise I don't want to take revenge on you. I'm perfectly happy like this.'

Perhaps he really was happier, which somehow only made me feel worse.

Amber asked: 'When they altered you... did it hurt?'

'It did hurt at first...' Oliver admitted.

'Good!' Amber said fiercely. 'After what you did to Mrs Whittle I hope it hurt like hell you...' and she added several choice biological obscenities to describe Oliver.

Oliver faltered for a moment, as though the insults had pierced his new metallic hide, then he regained his composure again and continued calmly: 'I understand your hatred, Amber, but you must direct that at the old me, and that Oliver Vance is dead. I have been reborn without fear or doubt and with a new purpose that's more important than any individual's suffering. The machines in the wreck accepted me as though it was meant to be. They have waited so long for a new living mind to direct them and I was glad take on that role. And in return I have been rewarded. I'm not weak anymore. Now I can live in a vacuum as well. I'm better, stronger, faster than I was before...'

I recognized where this was coming from. 'You're no bionic man, Oliver. He was a hero...'

Oliver laughed. It was a terrible sound; grating and metallic. 'It seems you have me cast in the role of a villain, Tom. I'd prefer to think of myself as a bringer of enlightenment —'

'Who's not above calling up first to gloat at us,' Amber pointed out.

'To give you a chance to surrender to the inevitable and invite me into the fortress,' Oliver corrected her. 'I know you haven't any weapons

204

and the place has been stripped bare. Apart from the exterior batteries you are defenceless. How can you resist? Believe me this is the only way, as you'll find out for yourselves soon enough, when you join the service of Janus. The transformation machine in this ship is still in perfect working order. It will be less painful if you enter it voluntarily. And then you'll help me in our great quest. There are six keys to unlock the Terracage scattered somewhere around this system. We'll find them however long it takes.' His eyes seemed to glow brighter. 'And then he will be free again!'

'How can you possibly want to free that thing!' Amber almost shouted at him. 'We saw what it was like! We felt it, even through a recording. It's evil!'

'You saw Janus through their misguided eyes,' Oliver countered. 'Propaganda! They made him look like a monster. You do not know him like I do.'

'Been talking to him recently, have you?' I said with a sneer. 'And your pet rock as well?'

'Are you saying he's still alive on Earth... Terra?' the Professor asked.

Oliver paused. 'Perhaps I feel a link to him in spirit. I know his will cannot die. But I have access to records of all he did in this system and it was magnificent!'

'That's not what I call it,' I said.

'You are just an ignorant child!' Oliver snapped contemptuously.

'At least I'm not a traitor to my whole species!'

'I'll never let you have the *Eclipse* for such a purpose, Oliver,' Cavendish said grimly. 'I'd rather destroy it first. It's badly damaged already and you'll never be able to repair it without me. And if you attack this base you only risk damaging it further...'

'We'll see about that,' Oliver said simply. 'If you won't hand over the *Eclipse* voluntarily then I'll send my warriors to take it... and then I'll have you anyway...'

His image blanked out.

I shivered. It was probably one of the oldest fears in the SF universe: to be taken over by an alien force; to lose everything, even your own will to resist and ultimately your very identity; to be assimilated and converted to serve another purpose.

The Professor took off his glasses and polished them severely. 'This is all most... unfortunate,' he said, which was probably the understatement of the year.

'Did he realize you were lying about how badly the ship is damaged, Father?' Amber asked.

'I hope not. It's not spaceworthy yet, but by making it seem worse than it is I was trying to buy us time enough to repair it and leave here before he makes his next move.' Then he frowned. 'But what can he do? He knows about the power of the fort's external defences. If he tries any kind of frontal assault his machines will be detected and destroyed, he must realize that. Let me see the wreck...'

I put up the magnified image of the wreck on the big screen and we all studied it. Nothing seemed to be happening. Nevertheless it somehow seemed more sinister than ever. What was Oliver... or whatever it was he had become... planning?

'Why does he want the ship so much anyway?' Amber wondered. 'If he had control of the Fort couldn't he use the transweb arch system to go anywhere he wanted?'

'Perhaps he can't use the arches for some reason,' the Prof speculated. 'Remember the filters set up on the airlock were designed to prevent Janus's machines entering the fort. There may be something similar on the arches. Or else he suspects that some of the keys are hidden on worlds without arch connections. We can assume that wreck is beyond repair and there are no ships in the fort so the *Eclipse* is his only means of transport."

'Or, once he's conquered this system, he wants the *Eclipse* to carry him and Janus back to our Earth,' I suggested darkly.

Amber went very pale. 'We can't let that happen.'

Cavendish suddenly said: 'Display all the views of the interior of the moat.'

I hunted through the camera options until I found a series of viewpoints showing the gloomy, blue-tinted depths of the moat from all angles.

'He knows that Janus's machines would be detected if they appeared above ground,' Cavendish pondered, 'I was just wondering if he had anything that could burrow beneath it. Hopefully not...'

'They must have records of the machines they were fighting,' Amber said.

A little research in the base archive called up displays of military recognition charts for both Janus's spacecraft and land forces, giving their basic dimensions and capabilities. Some of them we'd heard mentioned on the recording of the last battle. I doubt if the colourful names on it were those Janus had used when he created them, but the warriors who built this place had to identify them with simple and memorable tags, inspired by their monstrous and sometimes insect-like appearance.

'Looks like they had several machines designed for excavation and burrowing,' I said, scanning the charts. 'The question is did any of them survive the crash?'

'Maybe Oliver was just trying to bluff us into surrendering,' Amber suggested.

'We can only hope so,' her father said grimly. 'But we do now know he's out there and is dangerously deluded. We must get the *Eclipse* spaceworthy as fast as we can. You keep watch up here, Tom...'

But even as he turned to leave, Amber pointed at a screen. 'What's that there... down at the base of the outer wall?'

I expanded the view. There was a small ragged hole appearing in the moat wall spilling a slowly falling trickle of dust and gravel as it grew steadily larger. The tip of a drill head began to emerge from it, grinding away at the edges of the hole and throwing larger chunks of the fused rock aside.

Shrilling alarms suddenly filled the control room and a dozen boards began to flash urgently. A warning came up: *Enemy intrusion detected. Tertiary batteries activated.*

We saw the lowest ring of guns swinging about in their mounts and pointing downwards.

'Zap them!' I shouted, caught up in the thrill of expectation.

But nothing happened! No bolts or streams of electric fire. Nothing!

A message flashed up: *Target below minimum angle of fire.*

'The tower guns can't be depressed far enough to fire into the moat itself,' the Professor growled. 'Oliver was in here when the fortress schematics were on display and he had time to study them. He must have realized this was a weakness in defences. There may be too much risk of damaging the foundations of the fortress if they fired on it. They must rely on their mobile forces to handle an enemy if it got that close: the tanks and infantry we saw. And now Oliver has told the machines there are none. Even while he was talking to us that thing must have been on its way...'

And we didn't even have a peashooter between us to stop it.

I said to Amber: 'Are you sure you wouldn't say no to a few ray guns right now?'

'All right, you've made your point Tom,' she said coldly. 'Now have you anything more positive to contribute?'

But I hadn't. All we could do was watch helplessly as the drill head shouldered its way out of the hole in the wall. It was connected to a wormlike metallic body about three metres in diameter and ten long that squirmed about and flopped down into the floor of the moat. A dozen beetle-like things with hunched bodies the size of transit vans poured out of the hole after it had swarmed across the base of the moat. They surrounded the drill worm which sprouted dozens of short stubby legs with spiked tips and undulated forward towards the sloping revetment that skirted the base of the tower itself. As the other machines took up defensive positions around it the drill worm clawed its way up the revetment and began to attack the massive outer door of the hangar bay. A spray of white hot sparks erupted as its drill snout ground against the outer hatch of the airlock.

The recognition charts gave us names for them. I said: 'The beetle-shaped things are called *Light Attack Roaches* and the borer is a *Drillipede...*'

But it was not making much progress.

'I think the metal may be too tough for it to cut through,' the Professor said hopefully. 'It may have been able to burrow through loose lunar rock and soil easily enough but whatever material they made this fortress out of it must be far denser and tougher than that.'

But even as he spoke a ring of flexible nozzles extended from around the base of the drill head and focused on the metal around the drill tip. They flared with white hot lances of flame. As the metal softened around it the drill tip began to dig slowly but steadily deeper.

'Oh no,' Amber said quietly.

'Either they have no large explosive charges suitable for blasting the doors down, or else they don't want to risk damaging the *Eclipse*,' the Professor said. 'Drilling is slower but more precise.' He peered at the image intently for some moments, coldly calculating. 'Assuming its rate of progress is steady and allowing for the fact that it would have to cut through the inner door as well to enter the hangar bay, I estimate they will be inside in somewhere between one hour and ninety minutes.'

'Could you finish repairing the *Eclipse* before then?' I asked.

'No. The repair and rewiring of the drive circuits alone will take me another six hours at least. And even if it was spaceworthy we'd have to get it out past those machines. That's the only exit from the hangar bay large enough to take the ship, as no doubt Oliver realizes.'

Then both of them looked at me expectantly. Had I made myself the go-to person in situations like this after my success with the language machine and the trans-web archways? Of course this was SF territory, which was kind of my speciality. My mind raced desperately until a thought occurred.

'Professor, can the fabricator units make weapons?'

'It has menus of basic standard components, but I didn't see any weapons amongst them. I'm not sure we could design anything as complicated as a fully functioning gun in time. The basic mechanics might not be too hard to design but to create the right mixture of explosives would take a lot of trial and error. You need a percussion cap of something like mercuric fulminate to trigger the main propulsive charge and both must be carefully balanced against the size of the projectile you wanted to propel or else the weapon will be useless or simply burst its breach. And to be effective against those machines I imagine it would have to have an explosive charge in its head which would mean designing some kind of impact trigger arrangement… it all might take days to perfect.'

And we only had an hour…

'What about the machine tools you were using? Are there things down there like oxyacetylene cutters or laser drills or something?'

'Everything like that has a very short operating range,' Amber said. 'To use them we'd have to be standing right next to those things. Would they let us do that?'

There had to be something we could do! On the ancient recording we had seen infantry fighting those machines out on the surface. Obviously they had advanced hand weapons and grenades but it showed it was possible in principle to take them on like that. We needed something we could use at a distance, although if they got inside the fortress then that wouldn't be any great range. I looked about me at all the display screens showing the amazing interior of the fortress, hoping for inspiration. For some reason the idea of games came into my mind…

'We've got time to convert to vacuum metaforms and leave by the bridge entrance,' Amber suggested. 'If any machines tried to follow us out on the surface then the fortress guns would be able to target them.'

'Yes, but we'd have nowhere to go,' her father pointed out. 'And while we were away Oliver could still take control of the fort. Then we'd have nowhere to come back to.'

'Then we must use the trans-web system to get right away,' Amber said. 'We know it works, at least for short ranges on the moon. It would be taking a risk but we'd have a chance of surviving on another world.'

'But we couldn't take the *Eclipse* with us,' her father pointed out. 'We'd never be able to return home…'

Amber took a deep breath. 'We're responsible for Oliver being here, Father. We may have to pay that price.'

I said nothing, just wishing right then that I was as brave and mature as she was and not just sitting a big chair pretending. Was I ready to give up any hope of ever getting home again?

'I am aware of what we've done,' her father replied solemnly.

'Would you really destroy the *Eclipse* to stop Oliver getting his hands on it?' Amber asked.

'I wouldn't need to destroy the whole ship. I could take away some essential component of the drive system that he could not possibly understand or duplicate. The main field sequencer unit for instance. I could easily carry that with me. Who knows, we might have a chance at some time to recover the rest of the ship again…'

Amber forced a wry smile. 'Now you're only trying to give me false hope, Father. If the ship was left intact Oliver would know we would try to come back for it. He'd be waiting for us and have the fort as a base. And while he was here we could never return… because he'd want to convert us as well…' She paused and bit her lip, and then asked quietly: 'Please don't let him do anything like that to me.'

'I won't…' Cavendish said simply.

But listening to them turning the problem over had helped. Like with the puzzle of the arches, all the bits began to fall into place and suddenly I had a plan! It was desperately risky, but then what wasn't right now?

'Before we just run away, are you ready to fight?' I asked them.

'If there is no other choice then we have nothing to lose by resisting,' the Prof said simply.

'Of course I'm ready to fight, but how?' Amber asked, pointing at the war machines on the screen. 'How do we fight them?'

'We have an edge. Oliver wants us captured alive to turn us into more of Janus's disciples so his machines won't use lethal force if they can help it. But if they fail he'll come after us in person because he has to live up to his boasts about how superior he is now. And he badly wants the *Eclipse*... but he never saw the arch rooms functioning... and we're still human while I'm not sure he is...

'What?'

'Sorry, I'll explain as we go. Can you make something simpler than a regular gun but which does the same job? And things like vacuum flasks? And I'll need a screwdriver...'

Chapter 15
Under Siege

It was an hour and ten minutes after the drillipede had begun chewing its way into the fort that it finally broke through the inner door of the hanger airlock. By then, after an hour of frantic activity, we were as ready as we ever would be. Amber and the Prof had worked away in the hanger with the fabricator and advanced machine tools, which made my plan possible, while I had taken care of things upstairs. I hoped it would work… It had to work…

The outer door had resisted for forty minutes before a hole had been cut through it large enough for the drillipede to wriggle through into the lock space between the two sets of doors, followed by a couple of the roaches. Then it had begun attacking the inner door. The roaches had not only been guarding it while it worked they had been ferrying a steady supply of silver cylinders from out of the moat tunnel which they had been plugging into the tail of the millipede and then discarding. Top ups for its power cells or fuel for its cutting torches, presumably, like our ration packs.

Now, from our positions in the bay we could see the lock door's inner face begin to glow red and spit sparks. It made me think of a classic SF movie with a howling Id monster on the other side of a massive portal unleashing the energies of a lost civilization to burn its way through. Well, there was a monster involved now and I didn't mean the machines. Oliver was out there somewhere, directing them over some kind of radio link. And like any prudent general he was sending in his troops first to test the defences before he risked his own shiny new skin.

Even if the drillipede had been howling as it cut through the lock door we could not have heard it though, because we'd exhausted all the air in the base, sucking it back into its storage tanks. We were all wearing combat uniforms and were adapted for vacuum conditions. The professor looked very strange with a silver face. He'd had to give up his glasses but said that his sight in his adjusted form seemed greatly improved. Ration bars of suitable kinds were stuffed into our belt pockets and, looking more like soldiers than ever, we also carried our improvised weapons. Hasty tests had proved they functioned but would they be *effective*?

I'm not sure if it was possible to be sick in a vacuum adapted form. But my stomach was doing its best to give that impression. I just hoped I could be as brave as the original garrison of the fortress had been in the face of the enemy. I knew I was no soldier but then Oliver, or whatever he had become, was not one either. We were all amateurs in this game using technology beyond our imagination only twenty-four hours ago. And if we could not stop Oliver and his machines down here, had I the courage to do what came next?

A great plug of red hot metal collapsed inwards as the inner door gave way and there was no time for doubts or fears anymore. It was time to fight back...

The Professor and I threw the insulated flasks of liquid oxygen and hydrogen we had been carrying through the glowing red tube of freshly cut metal into the space beyond. Then we ducked into the shelter of the side bays.

The flasks burst, vaporizing into a misty cloud and then exploded. Explosives don't necessarily need to be chemically complicated to have punch. Liquid hydrogen and oxygen are used to fuel rockets and when they combine they release a huge amount of energy and the drillipede had been good enough to light the fuse. We couldn't hear the bang, of course, but we felt the shudder and saw the results.

The confined space of the lock filled with blazing light and then twenty metre long tongues of fire blew inward and outward through the holes in the airlock doors, blasting the drillipede and three of the attack roaches to pieces, some of which showered out of the lock across the hanger floor. It was doubly spectacular because the light was dim. The bay ceiling lights had been turned out, leaving only small lights in the empty side bays. If Oliver had seen that blast I hope it had shocked him out of his complacent certainty.

But even as the flames died away more of the roaches scrambled in through the shattered airlock, clambering over the twisted remains of their comrades and into the hanger bay. They had huge snapping mandibles that could have picked us up whole and coiling jointed tentacles that lashed out like whips, trying to snag us.

At least we did not have to be so inhibited. We fired back

No, we had not been able to synthesize real guns in an hour, but we had been able to make some pretty lethal substitutes.

217

They resembled oversized paintball guns driven by pressurised gas cylinders which fired tennis-ball sized and eggshell-thin ceramic capsules lined with a film of platinum and containing Aqua Regis mixed with synthetic grease to keep it from boiling off too quickly in the vacuum. Aqua Regis is a mix of nitric and hydrochloric acids and is one of the few acids that can dissolve pure gold. Would it work against alien war machines?

Oh hell yes it did! The capsules burst against the attack roaches, splashing across their camera eyes and what presumably were their sensory antennas, burning into their metal skins. Where it hit their thin legs they softened, bent and then snapped off. The machines wheeled around in circles, flopping and kicking and scrabbling ineffectually.

But still more came on.

We retreated back through the communicating doors of the side bays, using them as shelter while we continued to fire our acid bombs into their advancing ranks. As they divided to follow us, from the head of the bay Amber, who had been hidden out of sight when they burst in, began to fire thermite grenades into their flanks from her gas gun. These were tacky gel cases surrounding packets of aluminium powder and ferric oxide triggered by magnesium ribbon with oxidized friction strip fuses that Amber had concocted: simple chemistry that gave spectacular results.

They stuck where they hit the roach's shells, burning with blue white fire and melting their way into their insides. Fire flashed through them as their power packs were shorted out and a couple of the roaches exploded in the showers of sparks, scattering twitching limbs and fragments of their casings across the bay floor.

And yet still more came.

The Professor and I joined Amber and, firing the last of our bombs and grenades, we retreated through the lower-level doors at the back of the bay into the base's main vertical access shaft. Above us ramps coiled their way around the cluster of lift tubes for floor after floor to the top of the tower. We shut the blast doors of the hangar bay and started upwards.

The doors were not as heavy as the outer lock and only stopped the roaches for a minute. At first they battered into them but they held. Then they used some kind of cutter to slice into the locking bolts and then they were forced open. With a grating of metal the roaches shouldered their way through the doors. As they milled about on the lobby we fired fresh acid and thermite bombs down onto the tops of their glittering casings from the stocks we had stashed on the ramps for reloading. As they thrashed about, burning and melting, we continued on up.

The next machines had to scramble over their remains. They were so bulky that they could only move up the ramps in single file. We retreated upwards, bypassing each other as we went, holding a position at the top of a ramp just long enough to fire on the leading machine and then retreating again.

If Oliver was seeing all this through their machines eyes, which in some way I was convinced he was, by now he must be wondering where the

Eclipse had gone. Clearly it was not in the bay. Therefore we must somehow have moved it. That made it even more important to catch us. Hopefully it would also make him careless...

From the main control room we had remotely shut the lift tubes down and locked all the stairwell shaft side doors. The roaches had to follow us upward to their disadvantage. Almost like in a true mediaeval keep we were fighting the advancing enemy up a spiral staircase, designed so they could only attack us one at time. Not that it was easy. If we had not been unencumbered by spacesuits with our breathing requirements supplied by our ration bars we would never have made it. As it was after ten floors we were aching and getting tired. But quitting was simply not an option so as we fell back in leapfrog stages we gobbled down ration bars to boost our strength. It seemed insane to be stuffing something very like a chunky cereal bar down my throat even as I was waiting for my next target to appear, but then today what wasn't at least slightly crazy?

And so we stumbled on, drawing the machines out up along that seemingly never-ending spiral of ramps, pausing only to reload from our stashes as we came to them, picking the roaches off one by one as they snapped at our heels. They melted and exploded in showers of hot metal droplets, collapsing into heaps of twitching, smouldering slag. But always fresh machines clambered over them and they kept on coming.

And then, just two floors beneath the control room level, there were no fresh attackers. Cautiously, with our guns and our few remaining grenades at the ready, we peered downwards. But we could see nothing moving past the remains of the last roach.

'Is that all of them?' Amber asked.

'That was more than we saw in the moat. Oliver must have had reserves hidden in his tunnel. But perhaps even they're gone now...'

And then we heard him through our radiohead ears, even as we felt through the floor the steady thud of approaching feet up the ramps.

'Congratulations, you really have been most ingenious,' he said, managing to sound pitying even as he complimented us. 'I admit I underestimated you. But you can't keep this up much longer. Are you getting tired now? I'm not. I don't get tired anymore. I supposed you used the base synthesiser technology to make those crude weapons? Janus's database references them. Still I'm certain you haven't had time to make an indefinite stockpile of munitions. Are you running short now? It will be easier if you surrender. Show your contrition and Janus will be merciful. You can begin by telling me where you have hidden the ship.'

He hadn't found it yet!

'You should have looked at the base specs more closely when you had the time,' I taunted him.

We scrambled up another couple of levels and then went through the blast doors at the end of the control room corridor. We cranked them shut leaving only a narrow slot, through which we peered intently. And then Oliver appeared.

In his new metal body he looked a lot bigger than he had on the screen. Over two metres tall, massive, grotesque, powerful and terrifying. Where earlier he had a claw in place of his left-hand, there was now some kind of energy gun with a glowing nozzle.

'There you are,' he said: his red eyes shining at us. 'Why don't you give up now?'

'This is your last warning, Oliver,' Professor said. 'Leave us now or well have to destroy you...'

'But you can't,' Oliver said, taking a step towards us.

I don't think any of us found it easy to fire at him through the slot in the doors. He was not some mindless machine like the roaches; he was still a person of sorts. But this was a matter of life or death... or worse!

Except that we could not hit him! Oliver dodged the grenades, even smacking them aside contemptuously, like swatting flies. They burst about him, hissing and bubbling, so he was illuminated in a haze of blazing thermite and acid vapour.

He laughed mockingly. 'I said I was stronger and faster now. Human upgrades get far better equipment than common soldiers. As you'll find out soon enough for yourselves...'

'In your dreams!' I shouted defiantly, with more bravado than I felt.

Then we slammed the double doors shut and locked them from our side — I'd found the keypad codes to do that in my earlier researches. We had not stopped him with Plan A so we had moved onto Plan B. I really hoped that would work because there was no Plan C...

Everything was reversed from the morning. Now we were on the inside of the door trying to

222

lock Oliver out. The blast doors were not as thick as the hanger doors. How long would they hold him?

We retreated along the wide corridor with the control room doors at the far end and the harness and arch rooms on each side. We knew what we had to do now and Oliver might be able to overhear us so we did not speak. The Professor clapped us on the shoulders and went into one of the arch rooms.

The ramp blast doors shuddered as Oliver pounded on them. But even he could not simply break them down. Then a dazzling lance of flame burst through the metal and cut out one of the locks. The cutting was repeated at the top and bottom of the doors, slicing through the locking bolts. Then the doors were pushed wide and Oliver strode through them, terrifying and determined.

'Get after the Prof to Fort Resolution!' I shouted to Amber. She dashed through the archway marked: *Lunar Transweb Terminal.*

'You can't follow us, can you?' I taunted Oliver. 'I don't think you can use the arches like you are now. They'll detect you're a monster. Of course you always were one on the inside but now everybody can see it. That's why you need the *Eclipse*! Well if you want to find out what we did with her then try to follow me. I dare you!'

'You will give her to me!' Oliver roared.

He broke into a thudding run that I could feel through the floor, bounding along the corridor in huge strides. I had just made him very mad. I dashed after Amber.

223

In the room before me the arch was already active with its rim illuminated in inviting green and its arrows flashing, indicating it was clear to pass through. Framed by its far end was a slice of landscape under a black star-spangled sky showing ruined walls with jagged rocks beyond them. As I reached the mouth of the archway Oliver turned off the corridor and plunged into the arch room.

He could have taken a shot at me then but he wanted to take me alive. And if I'd had to run another ten metres in a straight line he would have caught me. But ten metres on was the far side of the archway...

The metamorphic field of the arch took hold of me, clawing and twisting at my insides, seeming to send a thousand little electric shocks through me as it rearranged my entire metabolism. This was worse than before. Maybe two transformations, one on top of another was a bad idea, but it had to be done. I had to struggle not to cry out or fall over as the arch distorted my body, remaking it into something that could survive at the other end. So I kept putting one foot in front of the other and stumbled on.

Oliver was at my heels, pounding remorselessly forwards, by now building up such momentum that I don't think he could have stopped even if he'd wanted to. That was the idea...

I almost fell over as I staggered out of the other end of the arch and ran into twice the gravity field I had been living in for nearly a day. *Gravity step plus two* it had warned on the console when I had called this destination up earlier. I hadn't had time for much research but I should have remembered that…

Behind me I heard Oliver howl in pain as the field tried to rearrange his body, or else reject it. Miniature lightning bolts stabbed inward to earth through his metal form, framing him within the arch in a corona of blue fire. It was keyed to humans and after what the machines had done to him Oliver was not human any more. I was counting on it being hard to get through. Maybe it was trying to lock him out or maybe even kill him, but whatever the reason it seemed as though he had an even rougher transition than I did. But he also stumbled on out the other side of the arch, took a couple of steps and then sank to his knees, clutching at his chest.

Dull diffuse reddish light edged with a few reflected white highlights illuminated a small clearing amid the jumbled ruins of what once had been a structure smaller than the lunar fortress. Now only a partial roof remained over what had been its arch room while other walls were just broken stubs. A frosting of what looked a little like ice clung to the sides and hollows of some of the fallen blocks. The ruins were set on a hollow in the top of a low rocky hill overlooking a level plain crisscrossed by a network of deep cracks and pitted with a few meteor craters. This plain rolled away clear to the horizon where a humpback rocky mesa was outlined by a ruddy halo like tattered butterfly wings, which cast a long dull red shadow back across the plain to envelope the ruins. On either side of this band of shadow, very low but harshly brilliant sunlight picked out every detail of the plain, stretching out the shadows of every pit and boulder and casting it into sharp relief.

Behind Oliver the image of the control room at the other end of the arch thinned and became translucent and ghostly as it shifted to electromagnetic transmission only. He looked about him, his metal-plated features contorted into an expression of pain and bewilderment as he realized something was very wrong.

'Welcome to Mercury,' I said.

Chapter 16
Into the Twilight Zone

I stood well clear of Oliver as I made my announcement, holding my acid pop gun ready. He was still too close to the mouth of the arch to risk trying to get round. I'd been hoping, if he survived the transition, that he'd either be knocked out or too stunned to stop us getting past him and back through the arch. Now I had to convince him his holy crusade ended here...

·   'You thought we were going to Fort Resolution,' I said. 'I bet you could have walked back to Adamant from there if you had to. But not from Mercury. I swapped the door sign plates over. We went through the *system* transweb room that links with all the other planets. Yes, that's why there were two of them. The Prof was hiding in the local·one across the corridor. He's controlling the arch now and he'll never let you back through. This is Twilight Base close to Mercury's North Pole. As you can see it was abandoned a long time ago and it has no other links to any other world except the moon which we control. That makes it a good prison for you...'

Oliver was recovering a little. 'It seems I underestimated you once again, Tom,' he said grudgingly. 'You really are full of surprises aren't you?'

'Maybe you inspire me,' I retorted, starting to edge sideways towards the arch while keeping my gun pointed at him. 'Now you're going to stay here and we'll give you what you need to survive. In case you hadn't picked up on it this version of Mercury has a less eccentric orbit than our own and it really is locked with one face to the sun, so the climate in the twilight zone is pretty stable. But until we can work out what to do with you, you're never going back to the moon again or start recruiting any more disciples for Janus!'

'Never!' he roared and heaved himself to his feet. 'Janus shall be freed!'

And so Amber, who as planned had been standing on top of the arch out of sight while Oliver's attention was focussed on me, shot him in the back with the last of her thermite shells.

No, that doesn't look pretty written down does it? Shooting up the attack roaches had been a desperate kind of fun, but this was different. Shooting somebody in the back seems like cheating even if it's your only option. And it doesn't help if you used to know them as a living person before they had been changed into a fanatical cyborg.

I'd checked with Amber earlier, during our frantic planning for this possibility; if it came to it could she do it? Yes, she said, but we should give him a chance to cooperate first. That was the civilised thing to do. And so I had. But Oliver had thrown it away and so Amber had shot him coldly and efficiently as she had promised.

The shell stuck to Oliver's back and blazed and spluttered, throwing off sparks and blobs of molten metal. As Oliver screamed and clawed at his back I shot him in the chest with my last acid rounds. His body almost disappeared in a brilliant fleeting haze of thermite smoke and acid fumes.

As Amber dropped to the ground from the arch top in one third gravity slow motion on one side, I made my dash for its mouth from the other, both of us trying to keep clear of Oliver's flailing limbs. The arch came on, its lights flashing green in welcome as the Prof, several million kilometres away, saw what was happening and opened it up again to let us through. Half a dozen strides and we'd be safe! Then Oliver, writhing about and roaring and moaning, though whether in pain or outrage I'm not sure which, twisted around and fired his arm gun... not at us but into the mouth of the arch!

We heard the harsh crackle of its discharge through our radio ears as the interior of the arch lit up with crawling tendrils of electric fire like Oliver's body had earlier. The eye-watering swirls engraved on it seemed to twist and swirl about. Then the image of the fortress arch room on its far end flickered and went out, leaving just a hollow arch with the shattered remains of the base showing through it.

The transweb arch was dead!

As the thermite burned out and the fumes dissipated, Oliver swung his gun arm round unsteadily to point at us. His shiny machine body was scarred and blistered and he was swaying about but his red eyes still blazed with life!

I'd been wrong earlier. There was always a plan C and it was always the same one: '*RUN!*' I shouted.

Amber and I bounded over the jumbled rocks with less than lunar agility but still far faster than we could have done on Earth with Oliver stumbling after us. His gun cracked and bolts of blue fire zipped and zinged around us, splashing off rocks and kicking up showers of dust, sending us ducking and crawling and scrambling behind rocky outcrops for cover.

The ground fell away ahead of us and we dropped down a rubble-strewn slope, setting off a few small slow motion avalanches of loose scree. There were the remains of a wall at the bottom of the slope which seemed to enclose the outcrop on which Twilight base was built. Where it remained intact it was five metres high and half that thick, but it had collapsed in several places. We leaped through one of these rents and sprinted out across that cracked and ancient lava plain in long, low-g strides, skipping over the web of cracks under our feet that made it look like a crazy paving patio for giants. More electric bolts flashed and cracked about us but at this range they were losing their coherence and dissolving into puffs of sparks.

Then the gunfire stopped and we heard Oliver's voice over our radio ears, getting fainter as we ran. I think he'd been overtaken by murderous rage for a few moments, simply wanting to lash out as payback for the trick and ambush. Now he sounded a little more in control.

'If I'm marooned here then so are you, Tom and Amber. You can run if you want. I'll stay by the arch while I repair myself. And don't think you can sneak past me because I don't need to sleep anymore. I'll just wait until Cavendish resets the transweb systems. I'm sure he's smart enough to work out how to do that. After all he's got plenty of motivation. He'll have to fix it if he ever wants to see you two again!'

We ran out of the long shadow of the mesa into the brilliant direct sunlight. The stars and the ruddy coronal halo was washed out by contrast as the cloven disk of the sun was revealed, appearing almost three times larger than it did from Earth as it sat on the horizon like a glowing golden dome.

I felt its heat on the side of my face and I'm sure it would have burned our eyes out if they hadn't been adjusted for this environment. As it was I could actually see great arching prominences hanging above the sun's limb. It would have been an incredible spectacle had I the time to admire it. Right then I just wanted to get as far away from Oliver as possible. Amber didn't say anything so I assumed she felt the same.

We ran on until I saw ahead of us one branch of the net of cracks deep enough to drop a car into with an almost level floor. It was a ready-made slit trench.

'Let's get out of his sight,' I said.

We dropped down into its shady depths, which would hopefully mask our own radio voices from Oliver's ears.

I slumped down with my back to the wall of the crevice and Amber slid down beside me. The rock from which it was formed was generally lighter than the surface of the plain with pockets of frost in the corners like there had been in the base ruins. Some of the "frost" was actually frozen water while the rest was low melting point elements vaporised from the inferno of the day side of Mercury and deposited here on its twilight zone between its opposing hemispheres of perpetual day and perpetual night, which formed a pretty near perfect ring round the planet.

Amber took out a ration bar and peeled it open. I realized I was desperately exhausted and had to replenish my own energy levels. Also I needed a chance to think, struggling not to let panic get control of me. We were marooned on Mercury millions of kilometres and another universe away from home! Yeah, so what, my stomach said. You still got to eat...

I pulled a red-labelled Type Three ration bar from my pocket. It said it was for high temperature range metaforms and suitable for Mercury twilight zone with limited ingress into both hemispheres. It didn't really taste like anything much, which made me think I'd left my taste buds behind with my human form, but it was still reassuring to consume something.

'Well, it nearly worked,' I said to Amber as we ate, staring at nothing and trying to sound philosophical rather than despairing.

'Very nearly,' she agreed, taking another bite. 'Now aren't you glad I suggested we should bring more of these just in case?'

'I'm very glad,' I conceded stiffly. Then I loosened up a little. 'Actually I'm amazed that your father let you come with me.'

'Oh, Father gave up arguing with me years ago when he knows my mind is made up,' she said. 'And it was obvious that you'd need help if Oliver didn't simply collapse as you hoped. I didn't think it was going to be that easy.'

'Well you were right, it wasn't. Nice shooting though.'

'Thank you.'

'Pity Oliver didn't just burn up.'

Although that would have made us killers, I thought. What would that feel like? I really wished the arch had done our job for us.

'Yes, it's a pity,' Amber agreed. Then she added with slightly sinister determination. 'Next time we'll need something heavier...'

I glanced at Amber, seeing her face properly up close for the first time.

'Wow! Do I look like that?'

'Of course you do.'

Imagine a simple wire frame simulation of a face with all its polygonals filled in with gold tinted glass and the eyes golden marbles. That was us now, pretty much. Apparently our lunar silver skin option was not good enough for the extremes of Mercury. I hadn't noticed until now because it felt normal. Well, no worse than my first transformation anyway. Still if Amber could live with it then so could I. If you did this kind of thing often enough, would you get used to all these freaky changes? It was only temporary, I reminded myself... as long as we could get back through the arch again.

'Any thoughts on what we do next?' I asked. 'I think I've used up my supply of smart ideas for the moment.'

Amber gave the matter her typical studious consideration. If she was as nervous as I was she wasn't showing it right now. 'Well, the only way back to the moon is through the arch. Even if

Father gets the *Eclipse* spaceworthy he couldn't fly it here to pick us up. It would only take a few days to cover the distance but it was never designed to get this close to the sun. So we'll have to wait until he can repair the arch.'

'I'm sure he can fix it,' I said, trying to reassure myself as much as Amber. 'He's got all the resources of the base to help him and the help files from the arch console.'

Amber looked at me coolly, as well as I could judge her golden multifaceted expression. 'I *know* he can fix the arch,' she said simply. 'It's afterwards I'm worried about. Oliver will try to use our safe return as a bargaining lever to get himself back. And we can't let him get back to the fortress or find the *Eclipse*.'

'So we must make sure we don't get caught for a start,' I said. 'If Oliver hasn't got us to show your father then he's left with nothing but empty threats. Your father knows we took a supply of ration bars so as long as Oliver hasn't got us we can survive. And given enough time I bet your father can come up with some weapon powerful enough to take Oliver out.'

'Which Oliver will also realize. That means as soon as he repairs himself, he's going to come after us,'

'He might just wait around the base and set a trap. He knows we've got to go back at some time.'

'No, he's got a window of opportunity while the arch is dead. If he's fixed before it is he'll come after us. He'll need us as shields and bargaining chips if he ever wants to get back to the moon.'

It made sense. 'So we can't stay here very long,' I said. 'Any ideas where we should go?'

'I thought you researched this place?'

'We were a bit tight on time, if you remember. What I got was that this version of Mercury is mostly flat plains with scattered mountain chains so the twilight zone is pretty narrow. A few kilometres in either direction, depending on the degree of shade or exposure, there are glacial moraines flowing from the dark side... the ice comes from ancient comet impacts... or on the sun side rocks so hot that lead, zinc and sulphur began to melt and flow like water. They built Twilight base to research conditions here but it was abandoned years ago. What with the war I don't think they could afford to keep it going. They never built any kind of colony here as far as I know. I stopped reading there when I realized it would be a good place to trap Oliver.'

'And now us,' Amber observed.

We finished eating, stood up and peered over the lip of the crevice at the low isolated mound with a few jagged teeth of rock jutting up through it on which Twilight Base had been built. We'd run over a kilometre from it before we'd taken cover and could see it in its entirety. It was built on an isolated rocky hillock in the middle of the huge lava plain in the more or less perpetual shadow of the distant mesa, cast by a sun that would remain fixed on the horizon, never rising or setting. There was very little cover on any side of the base apart from the cracks, which got sparser and shallower the closer they approached the rising ground on which it stood.

We dropped back down to the floor of the crevice again.

'First let's use these cracks to get further away from the base,' Amber suggested. 'Then we can circle round the plain towards the night side. It's even darker there so we should be harder to spot. Then we'll have to get close enough to be able to watch Oliver and the arch. We must know when my father gets it working again. He'll use the sight and sound settings first to keep Oliver out and find out what's going on. We might be able to hear him calling us.'

'Once the arch is active, Oliver will keep close to it,' I said. 'If he hasn't come after us by then he'll simply wait for us to come back and try to capture us.'

'So we'll have to arrange some sort of diversion to draw him away long enough for us to get through the arch.'

'What if Oliver simply keeps out of sight of the arch and leaves the ruins looking deserted?' I wondered. 'If we can't contact your father, he'll come through to find out what's happened to us. We don't know how much he saw before Oliver blew the arch's fuses. Then Oliver could jump him or get past him back to the moon.'

'My father won't take that kind of risk,' Amber said, almost sounding affronted at the possibility. 'He knows the future of this whole solar system and possibly ours as well is at stake. We're talking about the lives of billions of people.'

'Can you be sure? I know my Dad would.'

'But that would be stupid. It would obviously be a trap.'

'Yes, but he'd do it anyway. That's what being a parent is about. They'd take any risk for me. Arithmetic doesn't come into it...'

This is one of those things I'd just always known, even if it was only recently that I could put it into words. I was surprised I had to spell it out for Amber.

Just for a moment Amber looked at me oddly, but with her altered features I could not be sure what she was thinking. Then she appeared to reach a decision. 'Come on, we've got a long way to go...'

We slung our empty gas guns over our shoulders and set off along in low gravity bouncing strides along the meandering crevice in the same direction we had been going, putting as much distance between us and the base before we swung about. The light of the low unmoving sun caught the lip of the crevice so we could both see and orientate ourselves by its scattered light, tinged with red from the coronal glow. In a few places there were puddles of maroon coloured tar-like stuff we tried to step round or heaps of debris where the sides of the crack had collapsed we had to scramble over, but generally the floor of the crevice remained quite firm and level so we made good time.

We were silent for a bit. Then Amber said: 'if my father opens the arch up and sees nothing, then he'll be sure to arm himself properly before coming through himself. He won't take any foolish chances... '

I didn't argue. 'Yes that sounds very sensible. I'm sure that's exactly what he'll do. Come to rescue you, but do it without taking any foolish chances.'

We went on for a little longer and then Amber said: 'you realize we made the transition to Mercury through the arches instantaneously. That means we travelled here faster than light!'

The speed of light is one of those inviolate things that seemed to be built into the fundamental structure of everything to make the universe work as it does. So far nobody's found anything that can go faster.

'Then why did the interplanetary links we saw on the control room screens have to be made at lightspeed first before the arches could work?' I pointed out.

'Perhaps the arches at both ends have to be synchronized to pinch space together between them to form a bridge that material objects can cross. You have to have two arches to make the transition.'

'So calling out: "Beam me up, Scotty" won't work here?'

'What?

'Don't ask me to explain that one! Everybody knows that one! Anyway, I accept that we went faster than light... effectively.'

She sounded a little disappointed. 'What is the matter with you, Tom? I thought you of all people would appreciate that. It's amazing! It's revolutionary!'

'Well, you know on any other day I agree that breaking the light barrier would be worth a banner headline. But since we've been turned into creatures who can walk about without protection on the surface of Mercury because we're fighting an ex-crewmate who's been turned into a fanatical cyborg in the service of a trapped mega mind in a parallel solar system following a thousand year old war, then afraid it can only rate a footnote...'

There was a long silence. And then Amber said tetchily: 'Well if you put it like that...'

Then I laughed. And then Amber laughed, letting her shield down a little once again. It felt pretty good us both laughing together while jogging along that crevice in the surface of Mercury. Yes, we both knew we were in a life or death situation and even if we won through and got back home safely there was more misery to come. But right at that moment it was good to know we were both alive and we had done some incredible things together. I only wish that moment had gone on a little longer...

But we both stopped laughing and skidded to a halt because just then something moved across a branch in the cracks ahead of us that was a lot bigger than Oliver. I got an impression of a long dark body with undulating ribbed sides moving at some speed in a sort of bobbing, rippling shuffle.

We were not alone...

Chapter 17
Hot Blood

'I think there's something living down here!' I said, stating the obvious as I clutched hold of my gas rifle again. Even empty I could use it as crude sort of club and right then having any kind of weapon in my hands gave me a little reassurance.

'Oh... no... I should have realized!' Amber exclaimed angrily, looking about her. 'It's obvious! The bottoms of these cracks are all smooth and rounded and compressed. That's not natural. Something's been moving along them compacting the soil. It must have taken years. These aren't just cracks, they're animal trails!'

Suddenly the network of crevices seemed cramped and confining and above all very dangerous...

'Maybe we should get back on top again...' I suggested.

We leaped out of the crack back into the heat and brilliant sunlight and landed on one of the huge irregular slabs that made up the shattered plain. Then we saw them...

Flashing in the sunlight were dozens of pairs of serrated fan-like in-line fins arching up out of the cracks and dipping down again, like a school of dolphins showing their dorsal fins as they briefly broke the surface. And the advance scouts of this school were already between us and Twilight Base. These did not dip back down immediately. Pairs of huge large black eyes like twinned periscope lenses with a funnel between them like the mouth of a

240

trumpet rose up on stalks between their fins and twisted about, scanning their surroundings independently. The periscope analogy wasn't a bad one. What we could see of their torpedo-like bodies suggested they were about the size of miniature submarines. Then the eye stalks folded down and the creature vanished again.

'Didn't you know there was life on Mercury?' Amber said accusingly.

'I never got that far reading through the notes about this place,' I protested. 'I was worried about human occupants, not these... these...finworm things! Let's get going...'

'Wait a minute,' Amber said. 'Just because they're not pretty doesn't mean they're dangerous. Maybe they use their fins to collect energy from sunlight using a thermocouple effect with their bodies in the shade where it's cooler. The light would be constant here. And having their eyes on stalks makes sense so they can see further. If crack systems like this cover most of the planet they've adapted to make use of them, that's all.'

'That sounds fascinating,' I said anxiously, 'now please tell me you can also deduce that they're vegetarians...'

I saw one of the periscope trumpet eye stalks suddenly rise up from a crack not twenty metres away and survey us intently. Then it folded up and vanished for a couple of seconds only to reappear again even closer. It folded and disappeared again and suddenly it popped up right up beside us, which made us flinch back from the lip of the crack.

It stared at us and we stared back. The eyes had a double set of lids, the outer silver and very heavy and the inner, closing in the opposite direction, tinted and thinner. The horn set between them was silver with a black centre. I noticed that the ribs supporting its fins had sharp curved spines on their ends.

'Do you think it's got radio ears as well?' I wondered. 'Can it hear us?'

'No idea,' Amber admitted. 'But keep your voice down just in case. No loud noise or sudden movements. If we just stand still and don't threaten it there's a good chance it will ignore us. Very few animals will attack unless they're provoked…'

'On Earth,' I pointed out. 'Who knows what the rules are here…'

The eyes suddenly turned away and the fin folded up again.

'There,' Amber said. 'No need to panic. It was just curious about us, that was all…'

Then the eyeless wormlike head of the finworm reared up out of the crevice. In the full sunlight we could see that its hide was only black from certain angles. From others it rippled and shimmered iridescently. Its front end flopped down on the slab we were standing on and it opened up a mouth large enough to swallow us whole filled with rows of dagger-like teeth. Its mouth was fringed with pairs of sharp feeding mandibles on either side of it and softer twitching feelers above and below. We hopped backwards.

'I don't think it's a vegetarian…' I said.

The feelers extended forward, weaving about like snakes, while the mandibles opened wide. Then it lunged and I smacked it with the butt of my rifle. It jerked backwards, coiling its feelers up and then snapped at us again.

'Run?' Amber said.

'Run!' I agreed.

We ran away from the sun. The bobbing, plunging school of finworms was already between us and what by now looked to be the very distant hill of Twilight Base. Even if we wanted to head back to it that would have meant crossing their path, and leaping over those big spine-tipped fins looked about as comfortable as trying to hurdle a random obstacle course of circular saw blades. As they dived down I saw flicks of whipping tails bristling with long spikes. They seemed to be digging them into the sides of the cracks to help thrust them along, but of course they would also serve as fearsome weapons.

'We need high ground where the cracks run out!' Amber said. 'Maybe they can't move so well on the surface...'

The nearest accessible high ground I could see was a rocky knoll rising up above the plain almost on the horizon about five kilometres away. It was not as large as the hill on which Twilight Base rested, but it was at least crack-free. Could we keep running that long? We had to.

And so we ran with the sun and the flashing fins of the worms at our backs, leaping the cracks as we came to them, seeming to be chasing after our own immensely long shadows which it threw out before us. Every so often one of the worms rose up and snapped at us. Whether it was the one I had smacked on the nose or some of its pals I didn't wait to find out.

The shadow of every crater and boulder lengthened on the plain ahead of us as the angle of the sunlight became even shallower. Even though Mercury is a small world, we would have had to have travel over thirty kilometres from Twilight Base to lose the half of the sun showing over the horizon by putting its curve between its globe and us, but we were gradually diminishing its blazing surface area from the bottom up. Ahead of us distant mountain peaks rose over the plain, their summits tipped with brilliant sunlight but with their lower levels lost in the red gloom of the coronal glow. We were crossing the terminator between perpetual day and perpetual night. Beyond those distant peaks was the frozen half of sun-locked Mercury that had never seen the sun for who knew how many million years.

'If these things like heat and light so much, maybe they'll stop chasing us when it gets too dark,' I said.

'I hope so,' Amber replied.

We could never have kept up that pace on Earth but in Mercury's one third gravity it was possible, aided by our adjusted metabolism's supplying us with energy from within and not sucked out of the air. Also I can confirm that having a hoard of monsters with huge teeth snapping at your heels greatly inspires you. Perhaps we broke the Mercurian all-comers five thousand metre record on our run through that eternal twilight or just got lucky, but the fact was that we stumbled at last onto the slopes of that rocky outcrop just ahead of the advancing wave of finworms.

We clawed our way up to the jumble of rocks, forcing our tired legs to make one last effort, leaping like weary grasshoppers onto to their upper slopes. And there, exhausted, we sprawled across the topmost boulders and looked back at our pursuers.

A few lunged up out of the cracks onto the lose sand and rubble slope that fringed the rock pile, following in our footsteps with their mouth tendrils weaving about. But we were out of their reach. They wriggled backwards and down into the cracks once again and joined the rest of the school as it divided about the outcrop and streamed past it.

Below us in the shadow side of the outcrop was a frozen drift of real snow and ice. The sun worms slithered and plunged about this and merged into a single mass once again.

'They don't want us so where are they going?' I wondered.

From our new vantage point we looked out the across the gathering gloom of the broken plane into that freezing eternal night. Then Amber said: 'Look, there's something coming this way…'

I squinted at the network of cracks fading in the distance. There was something moving along them heading in our direction, like a pale wave a kilometre wide with its fingers rolling along dozens of branching and merging cracks.

'It almost looks like rolling snow… like a horizontal avalanche,' Amber said.

Then the truth dawned. 'That's not an "*it*",' I said, 'it's a *them*! Animals moving along the crevice network like the worms do.'

They were things a little like huge white fuzzy balls, large enough to fill the cracks from side to side, rolling forward smoothly by comparison with the worms' leaping, bobbing motion, propelled by a blur of short stumpy limbs.

The worms had halted their advance just beyond our rocky outcrop, as though waiting for this new wave of creatures to reach them.

'It's almost like they knew they were coming,' Amber said. 'What's it all for?'

'I don't think it's a social call…'

The hoard of white things smashed into the finworm line. Teeth, tails and talons flashed as bloody combat filled the crevices. One of the white things rolled past the outcrop chasing a worm and we saw it clearly for the first time.

It was an oblate ball of long white bristling fur over two metres across with two rings of four short spike-tipped arms on each side of its body that jabbed into the rock and tumbled it along. Its middle was divided by a recessed black groove in which four heavily lidded eyes were set that flicked open to look ahead as they faced forward. Between each of these eyes was a vicious snapping beak-like mouth and the aperture of silver rimmed horn like those on the sunworms.

The worm it was pursuing arched his back and smashed its spiked tail down onto its pursuer. The ball-thing jerked backwards so the blow only grazed it and then lunged, stabbing at the worm with its spiked arms. It caught worm's tail in one of its beaks and tore a chunk out of it the size of a dinnerplate, sending out of a jet black stuff that must have been its blood. The worm squirmed about trying to escape but the ball rolled on top of it, stabbing downwards with its spiked limbs as though it was stamping, again and again. The worm's trumpet eye-stalks twisted about desperately and then they were crushed and broken. As the ball-thing rolled over its body its lower beaks extended and it began to tear great chunks out of its flesh...

We both looked away at that point.

'I suppose you've got a name for them as well?' Amber said.

'Slashballs,' I suggested.

'That's a really gross name,' she said in despair.

'I know, but then under that fuzzy white fur, that's what they are. Admit it: neither of them would make great house pets. But at least this explains why Twilight Base was abandoned and had a big wall round it...'

'Because they built it right on the front line between the finworms and the... slashballs,' Amber concluded. 'It's the only place they can meet. Not too hot for one or cold for the other. We've run into a war zone!'

All about us the crevices were filled with the writhing, churning bodies of slashballs and finworms locked in a fight to the death. Ripped shreds of slashball fur mingled with the shredded remains of iridescent finworm hide. Tail clubs thrashed and spiked arms hacked and stabbed. Finworm teeth lacerated slashball flesh while slashball beaks tore back. Dark blood and shreds of flesh were scattered across the seared Mercurian ground. The one thing that was missing was sound. If they made any noise we could not hear it. The terrible primitive combat all took place in total eerie silence.

'It's like they're caught up in a feeding frenzy,' Amber said. 'Of course we've no idea how often they normally eat. Perhaps this is their only chance to gorge themselves and then they may go without food for months...' Then she paused and clapped her hand to her forehead. 'Oh! Of course, that's why they attacked us earlier!'

'Why?' I asked.

'The tar puddles we crossed in the cracks earlier must have been old slashball blood. We must have got some onto our boots. And that's what those open horns between their eyes must be for: not to catch sound but fast scent molecules and direct them to their olfactory receptors. We smelt like their enemy and food. That's why they chased us and even tried to follow our tracks onto solid ground. They were following our scent trail. It must have been old blood so it wasn't strong enough to get the whole herd of them after us.'

'This is pretty close to being a hard vacuum,' I pointed out. 'Could they smell anything in it?'

'They'd have to be sensitive. The scent molecules would disperse very quickly but that would also make it more long range and directional, which could be an advantage. They're body chemistry must be pretty extreme to survive here. If the slashballs normally live in intense cold their blood must contain a lot of volatiles to keep it active. Those puddles were in freezing shade and yet they were still fluid. When we moved back out into the sunlight the old blood on our boots warmed up and started giving off its scent.'

'That makes sense, but it also means we're stuck up here until we can get ourselves cleaned off!'

'Be grateful they've got something else to distract them,' Amber said.

Feeling sick but fascinated we watched the desperate struggle about us as the slashballs and the finworms surged back and forth along the crevices about the outcrop. How long could it possibly last? Did they fight on until they'd eaten enough or there was only one beast left?

And then we heard it, faintly but clearly: 'Amber! Tom! Can you hear me?' It was the Professor's voice amplified through the arch speaker system radiating out across the plain.

'He's fixed the arch,' Amber exclaimed. She shouted back: 'Father, we can hear you! We're all right but don't come through the arch. Oliver is waiting for you!'

The call rang out again: 'Amber …Tom can you hear me?'

'It's no good,' Amber said. 'There's no clear line of sight like there was on the moon. We're being blocked by the rocks around the base. But at least we know the arch is fixed again.'

'And so will Oliver.'

The call came again: 'Amber, Tom, can you hear me?'

'We've got to get back there before he risks coming through,' Amber said. 'At least if we get close enough we can warn him about Oliver. Then he might be able to make some weapon powerful enough to stop him.'

'How do we get back without getting eaten? We must get ourselves cleaned up first so the worms and slashballs can't smell us.'

Amber pointed down into the shadow side of the outcrop. 'Maybe we can scrub our boots clean with that snow down there. Then we can get away while they're still distracted fighting each other...'

And then I had my idea. The pieces were all there around me. They just needed to put together in the right way.

'You said we needed a diversion to get past Oliver...'

* * *

Half an hour later we marched back across the plain towards Twilight Base. We did not sneak along the crevices we walked across the surface, leaping lightly over the cracks as we came to them. We did not try to conceal ourselves. In fact we positively wanted Oliver to see us.

'Oliver! Come out, come out wherever you are!' I called.

'You want us so you come and get us!' Amber added.

'That is if you haven't blown a fuse yet!' I taunted.

'We're going back home and you're staying here!' Amber said.

As we marched we could hear the Professor's regularly repeated calls. But it was not until we were within a few hundred metres of the base's shattered walls that he heard us replying.

'Is that you Amber? I can hear you now. Are you all right? And Tom?'

'We're fine, Father,' Amber called back. 'Can you see Oliver through the arch?'

'No, he's nowhere in sight.'

'We think he's probably hiding, waiting for you to come through after us. Don't worry we'll take care of him. We'll be with you in a few minutes. Just be ready to let us through...'

Of course Oliver would have heard that exchange as well. I wonder what he made of it? It didn't matter really. He was going to have to confront us so he could catch us and use us as bargaining counters with the Professor. As far as he knew we were out of ammunition. At this range even if we still had thermite and acid shells, he could dodge them. Physically we were no match for him. Of course he could see we were holding our guns but what did that matter? So there was no reason for him to be particularly subtle. Or so I desperately hoped...

We reached one of the gaps in the base wall. I thought it had simply fallen down from decay or perhaps some seismic event or meteor strike. Now we knew better, but I hoped Oliver didn't...

Oliver appeared in the gap, standing in a masterful pose with his legs spread wide blocking our way. The signs of the damage we had inflicted on him had almost completely disappeared and he looked dauntingly impressive and powerful once more.

We raised our guns. He laughed. 'What are you going to fire at me, Tom? Snowballs?'

'Funny you should say that,' I said. 'Because that's just what we are going to do...'

The advantage of smoothbore gas guns was that they can fire more or less anything that fitted into them. It hadn't been too hard to roll up some firm snowballs out of the drift in the shade of the outcrop. They were not perfect fits so the range was not great, but it was quite enough to pepper Oliver with them at thirty metres.

Oliver batted the first few aside which of course only made them burst, showering him with ice. When he realized they contained nothing more substantial than that he let the rest shatter against his hard body.

'You really are firing snowballs at me!' he exclaimed. 'Do you think you can freeze me? It this some kind of bluff?'

'Come and find out!' I called. 'I dare you! If you're so superior catch us if you can...'

Oliver stepped out from the gap in the wall, striding forward purposefully. He slid down the rubble slope and onto the hard cracked floor of the plain.

We turned and ran and he ran after us, out of the shadow of the base hill and into the low stark sunlight.

The ice we had showered him with began melting, leaving the sticky black blobs of finworm and slashball flesh which we had carefully encased within them behind. As they warmed and boiled off they radiated their invisible molecules out across the almost airless void over the plain, carrying the silent message: *'Food! Enemy!'*

In the distance I saw flickers of fins and furry white backs advancing in a wave towards us.

Amber and I split up, going left and right and leaping the cracks. The beasts rolling and slithering along them under us took no notice. We did not smell like the enemy any more. Oliver slowed, uncertain which of us to follow and wanting to be sure we weren't trying to get behind him.

A finworm reared up out of a cleft beside him and closed its huge jaws about him. Its dagger-like teeth broke across his body even as he fired a blast from his gun which tore its head half off while showering him with its sticky black blood. Even as the worm flopped about in its death throws a slashball seemed to bounce out of the cleft and crashed into Oliver, knocking him to his knees as its beaks scraped across him, snapping wildly as its spiked legs stabbed. He punched out one of its eyes and snapped its stabbing arms. More blood splashed over him...

'You think these things can stop me!' he roared.

And then a dozen worms and slashballs erupted from the cracks about Oliver and threw themselves upon him and each other, joining the feeding frenzy which did not distinguish between their prey and metal covered in Mercurian flesh and blood.

I don't think Oliver suspected how many of them there were at first. Or maybe he did but his arrogance refused to see them as serious enemies. How could mere beasts stop him: a superpowered cyborg and Janus's chosen one! By the time he realized the truth it was too late.

The sheer weight of alien flesh toppled Oliver over and he fell into one of the clefts, vanished in a heaving mass of fur and iridescent hide even as it was being blasted through by flashes of electric gunfire and shaken with the impact of mechanical fists. I tried not to look at it as we sprinted back to Twilight Base. Maybe Oliver would survive and maybe he wouldn't. We had our diversion which was all we wanted.

We scrambled through the gap in the wall and up the slope to the ruined basin in which the arch lay.

'It's us, Father,' Amber called out. 'Open the arch...'

The arch sprang into life ringed by welcoming green lights. We darted through it, feeling our bodies once again being twisted and re-written from their molecules up even as we crossed millions of kilometres of space in a few strides. And then we tumbled out of the far end onto our knees, gasping for breath as our lungs began to work again and our ears rang with sound. Fort Adamant was filled with air and we were human once again.

The arch shut down and the Prof ran forward to help us onto our feet.

He hugged Amber tightly and she hugged him back.

Then Cavendish looked around at me and then at the empty arch. 'What happened to Oliver?'

I thought of that Mercurian twilight zone between eternal burning day and frozen night populated by its nightmare beasts and suddenly it seemed very much like a medieval visions of Christian Hell, with its rings of ice and fire and torments by demonic creatures. Was Oliver still fighting them or had they finally done to him what we could not? I might never know.

'He's where he belongs,' I said simply.

Chapter 18
The Voyage Home

Did we celebrate then? No...

We had fought a running battle against alien war machines up the equivalent of a skyscraper, Amber and I had been to Mercury and back and had a skirmish with cyborg Oliver and another with some local wildlife while the Prof, left in the fort alone and out of touch, had somehow mastered the transweb systems' diagnostic programme until he could reset and reboot the arch link. When we had not replied he had begun working on new explosive shells for his gas rifle ready to take on Oliver when he came through the arch to search for us. Fortunately we managed to get back before his new shells were ready. Yes, he would have come after Amber despite what was at stake. There was an odd look on Amber's face when she found that out...

So what did we do then? We all slept for another eight hours, that's what we did. Because we were all totally and completely exhausted!

* * *

After that we spent another day on the moon before we headed back home. Of course we all desperately wanted to go back as soon as possible even though we dreaded what faced us. The Prof and Amber would have to come to terms with a firebombed house and the horror of Mrs Whittle's death and I would have some serious explaining to do to my parents who must be getting desperate by now.

But some things could not be rushed. The Prof and Amber had to finish repairs to the *Eclipse* and test she was spaceworthy while I cleared up the fort as well as I could, cutting up and dragging the remains of the attack roaches off the ramps with the help of a hand cutter and a power winch from the hanger workshop. In the process I also harvested some of their parts for a special purpose we needed them for later.

Then I helped patch up the damaged hanger airlock doors with materials synthesised by the repair shop machines. There was a sort of molecular welder tool that fused the segments smoothly back into the gaping holes that had been bored through them by the drillipede. Car body shops back home would have loved it.

We wanted to leave Fort Adamant secure and in the best state of repair we could manage. It was not simply because we had been responsible for much of the battle damage. If the *Eclipse* got us safely home, we would be coming back one day, perhaps as part of some much larger expedition, and we wanted it to remain safe and secure.

With all the official attention the destruction of Continuum House must have attracted and the hunt for us that must even now be going on, it would be impossible to conceal our return and serious questions would be asked. So the Prof decided that he would hand the specifications of the Cavendish drive over to the government. This would also be his best protection against Oliver's mysterious backers if they still wanted the *Eclipse's* secrets for themselves.

Oh, yes, where had we hidden the *Eclipse* before Oliver's attack?

It never left the hangar bay, of course. It was suspended from the big travelling roof crane high up out of sight and harm's way. That was why we had turned the ceiling lights off and left the side bays illuminated. A little misdirection, that was all. Oliver must have walked in right underneath it.

Finally the Prof declared the *Eclipse* spaceworthy and we were ready to leave.

We moved the ship back up onto the surface, sealed the hangar bay, exhausted the air in the base and shut down all but essential maintenance power. Then, back in our original spacesuits with freshly synthesised helmets to replace the ones Oliver had dropped down the moat, we went back through the crater floor level triple airlocks and crossed the bridge that I had previously strode across so impetuously.

You can't cross the same river twice, they say. Well I don't think I was quite the same person going back in the other direction of that chasm of a moat.

We boarded the *Eclipse* and prepared for take-off.

The Prof was in the pilot's chair of course, while I sat in Amber's seat before the environmental, sensors and communications controls. She took Oliver's old position at drive and power. Amber had given me an intensive briefing on how to monitor the most important systems and the operation of a few key controls so I could make myself useful.

The ship was powered up and Amber reported that the batteries were charged and the drive was functioning. Gently we lifted off from the moon. It was 10:02 GMT on Monday morning at the end of the longest weekend of my life.

At five hundred metres we levelled out and the Prof flew the ship across the plain to hover above the wreck of the Hydra carrier. We had one last task to perform.

Hanging beneath the *Eclipse* by wire rope loops hooked about its landing gear, which had not yet been retracted, was a large heavily shielded isolation carton that outwardly resembled a segment of our outer hull. It was packed full of the parts I had salvaged from the remains of Oliver's attack roaches.

'Retract landing gear,' the Professor commanded.

I pressed a button and heard the whine of motors. The ship bobbed as the rope loops slipped off the landing struts as planned. There was a clunk. 'Landing gear retracted,' I said. As the carton tumbled slowly downward in one sixth gravity the Prof flew the *Eclipse* up another five hundred metres and then turned it about so we had a view through the forward ports.

The tumbling carton struck the twisted hull of the ancient warship and split open, scattering its contents in a fountain across it. Until now Adamant's sensors had registered it as part of our ship, which they must have decided when we had first approached the crater was not of enemy construction. But suddenly it detected multiple fragments of Janus's machines in apparent rapid motion...

Adamant's lower ring of guns came to life, swivelling about and pointing at the wreck.

Brilliant bolts and pulses of blue white plasma and electric fire zapped across the plain and vaporised the tumbling wreckage, gashing great holes in the sides of the wreck as they did so, exposing more previously hidden machine parts that tumbled and collapsed, their motion now registering as fresh targets. The wreck vanished in a withering hail of energy that filled it with a surge of incandescent vaporised metal. It burst into red hot fragments that tumbled across the plain in great slow motion arcs. Still the guns fired and the structure of the ship's sides caved in, collapsing into molten droplets. The ground underneath the wreck gave way, falling into the excavations that the machines had dug underneath it. A stream of liquid metal poured into the tunnel the drillipede had bored and thundered along it under the plain towards the hole in the moat wall, blasting a plume of vaporized metal ahead of it. It spilled out of the tunnel mouth and began to pour like a shining boiling waterfall. But by then it was cooling rapidly. As the tunnel was plugged and flow diminished it slowed and hardened into a petrified metal arch, like melted candle wax.

By the time Adamant's batteries ceased firing there was nothing left of the wreck but a great fuming lake of swirling green and bronze molten metal framed within a sparkling kilometre-deep halo of a billion molten beads scattered like metal hail, mingled with a few shattered spars and twisted fragments of hull plate. If any working machines had still been hiding in the wreck they were dead now. Adamant's guns had at last finished the job thcy had begun a millennia ago.

As we stared at the incredible sight, Amber said mournfully: 'If only they had destroyed it when they had the chance.'

'They were sure they had won,' the Professor said. 'Perhaps they left it as a monument to their suffering.'

'I think they were sick of fighting,' I said. 'The guns had to stop firing at some time. They didn't know it was just a few shots too soon...'

The Professor tilted the *Eclipse's* nose up once more and we set off for home.

* * *

We didn't talk much on the way back because we were all wrapped up in our thoughts. This should have been a triumphal return after a fantastic adventure but now it felt dismal and strangely anti-climactic. And there would be worse to come.

I began working out what to say to my parents. They'd be overjoyed to know I was safe and well, of course and I'd be famous for producing the most incredible school newspaper article ever written. But thinking about what had happened to Oliver and his treachery and what he'd done to Mrs Whittle, none of it seemed to be that important.

There would have to be some kind of police enquiry about Oliver with him not coming back. We'd have to make statements and give evidence at an inquest or something. I'd have to say how he'd tried to kill us and we'd tried to kill him. Okay, so it was in self-defence but we'd still used improvised lethal weapons that I had sort of helped create. And how were we going to explain how we left Oliver stranded on a parallel version of Mercury and don't know if he's alive or dead? It could take months...

We approached the boundary of the shimmering Terracage that in our version of the solar system corresponded with the boundary of the outer Van Allen belt. Within it I could see Terra's phase had changed slightly over the days since our outward journey. Then both it and the moon had been half full, the moon waxing and Terra waning, matching the phases in our own universe. Now the moon behind us was edging towards gibbous and Terra was shrinking to a crescent. I looked at the still dark globe. Was the mind of Janus, whatever that meant, still alive down there, or had it died long ago?

The great multicoloured insubstantial jewel of the energy field grew larger and larger. At 13:26 the Prof warned us: 'Contact in five minutes. Make sure everything loose has been stowed away...'

We were well strapped in this time but otherwise everything else was as it had been on the way out, including our velocity. Hopefully that would cause the interdimensional transition to work exactly in reverse. Except of course there were only three of us on board now. No Oliver pouring his drugged champagne this time. No Oliver... Could his weight make the difference between a successful transition back to our own universe and smacking into the barrier of the terracage? What would happen if we did?

Too late now because the shimmering wall was swelling by the second...

'Brace yourselves,' Cavendish said.

We hit the terracage.

The background hum of the drive rose to a whine as the instrument displays flickered. Bluish light flashed across the ports and I felt a tingle of static. Then the drive cut out and we tumbled end over end. As the stars, Terra and Luna all seemed to swirl together I felt something twist inside me almost like going through a transweb arch.

Then the instruments came on again. We were still tumbling. Cautiously the Prof cut the drive in and stabilized the ship. Ahead of us was a blue-white globe. But was it Earth?

'I can see city lights,' Amber said excitedly

Instead of the dead world we had seen under the cage wall only minutes earlier there were strings of city lights showing in the night. A rear camera showed the moon as should look from our Earth.

I saw Amber's face light up and grinned back at her in foolish delight. We really were back home!

But the Prof was frowning. 'Something's wrong. The Earth's phase has changed...'

I blinked. He was right.

Extending the course we had been on through the barrier and out of our own van Allen belt we should have emerged somewhere above night time Indonesia with the terminator visible over the Indian Ocean. Once there the Prof had planned to go into orbit until it was night over Great Britain and land then. But now below us was the outline of the African continent with what looked like the brilliantly illuminated cities of the Mediterranean coast to the north and the terminator cutting across the Atlantic

How had it all shifted like that?

'This may not be our world,' the Prof said grimly. 'Check for radio transmissions...'

263

With a little guidance from Amber I managed to open up the ship's radio receiver and began scanning the frequency bands. There was a babble of channels across the whole range in many languages. Then I found the BBC World Service right where it should be. It was so reassuring to hear its measured familiar tones even if it was talking about a scheme to improve sanitation in isolated African villages.

'That's sounds right,' I said.

'Maybe the *Eclipse*'s control system clock was damaged in the crash,' Amber suggested.

'But then why do our own watches agree with it?' the Prof wondered.

'Tom, go to *System Settings* then *Timebase Reset*,' Amber said. 'That automatically links the onboard clock to the National Physical Laboratory time and date signal. That will correct it...'

I followed the links and pressed the reset. A new time and date flashed up. 'The ship's clock was off,' I said. 'The correct time and date is 23:11 GMT on Friday the Twelfth...' then I trailed off as my brain caught up with what I'd been saying.

That was a little over two hours after we had taken off from the back garden of Continuum House and within a few minutes of the time we had crashed through the van Allen belt and got thrown out of our universe! Allowing for the time I had taken to call up the time signal, we'd come back through into our own space and time exactly at the moment when everything had first begun to go wrong!

264

It was Amber who realized what that meant. 'Father… if this is still Friday night, Mrs W's still alive!'

* * *

We were pressed back in our seats as the Professor drove the *Eclipse* towards the Earth at full acceleration. He'd abandoned the flight plan and he was just using the ships raw power and point-and-go capability to its maximum to get back to England and Continuum House by the most direct course possible. Amber was calling out our falling battery charge. I think he was prepared to run it down to zero if that put the ship on the hangar lawn in time. Oliver had said he'd set the fire bombs to go off at "one o'clock". If he meant BST then that was midnight GMT. We had a little over forty five minutes to get back home…

We hit the upper atmosphere at a dangerously steep angle. The ship shuddered as a whisper outside swelled to a moaning roar. The bow wave of compressed air in front of us began to glow and the hull began to heat up. I began relaying frightening temperature readings. The Prof nodded but did not seem to slow down.

As we descended he began snapping out instructions to us.

'As soon as we touch down you and Tom get Mrs Whittle out of the house as fast you can. I'm going to try to find the bomb in the hangar first and then one in the house if I can. I don't imagine Oliver hid them too well… probably in the back of the workshop and the cellar. He wouldn't plan on anybody searching for them and they had to be accessible in case he had to get at them if our test flight had to be aborted…'

'Father, don't be silly!' Amber said. 'You can't take the risk.'

'I'm not losing anything else to him! Oliver is not going to have the last laugh…'

Apparently Amber was not the only Cavendish who could be stubborn. I looked at the time: 23: 47 GMT.

Still supersonic we flashed across the skies of central England towards Fulchester. I hoped no aircraft got in our path because right then the Prof was in no mood to give way.

Then there was the familiar triangle of town lights ahead of us which I had last seen when we had lifted off: Leahampton, Wychford and Fulchester. We were hurtling towards the hilly end of Fulchester…

'Deploy landing gear!' the Prof snapped and I punched the button.

We dropped down out of the night onto a corner of the big back lawn of Continuum House and hit almost as hard as we had on the moon when Oliver and I had been fighting in the cabin. As we bounced on our shock absorbers security lights on the back of the house and hangar came on automatically, flooding the lawn with light. Suddenly I felt very heavy as full Earth gravity tugged at me one again.

Amber had already unstrapped herself and was running for the rear hatch. Her father was at her heels. I stumbled after them. He practically tore the air lock doors open and leaped from the ramp towards the hanger. Amber made for the house and

I dashed after her. There was a light on in the kitchen.

It was 23: 56.

'Mrs Whittle, we've got to get out of here!' Amber was shouting as we burst in through the back door. But there was no reply. Mrs Whittle was sitting slumped over the kitchen table with her head resting on her arms. Beside her was a half-finished mug of cold cocoa.

We hooked our arms under Mrs W's shoulders, lifted her up between us and half carried her out of the kitchen door onto the back lawn and across to the *Eclipse*, where we sat her down with her back propped up against one of its wheels. Amber examined her anxiously.

'She's not hurt, just very deeply asleep,' she said.

The Prof burst out of the hangar workshop door. He was carrying something about the size of an attaché case that he put down in the shrubbery on the far side of the lawn. 'No time to disarm it,' called out. 'Keep clear. I'm going for the other one...'

'There's no time, Father,' Amber called out. But he had already dashed into the house.

It was 23:58.

As the seconds ticked by Amber stared at the house, clenching her fists. There was no sign of the Professor. Then she said: 'I'm going in to help him...'

'No,' I said, grabbing her by the wrist. 'Time's up...'

It was midnight GMT.

The Prof ran out of the house and threw another case into the shrubbery. Then he dashed over to us in a crouch. We all hunched down expectantly.

Nothing happened. We stared across the lawn at the cases in the shrubbery.

'Perhaps he meant one o'clock *GMT*,' I suggested.

Then the bombs exploded into harsh brilliant light with a booming double whooph; hissing fiercely and sending up showers of sparks and splashes of liquid fire which ignited the flowerbed. A cloud of smoke billowed up into the night sky.

For a moment it reminded me of cyborg Oliver on Mercury writhing about with the thermite blazing on his back. Yet here I was back on the same night we had set off so that had not happened yet. I felt dizzy and disorientated. Forget jet-lag. I think I had just discovered time-shift lag...

Mrs Whittle stirred and opened her sleepy eyes. 'Oh my... did I drop off? What are you doing back here, dears? Did something go wrong?' She looked about in confusion at the brilliant showers of sparks the fire bombs were still throwing up. 'How pretty... are we celebrating something?'

'Just being alive, Mrs W,' Amber said, hugging her.

* * *

So, no need for incredible explanations to my parents, no police interviews or enquiries to face. As far as everybody in Fulchester was concerned nothing strange had happened to me or Amber or the Prof because there had been no time for it to happen in. We had only been gone a few hours.

Reset to mundane reality once more. That also felt pretty weird. A double anti-climax...

Actually I did have to explain to my parents why I came home on Saturday rather than Sunday as arranged.

'Well, Professor Cavendish's experiment didn't quite work out as he planned,' I said, possibly committing the biggest understatement of the decade. 'It was a bit embarrassing for him really. He says he needs to think things over before he tries it again. Meanwhile he asked me not to talk about it in detail...'

The Professor had decided, during a conference with us in the early hours, on the story he was going to tell, which did not include a trip to the moon. 'In a few days I'll report to the police that Oliver is missing. I'll imply that he'd been behaving a little oddly recently and asked for some time off. Hopefully his backers will think he could not see his plan through and ran away to avoid their reprisals.'

'But they're still out there somewhere,' I pointed out. 'Will you be safe?'

'I'll increase my security of course. They may believe that Oliver gave their existence away to me before he disappeared, which I suppose he did in a way. That might put them off trying again. In the meantime I must reconsider the implications of revealing the existence of the Cavendish drive, even confidentially to the government. After all it's not just the key to the exploration of our solar system, it opens a door to other universes, and perhaps even time itself...' I could see him swelling with the thought that one day he'd make a clean sweep at the Nobel prizes. His hall would be stuffed with award

269

photos... Then he frowned. 'But it might be misused. I think I may have been underestimating people's greed...'

When I finished telling what had supposedly happened at Continuum House to my parents, Dad said: 'That sounds just like Cavendish. A proper eccentric scientist. Bet he wasn't easy to interview.'

'He was a bit touchy at first,' I admitted. 'But we got on better later.'

'Well I'm sorry it didn't work out as planned,' Mum said. 'Will you be able to write any kind of article?'

The Prof's decision meant my article for *The Gazer* was also metaphorically stamped top secret and locked away. I might never be able to publish it.

'The world's not yet ready to hear what really happened,' I said with mock solemnity, just to show I was joking.

'Will you be reporting on his experiment if he tries it again?'

'Oh yes, I've got a front row seat already reserved,' I assured them.

That bit was true enough. The *Eclipse* needed an environmental, sensor and communications operator and there are not that many of us experienced astronauts around with an interdimensional moonflight under our belts. Amber, now promoted to power and drive engineer, had promised to tutor me on the ship's systems, which was something to look forward to.

'Well, did you enjoy yourself anyway?' she asked.

270

'Bits of it were fun,' I said.

'And what about Amber Cavendish?' Dad added with a knowing grin. 'Did you spend much time with her?'

'Some,' I admitted. 'We went for a bit of a run together, actually…'

* * *

And so I dropped back into ordinary life, trying to act as though my three days in space in another universe had not happened. I cleared the garage as I'd promised and wrote my essays. And on Monday morning I went back to school as usual. Well, not quite usual. The high of returning safely and finding everything normal had faded and I walked in through Stapleforth's gates in conversation with Amber about something I could not get out of my mind…

'Was setting the slashballs and worms on Oliver any different to shooting him?' I said. 'Does that make us killers?' It'd thought I'd been so clever at the time, even coming up with that smart payoff line. I didn't expect I'd start feeling guilty…

'He gave us no choice,' Amber said simply. 'If we hadn't done what we did he'd have got back to the moon and we couldn't risk him finding the keys to the terracage or getting hold of the *Eclipse* and coming here. Besides, we don't know he's dead. We may have just put him in prison; if you can call a whole planet a prison.'

'As long as he doesn't escape,' I said darkly.

'How could he?'

'He's a cyborg with a self-repairing body and a store of ancient downloaded knowledge we can't even guess at. Maybe there are still tools and machines in Twilight Base he can use to…'

'Stop it, Tom,' Amber said, gently but firmly putting a hand on my arm before my imagination got into top gear. 'Soon you'll be blaming yourself for *not* killing him outright. We did the best we could with what we had. Leave it at that…'

It was only when we separated to go to our lockers that I noticed the envious glances from a group of my friends who had been watching our intense discussion from a distance. Even if they did not quite believe it they imagined something romantic was going on between me and Amber and pestered me for details. I mean she'd actually put her hand on my arm in a comforting kind of way and smiled…

Of course it was nothing like that and I knew it. My heroics had not melted Amber's heart or anything so rom-com-ish. But there was a kind of bond between us now. You couldn't go through what we had together without finding something out about each other. Even though she thought I was too juvenile at times, she knew I came through in a crisis and could sometimes be quite useful to have around. I could live with that…

Of course I didn't actually deny my friends' misinterpretation of what they had seen. I simply smiled knowingly, admitted nothing and basked in their envy. So this was what it was like to be popular…

One thing I'd completely forgotten about though was Madam Dupont's French test! I hadn't revised for it at all. It was an oral translation when she read out a text in English and we had to write it down in French. And yet I felt oddly confident as she dictated, not even having to struggle to recall the right words. Even my handwriting seemed be more than usually neat and flowing. Maybe all that exercise my brain had got during those lost days in another universe had an unexpected pay off. Well that was only fair after all.

Madam Dupont glanced at our papers as we handed them in at the end of the lesson. She saw mine and frowned.

'What is this meant to be, Tomas?' she said, holding it up in front of my face. 'Some sort of joke?'

It was not a joke. In fact it was a perfect translation of the passage she had dictated to us. The only problem was I'd written it out in thousand year old Terran System script...

THE END

AFTERWORD

Some readers may not perhaps recognize the references Tom made to "Bob", "Isaac" and "Arthur" while he was recovering from the effects of the linguagram in Fort Adamant. These were actually leading SF authors of the middle to late Twentieth Century and the creators of some classic books.

Bob is Robert Heinlein, author of a story called "Stranger in a Strange Land", a social satire about a human child brought up by Martians and then returned to Earth. In the Martian language is the word: *grok,* which has many possible meanings, including to understand or to know something deeply.

Isaac is Isaac Asimov, creator of the famous "Foundation" series and many stories about robots with positronic brains.

Arthur is Arthur C. Clarke, who co-wrote "2001: A Space Odyssey" and who lived for many years in Sri Lanka, once called Serendib, from which the word *serendipity* derives, meaning a fortuitous discovery made by happy accident.

The Author.